BABY
of the
FAMILY

TINA McELROY ANSA

❧   ❧   ❧

A Harvest Book • Harcourt, Inc.

San Diego   New York   London

Library of Congress Cataloging-in-Publication Data
Ansa, Tina McElroy.
Baby of the family/Tina McElroy Ansa. – 1st ed.
p.   cm
ISBN 0-15-610150-5 (pbk.)
I. Title.
PS3551.N64B34   1989
813'.54–dc20   89-7466

Designed by Ann Gold
Printed in the United States of America

First Harvest edition 1991

P R T V X W U S Q O

For Jonée,
whose love sustains me

ACKNOWLEDGMENTS

❧   ❧

To complete a book in the 1980s a writer needs more than a story to tell. She needs a fair amount of support — spiritual and financial — to keep body and soul together. I want to thank my family — the McElroys, the Kerrs, and the Jacksons — for making me a writer; Bill Diehl and Virginia Gunn for love and direction; Dennis (Buck) and Gail Buchanan for vital transportation; Robert Griffin for sailing and support; Joanna Allen for honey and cheese as well as friendship; Paul and Pam Christian for casseroles, cakes, and love; the local ladies at Mary House, who taught me so much about spirituality; Roy and Anne Hodnett for work and support; Dorothy Houseal at the library, who always answered my cry for help; my agent Pam Bernstein and the William Morris Agency, who showed their belief in me in concrete ways; Daphne Merkin and Elizabeth Harper, my editors at Harcourt Brace, who both guided me through my first experience in the world of publishing.

And I thank St. Simons Island, which continues to offer me the beauty, peace, and acceptance of home.

ONE

   ❧   ❧

BIRTH

A hush swallowed the hot little room as the mother shuddered one last time, pushed down hard, and bore her third child, her baby girl, into the world.

"Awww," the doctor's and nurses' sighs floated on the hot humid air of the room like a hymn.

"Well, well, well. You got you a lucky baby here." Dr. Williams was red in the face, as if he had been doing all the work himself. He held the newborn child up for the nurses and the mother to see. "Yeah, a mighty special child."

Nellie, the mother, wasn't a bit surprised by the doctor's words. She had known this child would be different the moment she felt its head break through her vagina and enter the world. It was a special sensation, unlike those of the births of her two sons.

Around the time her water had broken the evening before, the mild November temperatures had suddenly dropped into the thirties. But now it was torrid in the tiny delivery room. Everyone there was as soaked with sweat as the mother who lay panting and grunting on the hospital table.

To Nellie everything in the delivery room seemed to be covered by a spotless white material: the nurses, the doctor, the table she lay on, her own body. Even the walls and ceiling were painted a white white that reflected the sharp glare of the round overhead light. The glare made her eyes ache, but Nellie was so glad to be in the last stages of labor—a hard, long, wrenching labor such as she had never experienced before—that she didn't mind the light.

The labor pains had gone on all night, and with the rising of the sun her baby was born.

"Yeah, a mighty special little girl, Mrs. Mac," Dr. Williams repeated.

As if she weren't the center of attention already, the doctor's statement made all eyes in the small hot room fix on the newborn child even more intently. In her first seconds in this world, the little girl seemed to bask in the glow from the eyes of her mother, her physician, and two nurses—a tiny cynosure.

"This one came with a veil over her face. Yes indeed, it's a sure sign that she's a lucky one, yes indeedy."

Wide arcs of perspiration marked the doctor's armpits, and the white surgical gown he wore over his tight little round belly was stained front and back with his sweat.

When Nellie rose up on her elbows, the sweat at the roots of her auburn-tinted hair and on her brow rolled down into her eyes and stung them a little. But she was so anxious to see her little girl that she hurriedly blinked the salty drops away as if they were tears and craned her neck to see around the younger nurse who had moved in for a closer look. Still blowing and puffing from the exertion of the birth, the mother was forgotten in the excitement of the newborn child. She looked at her longed-for girl over the sparkling white cotton cloth draping her knees. At first sight of the infant, Nellie drew in her breath so sharply that the shot of oxygen made her a little dizzy.

The baby, whom she planned to call Lena after her own grandmother, lay in the doctor's outstretched hands. Her wrinkled skin was hardly any color at all and her tiny legs and arms made circles in the air as she wiggled about. She began a soft sweet whimper that made the doctor and nurses smile at each other as if the child had performed a trick.

It surprised her mother that Lena could cry at all. Over her entire head, as if draped there by a band of angels, lay a thin membrane that rose and fell away from the child's sweet face with each breath she took. It looked almost like the white stockings the nurses in the room wore.

Although at first Nellie's gasp sounded like one of fear, it was really an expression of wonder. She herself was an only child and had learned everything she knew about babies when her own children were born. She had never seen an infant with a caul before.

The veil over her daughter's face gave the little girl a ghostly appearance. Nellie almost expected her to rise from Dr. Williams's large rubber-gloved hands and float around the small steamy room like a newborn apparition.

"Oh, my precious, precious," she crooned to the child lying a few feet away from her in the doctor's hands. She longed to reach over and take the baby in her arms, but she was so fatigued that even the thought of lifting her arms made her eyes roll around in her head.

Everyone in the delivery room was still. The doctor and the two nurses, grinning under their white surgical masks, stood around as if they were part of a Christmas tableau. Arriving with a veil over her face, the child brought with her a touch of the supernatural into a place that owed so much to the scientific. The doctor was reluctant to break the spell that had settled on them all there in the hot, antiseptic little room.

The fact that St. Luke's Hospital existed at all in the small Georgia town of Mulberry in 1949 was spectacular in itself. Nellie had thought so each time she went there for a doctor's visit or a child's emergency or to visit a sick friend. She knew that when black people went downtown to the large county hospital, they had to use a back entrance and sit in a dingy back room until a surly white nurse got around to them and shunted them off to the colored ward and rooms, where everything, even the sheets, looked used.

But a stay at St. Luke's, no matter how serious the complaint, was a life-affirming experience. Nothing but black folks—the doctor, the nurses, the receptionist, the aides, the orderlies, the patients, the families—all black folks. And the sick and injured got nothing but the best the staff could give.

Being private it cost more than the public county hospital. Even a stay in the wards at St. Luke's cost almost as much as a private room on the colored floor of the public hospital. But Nellie didn't know anyone able to scrape up the money who didn't try to get into St. Luke's first.

Dr. Williams, once a poor ashy-legged boy in Mulberry, had made two promises to himself when he returned home from working and scuffling his way through medical school: one was that he would help another black Mulberry boy through medical school if the boy promised to come back home and practice there; the other was that he would have a real hospital in his hometown for his own folks one day. After years in a lucrative and busy practice as the only black doctor in town, he had fulfilled both promises. His first wife's nephew would be graduating from Meharry in the spring. And this little hospital—just a one-story white wooden building with a wide front porch, on a paved residential street in the black part of town—was the other.

And exactly as the doctor—now graying at the temples and thickening at the waist—had planned as a young man, his hospital had as much modern equipment as he could acquire. There was an old but functioning incubator in the delivery room, an X-ray room behind the nurses' station, and a small laboratory in the basement next to the laundry, where the hospital's nurses did all their own routine tests.

Dr. Williams only hired nurses from the top of their classes at Tuskegee Institute. The examining rooms and main operating room had such up-to-date equipment that he was sometimes reluctant to let the white doctors from the county hospital come for a tour, for fear of their jealousy.

For weeks the whole town had talked of the time Dr. Williams had stormed out the front door of the hospital in the dead of winter, leaving his hat and overcoat behind, in a fury about the death of another black premature baby. "That's the last baby we're going to lose because we don't have an incubator!" old Nurse Bloom told folks he had shouted as he jumped into his shiny black Ford and drove off into the night. Two days later a crate arrived from Boston, Massachusetts, with a used incubator inside.

"Don't be asking me a lot of questions 'bout this stuff," he'd tell his staff when a new piece of equipment arrived unexpectedly. "Just read those specifications and make sure you all know how to work it. You all smart people, that's why you're here."

But this early morning Dr. Williams gave no thought to the techniques he had learned at Meharry. Seeming to forget his usual delivery-room procedure, formed over nearly a quarter century of practice, he turned the next two minutes into a ritualized dance that had nothing to do with modern medicine.

Standing at the foot of the delivery table so the mother could see what was going on, the doctor turned with the baby in his outstretched hands to Nurse Bloom, the older of the two women in white, walked three steps over to her, and proffered his bundle, still steaming from the womb. Wiggling and squirming and fighting the air with her tiny fists, little Lena stretched her body out to its full length and threw her head back, seeming to strain against the veil.

Nurse Bloom, acting as if the gods were watching her every move, reached out, her elasticized fingers trembling a little. Starting at the base of the child's neck where the thin membrane began, the nurse gently pulled the caul from the baby's face until she had uncovered her miniature features, the crown of her round head, and her mat of thick tightly curled hair.

In the nurse's slim hands, wrinkled under her rubber gloves from age and innumerable scrubbings in hot soapy water, the veil gave no resistance. It came away from the child's head evenly, with a faint hiss, disengaging at the nape of the tiny girl's neck where her hair grew to a little V.

Now it was the young nurse who gasped as she watched the procedure for the first time. Old Nurse Bloom, feeling the gossamer weight of the caul in her finely etched hands, had to stifle a bubble rising in her throat and call on all her years of training and self-discipline to fight the giddiness that was about to overwhelm her in the windowless room. Turning away from the others, she walked to the far side of the room, dropped the limp membrane into a shining silver pan, and deftly slipped the receptacle onto a shelf under one of the white tables there. Beneath the white mask that covered her nose and mouth, her wrinkled lips moved to a chant she spoke in her head.

The sound of the caul hitting the metal pan and the pan sliding across the metal shelf were the only noises in the room besides the soft mewling of the baby squirming in the doctor's big hands. The atmosphere in the stark delivery room reminded Nellie of a joyous yet reverent occasion—a baptism or a wake. "Let's get this baby cleaned up and in her mother's arms where she belong," Dr. Williams barked. But when he handed the child over to the older nurse, it was with a gentleness that few of the staff of the small hospital had ever seen in the harried physician. And Nellie thought his whole stance, which had stiffened while he issued his order, had suddenly relaxed again as he watched the old nurse take the newborn baby into her hands.

Nurse Bloom hadn't giggled in years. Now, like a young girl accepting a prize at the county fair, she carried the child to the metal table and silver pan of clear water with a smile playing around the corners of her mouth. Lying next to the pan of warm water was a stack of bleached white towels neatly folded into squares by the younger nurse's aide.

The old woman dipped the baby's body into the pan of warm water, washing the blood and afterbirth from the infant's face, throat, chest, arms, legs, behind, and feet as she crooned softly to the child.

"Oh, what a special baby. What a sweet little lucky pretty baby girl. Yes, that's what you are, all right. That's what you are. A sweet little lucky baby girl. Yes, you are, 'cause you come to this world right to the person who know all about you, who know everything to do for you. Uh-huh, this old lady right here washing your new little behind know just what to do for a pretty, lucky little baby girl like you."

Nurse Bloom was standing on the other side of the room from where the mother lay on the cloth-covered table, her feet still in the stirrups; with her knees poking up in the air, Nellie looked like a capital M. She couldn't quite make out what Nurse Bloom was saying, but the old nurse cooed so sweetly to tiny Lena that to the mother's ear each word sounded like a tablespoon of rich warm Alaga syrup poured over the child's soft new body.

Dr. Williams and the other nurse looked on silently, smiling like godparents. They stood there at the foot of Nellie's table with their hands hanging limply by their sides as if they had nothing else to do but admire Lena.

Well, damn, they just gonna forget completely about me, Nellie thought, and let her elbows slip down the smooth sheet covering the surgical table and her tired body fall back on its padded surface. She closed her eyes against the bright light shining directly into her face, and before she knew anything she had fallen into a deep, peaceful slumber.

When she awoke, the first thing she noticed was the strawberry-ice-cream-pink walls. They were such a contrast to all the glaringly stark whiteness she had been surrounded by in the delivery room that for a moment she thought she must still be dreaming. But when she heard Christine Williams's rich throaty laughter floating down the hall outside her private room, she remembered where she was and allowed herself to drift back to sleep.

Christine was the reason her room was pink instead of the antiseptic white of most rooms in the small hospital. Even the narrow white iron hospital bed in which she had just spent nearly twelve hours of labor had been replaced by a brand-new pink one.

Christine, Dr. Williams's second wife, had insisted that some color was needed for the women's private rooms and wards.

"Ya'll just wait," the tall slender woman with the elegant pompadour hairstyle had promised as she stuck her head into each room one evening. "I'm gonna get your butts out of these old white iron beds and into some pretty pastel ones to match your new walls before this time tomorrow."

And everybody believed her, too. All the next morning, the nurses and staff could hardly do their work for running to the windows and doors each time they heard the gears of a truck grinding outside. The staff had been as excited about the promised delivery of the pink, blue, and peach beds as the patients were. If Christine Williams said they would be there, they would be there.

Christine was the type of woman whom people just naturally flocked to and trusted. More than one patient had teased Dr. Williams that the only reason his hospital did such good business was because his wife ran it.

When Edward, Nellie's second son, had been born at St. Luke's Hospital, Nellie had seen Christine send twice to the drugstore down the street for tobacco for an old man on the ward who couldn't even afford to pay for it. When he complained about it not being his brand, Christine just laughed at the old fool's crotchetiness and promised to get it right the next time.

Everyone knew that Dr. Williams owned the hospital. But they also understood that his wife, a woman much younger than he, who strolled the halls and rooms all times of day and night dressed to kill in taupe gabardine suits and neutral-colored silk blouses, was the heart of the private establishment that black people in Mulberry considered a privilege to get well in.

Most of the hospital—the wards, private rooms, and operating rooms—was laid out on one floor, but at the end of the hall was a staircase that led downstairs to the basement. This was Miss Sallie Mae's domain. She was the cook for the hospital and ran the large basement kitchen like a minor dictator. Reluctantly she shared the basement with the laundry, the lab, and the hospital's owner himself, whose office was at the very rear of the building.

"Leave this room the way it is," Nurse Bloom told the orderly the moment he entered the delivery room. "I'll take care of it myself."

TWO

❧ ❧

TOWN

When Jonah got the news that Nellie, his wife, had delivered a baby girl ("Mother and daughter are doing fine," the young nurse on the other end of the telephone line said proudly) he was still at the bar, grill, and liquor store he owned. As he settled the phone back onto the hook, he turned and grinned at his buddies seated around a makeshift poker table in the grill side of the juke joint. Its proper name was the Blue Bird Cafe, Grill, and Liquor Store, but everyone in town called it The Place.

After Jonah had taken Nellie to the hospital the evening before, chatted with Dr. Williams awhile, and seen that she was settled in, he had returned to The Place with the latest.

"Well, folks," he had said heartily as he entered the smoky crowded juke joint, "looks like Nellie's fixing to have that baby."

The crowd—winos, hustlers, small businessmen, working women and men, the waitresses, and the roustabouts—all let out a yell. Most of them had crowded into the bar to escape the sudden cold outside. And when they heard that they had chosen the night that Jonah McPherson and his pretty wife Nellie were

9

about to have another baby, they felt as though they had found money.

Patrons extended four or five half pints of spirits—Dark Eyes vodka, King Cotton wine, XXX bourbon—toward Jonah, the about-to-be new father. But he smiled and brushed the bottles away.

"Man," he laughed, "get that cheap liquor out of my face. Nobody's gonna drink that shit tonight."

The crowd laughed with him. Most of them had been around for the births of his other two children, his sons, and they knew what kind of celebration they were in for.

Jonah went around to the liquor store side of the joint and returned with a fifth of Chivas Regal in one hand and a fifth of Jim Beam in the other.

"Here, sugar," he said to a laughing woman in a dangerously tight dress sitting on a stool at the entrance to the bar with her legs crossed at the ankles, "twist off these bottle tops and throw 'em away. We won't be needing them again."

The woman giggled and leaned up into Jonah's narrow, handsome face, nearly grazing her cheek on the black bristles of his thick, shiny mustache as she uncovered the bottle caps and threw them into the air.

Then Jonah, grinning proudly, moved along the bar and weaved gracefully among the tables, pouring splashes of the expensive liquor into every glass he saw, including the ones held by the staff. Someone put more coins in the jukebox and honky-tonk music filled the smoky room.

"Well, what you think it's gonna be this time, Jonah? A boy or a girl?" Peanut, one of Jonah's poker buddies, asked as he drank down the scotch and held his glass out for more.

Jonah snorted a little laugh and said, "Hell, man, you know what Nellie said. She's not taking anything but a girl this time. Anything else, she's sending back!"

Even the town's one black policeman took a little drink to celebrate the occasion when he stopped in, swinging his nightstick, to see what all the commotion was about on a weeknight in the crowded corner bar.

"Don't mind if I do," he said in his booming voice and laid the nightstick on the wet counter to take the glass of ice proferred him.

When Jonah finally yelled, "Closing time," it almost started a fight, and a couple of the roustabouts had to threaten a couple of the revelers to get the last of them out of the bar.

"Let's all stay here till Miss Nellie have that baby," one drunk patron shouted.

"Shit, man," Jonah said, "you better get your ass on home. I know your old lady, she sleep with a pistol under her pillow and it's got your name on it as it is. Hell, it's past three o'clock." He checked the Miller High Life clock on the wall. "I don't give a damn where you go, just get your ass on out of here."

When the last unwanted patron had been pushed out the door, Jonah got another bottle from the whiskey store and sat down with four of his gambling buddies to play some cards and await the news.

"Well, here's to her, Mac," Peanut said, raising his glass formally when Jonah came back to the table grinning over the news of his baby girl. "Any daughter of yours is bound to be something else."

Then all the men stood and had one last drink to the new baby Lena.

Jonah grabbed his coat from behind the liquor store counter and felt in his pocket for his car keys. "Close up the place and drop the keys by the house," he shouted as he picked up his glass of bourbon and headed out the door into the crisp dawn.

Jonah started to go right to the hospital but decided to take care of a number of chores instead. He pointed his shiny black Cadillac right through downtown Mulberry, turning down Cherry Street and heading for the big funeral home four streets over. When he pulled the Cadillac up to the curb there, he saw that the florist next door still had a CLOSED sign hanging in the glass door out front. So he didn't stop at the front door, but headed around back through the alley that ran beside the business. Locked doors and CLOSED signs didn't stop him, especially in his town.

He met the florist taking chilled long-stemmed roses from a truck parked out back. "Send a bunch of those to my wife up at St. Luke's. She finally had that girl she wanted so bad." Jonah laughed to himself and went out the door without bothering to tell the man to put the roses on his bill, or that the next week he would bring him a box of rib-eye steaks he would get from the head waiter down at the DuPree Hotel.

In the early-morning hours there was little traffic in the narrow streets of the small busy town. Jonah drove slowly as he headed across town to his home in Pleasant Hill, casually cutting down little-used side streets and back alleys. The window was down despite the chilled air, and his arm rested casually on the door of the car.

He drove past the Gothic railroad station and down the street past his parents' former home, where he had grown up. He cut sharply down an alley and drove alongside the playground to the Catholic school behind the church his family attended. Two blocks over, he passed the deserted yard of the public elementary school on one side of the street and the house of his old music teacher on the other.

Every time he thought of his new baby girl lying in her mother's arms at St. Luke's Hospital, he couldn't help grinning. He knew she was pretty. Whenever anyone complimented a baby in the family, his mama said, "You know, the McPhersons ain't never had no ugly babies." It was a statement that always made his wife mad because she said her mother-in-law made it sound like she, not born a McPherson, had nothing to do with how her own babies turned out.

Jonah laughed again to himself when he thought of his wife and her determination to bear a girl this time. He even knew what her name was already.

"Lena"—he said it aloud to see how it sounded. Then he

repeated it again with a smile, "Lena," because he liked the sound of it.

Suddenly, out of the corner of his eye, Jonah caught the quick stealthy movement of an old tweed coat he recognized. Not even touching the brake pedal, he made a U-turn in the middle of the street and drove his car partway up on the sidewalk.

The man in the tweed coat hiding behind the big oak tree knew he was trapped. He stepped from behind the tree lightly. "Hey, Mac, I been looking for you."

"Yeah, well, you found me, baby, so give me my goddamn money."

"Well, that's what I wanted to see you 'bout," the man said brightly.

"No, you ain't got to see me. You just got to give me my goddamn money. Man, how many times do I have to tell you? Don't fuck with me about my goddamn money. You need to stay out the card game if you can't take the pain. Now, give me my money."

"Okay, Mac, I be honest with you."

"I don't want your honesty, motherfucker. Just give me my money."

"Let me tell you what happened," the man in the tweed coat said, talking as fast as he could. "I was on my way to see you last night, I swear to God I was, but I stopped by this house, you know Bessie Mae's house, and I got caught up in a skin game. Mac, you know how I am 'bout skinnin'. You know I can't help myself. Got caught up in that game, Mac, and lost every penny I have."

"Every penny, huh?" Jonah asked suspiciously.

"I swear, every penny," the man said as he turned his pants pockets inside out to show they were empty. "Every penny, except for these two dollar bills right here in my coat pocket. That's all I got in the world."

"Well, then," Jonah said, "hand them over."

"Mac! You gonna take my last two dollars?"

"You damn right I am. Man, my wife just had a baby . . ."

"Well, well, well, congratulations, Mac. What she have?"

"A girl, Nellie finally got her a girl." Jonah beamed proudly behind the wheel of his car. Then, "Now, give me those two dollars."

The man's face fell to pieces as the conversation came back to money. But he knew there was no use talking, and he handed over the two crinkled bills, shaking his head in disbelief. "You a hard man, Jonah McPherson."

"Yeah, you weren't saying that when the cards were falling right," Jonah shot back as he put the big Cadillac in reverse and backed off the curb.

Wait till Mama and the boys hear 'bout our new baby girl, he thought, grinning again, as he drove past the corner grocery store he had owned when he first got married, then turned down Forest Avenue toward home.

THREE

❧ ❧

VEIL

As soon as Nurse Bloom had seen that Nellie was comfortably on her way back to her private room with a nurse and the orderly by her gurney, she cradled the infant Lena in her arms and headed for the nursery and the process that all newborns at St. Luke's Hospital went through.

The old nurse never put Lena down, from the time she washed the newborn baby until she laid her in her bassinet among the other babies in the hospital nursery. Nurse Bloom saw to it herself that Lena was weighed, measured, and footprinted. Then the old nurse pinned her first diaper on her and set her down in her crib.

The whole process wouldn't have taken as long as it did if Nurse Bloom had been left alone to finish her business. But she wasn't. Every nurse, nurse's aide, and cleaning woman in the place kept slipping away from her duties to come get a look at the new baby, the one born with a veil over her face. Even Miss Sallie Mae from down in the kitchen hoisted her wide heavy frame up the back steps to see Lena and cluck her tongue over the special child.

"Would you look at that little one come to this earth with a veil over her face? Gon' be a wise child," Miss Sallie Mae pronounced, then headed right back downstairs, sniffing all the way as if she smelled something burning.

The cook's place was immediately filled by two young nurse's aides. "Oh, look, isn't she pretty? I've never seen one come with a veil over its face before. You can't even tell where it was," one young woman said.

"She already got a head full of hair," the other replied. "Lord, I shore hope she ain't tender-headed, 'cause I bet it's gonna be a chore and a half to comb it."

"I wish she'd open her eyes. You know it's supposed to be good luck for a child like that to look at you. That's what I always heard. She supposed to be a lucky child herself."

"My grandmama always said a child like that was kin to being a witch."

"A witch?"

"Yeah, but not a evil witch, just a person with special powers. I had a cousin who was born with a caul over her whole body that folks used to come to from all over south Georgia to see 'cause she could read 'em. Tell 'em they future."

"That's right, they do supposed to have special powers. They supposed to be able to tell you things. But the biggest power is they able to see ghosts."

"You right about that. I knew a woman in the country who had three children—a boy and two girls—who was all born with cauls over they faces. And she say they used to see ghosts all the time. Say they used to play with 'em as children."

"For real?"

"That's what she told me. And she didn't have no reason to lie on her own children. She said they used to play with them ghosts when they was small. But said as they got older, they grew real scared."

"All of you talking that silliness about ghosts and haunts and spirits," an older nurse cut in. "But you're overlooking the real thing that this child's caul is a sign of. It's a sure sign that this child is special. That caul is a gift from God, that's what it is. This little girl has been chosen by God as a special person on this earth. She can't hardly help but do something great in this life because God has touched her in the womb."

Nurse Bloom just let them talk. She didn't confirm or dispute what they said. She acted as if they weren't there and kept crooning to little Lena as she weighed and measured her, "Oh, yes, sweet baby, Nurse Bloom gonna take care of this sweet little thing. No need to worry atall. Old Nurse Bloom know what she doing, sugar."

The whole process took less than half an hour. Nurse Bloom kept an eye on the clock over the nurses' station to make sure. When she finished with Lena and laid her on her stomach in her crib, the nurse glanced at the clock on the wall again and shot the women gathered around the baby a meaningful look. They got the message immediately and scattered like baby chicks out of the nursery back to their duties.

Nurse Bloom stood in the hall and watched the women disappear into doorways. Then she turned to the left and headed back to the nurses' station.

"Let Mrs. Mac have her baby as soon as she wakes up," she told the nurse behind the desk. "And I don't want anyone to bother me for at least an hour. I'm taking a break." She turned with a slight smile on her wrinkled face and headed down the hall to the delivery room, where the piece of membrane lay drying out in its metal tray.

When Nurse Bloom had been a midwife in the country, she had never let a caul sit for more than a few minutes before preserving it for the child. Now that she worked in a hospital, she had to adjust her ritual to fit into the modern mode. But there were still some things that she would not give in on.

I'm not the one to be changing some things that have always been, she would tell herself when, on occasion, she bent hospital procedure and slipped a sharp knife under the bed of a narrow-hipped woman who was having a hard time having her baby.

The old nurse stopped at the door to the hot little delivery room. She was about to ask the powers who controlled such things to look on this newborn child kindly and let pass what

BABY OF THE FAMILY

must pass. She took the white starched cap off her head and the white leather oxfords off her feet and laid them on the black-and-white square-tiled linoleum floor by the door.

The atmosphere inside the room was alive. She glanced around quickly to make sure nothing had been disturbed. Satisfied that everything was as she had left it, Nurse Bloom padded over to the table against the far wall with the pan of water on top and pulled out the pan with Lena's caul resting there where she had dropped it.

Picking up the thin membrane sent shivers through the nurse's stocky body and set her teeth on edge. The caul had begun to stiffen and dry out a bit in the room's heat. Without hesitating, Nurse Bloom dropped the drying membrane into the still-warm bloody water in the round metal pan beside her on the table. The caul immediately loosened and spread out on the surface of the pinkish water.

With a satisfied little grunt the woman picked up the pan of water and headed out the door. She was surprised at first to find the hall deserted at this time of morning. But then, she thought, a child had been born in this hospital with a veil over her face. Nothing much that happened this November day was going to surprise her much. She turned to the left and hurried toward the back staircase, careful not to slosh the water from the pan onto the floor. At the foot of the stairs she made a sharp right and slipped into the laundry room.

The heat of the room nearly knocked Nurse Bloom off her feet. The big white industrial dryer in a far corner was kept running most of the time, and even the linoleum floor was damp and warm under the nurse's stockinged feet. The only person in the single large laundry room was Ted, the orderly who had helped take Lena's mother back to her room.

"Ted, I need you to go up and scrub the small O.R.," Nurse Bloom told the orderly, who sat with his feet stretched out in front of him taking a break. "Please see to it that that room is spotless and antiseptic before you leave it. You know what to do. And when you finish that, collect all the soiled linens from the closet upstairs and sort them for pickup. Then you can go to lunch.''

Ted pulled himself up from his comfortable seat and wondered what he had done to deserve Nurse Bloom's attention. Efficiency was a prized commodity at St. Luke's, and he had tried to keep in step with the hospital's policy since he had begun working there two years before. But all this jumping back and forth! First leave the O.R. the way it is, then clean up the O.R. right away. Don't touch those linens; collect and sort those linens right now. Ted frowned. I'll have to have a talk with Mrs. Williams, he thought. Still, all he said was, "Yes, ma'am." He was so steamed that he didn't even notice she wasn't wearing her cap or her shoes.

The nurse watched Ted leave the room, then walked over to the long wooden table where the aides folded the clean dry clothes and linens. Except for a large roll of white butcher's paper on a holder that was used to keep its surface clean, the table was clear. She put the metal pan she was holding down on the smooth paper surface. The caul, still floating on the top of the water, waved around in the pan like a jellyfish. She reached over the pan, pulled off a length of the heavy white paper, and tore it off from the roll. Then she spread the paper on the tabletop and smoothed down its curling ends with her hands.

She had to smile at her hospital efficiency. For years in the country, where she was called Mother Bloom, she had conducted this same ritual time and time again but not with all these conveniences.

"But I guess I been in the city too long," Nurse Bloom said to herself with a cackle. In her three years at Saint Luke's, she had found the most efficient way to preserve a child's veil. Until she returned to her people's home in the country when she retired, she planned to continue doing it this way.

She took the caul from the baby's bath water and spread it out as smoothly and evenly as possible on the paper. She didn't hurry. In all the years that she had done this—Must be forty at least, she thought—no one had ever burst in and disrupted her.

And she believed that events, once set in motion, continued on the road intended for them.

Carefully she picked up the paper with the caul, placed it on the hot clean surface of the dryer, and stepped back with an air of satisfaction. Now she had to dispose of the water she had first bathed Lena in. She had no intention of pouring it down the drain of the deep double porcelain sink in the corner of the laundry room. The pipes connected to that drain led to the city sewerage system, where the child's bath water would be mingled with all kinds of waste. And Lena's first bath water, in which Nurse Bloom had soaked her birth caul, was, like the child, special. It deserved special treatment.

The nurse picked up the pan, headed out of the room into the basement hall, and padded in her stockinged feet toward the back stairs leading outside.

The freezing temperatures of the night before, when she had come on duty, had mellowed into a crisp autumn day with a pristine blue sky and the smell of old leaves in the air. What a good day to be born, she thought as she walked over to the rosebushes lining the rear wall of the building beside the door. She clucked her tongue and shook her head sadly. Every time she saw the poor sickly-looking things, she got a picture of Mrs. Williams in one of her pretty suits squatting down in the dirt with Ted the orderly to see what was ailing the bushes that had looked stunted and yellow and refused to grow ever since the two had planted them.

Let's see what this baby's water can do for Mrs. Williams's poor little roses, Nurse Bloom said to herself as she sprinkled the base of the plants with the pinkish water. I wouldn't be surprised if those things aren't flourishing next spring.

Back in the building, the laundry room was still empty. When she reached the dryer, the air escaping from inside felt so good blowing on the front of her body that she stood there awhile with her eyes closed, letting the warm dry heat blow up under her dress on her thighs.

Before she knew it, she was singing to herself a rhyme she had sung as a girl: "Uncle Ted got this, Uncle Ted got that, Uncle Ted got a dick long as a baseball bat." She thought about Amos, a boy who used to live next to her folks' farm when she was a girl. He was the first boy she ever opened her legs to and he used to blow his hot breath on her thighs, too.

"Lord, have mercy," the old woman said aloud, as she shook herself all over and stepped out of the direct blast of the dryer's heat. "What's the matter with me? I hadn't thought about that little old nappy-headed boy in years. Must be this child's caul making me remember such things. There's all kinds of powers in this here caul. I can tell."

She reached over and touched the dried and wrinkled membrane and wasn't a bit surprised to see her hands shaking. Along the edges of the caul, the paper had turned a pale beige and left faint water marks. In the center the caul itself had dried and puckered into tiny peaks and valleys. The whole sheet of paper resembled an ancient map of some unexplored territory.

"It's done," the nurse said softly and lifted the caul with the paper and took it back to the folding table. Then she headed across the hall to Miss Sallie Mae's steamy kitchen that smelled of fresh vegetables—turnip greens and rutabagas and pole beans—cooking in a little fatback, and juices and roast beef and chicken baking in the oven. Nurse Bloom had the nose of a hound, Ted the orderly always complained.

No one paid any attention as she took down a pretty blue-and-white-flowered china teapot, just big enough to hold about two cups of water, and a small sharp knife from the shelf where the nurses kept their personal eating things. On her way out the door, she looked over at the stove to make sure the big copper tea kettle was whistling gently, as it usually was, on a back burner.

When she reentered the laundry room, she walked over to the dried caul on the table, swiftly cut a piece of it about the size of her palm away from the paper, rolled the stiff section of skin up, and dropped it in the teapot. Then she hurried back across the hall to Miss Sallie Mae's kitchen and poured a stream of hot water into the teapot from the steaming kettle. She was finished and out of the kitchen before the workers noticed her.

Returning to the laundry room, the nurse placed the hot teapot on the table and ran her hands over the dried caul once more. Then she deftly folded the sheet of white paper with the caul inside nine times, until it was reduced to a rectangle no bigger than her fist. She slipped it into her pocket along with the small knife and headed back up the stairs with the warm teapot in her hand.

When she nearly slipped on the freshly mopped floor that smelled of disinfectant, she stopped and looked down at her bare feet. Frowning at the dirty footprints she had left on Ted the orderly's clean floor, she turned in her tracks and went back down the hall to the delivery room. He won't like it one bit, she said to herself. But he'll have to go back over this floor again with the mop.

As soon as she had slipped her dirty feet into her white oxfords and set her cap neatly over the spot where her graying nappy hair was pulled back into a bun at the back of her head, she was ready to go.

"I'm back on duty," she told the nurse at the station near the nursery as she passed by on her way to the infants' supply closet. When she glanced at the clock over the nurse's head, she was surprised to see that only forty-five minutes had passed since her trip to the laundry room. It seemed like she had spent hours down there. But it always did. In the country, when she had dried babies' cauls over a red-hot brick, the ritual had seemed to take all day.

Now she was moving with such smooth efficiency that she could almost feel her body humming. She took a glass baby bottle down from the shelf and poured the warm caul tea into it. When the pot was drained of everything but the wet, limp piece of caul itself, Nurse Bloom put the pot back on the table, screwed the nipple lid on the bottle, and held the bottle up to the light.

Ignoring the nurse who sat at the station pretending to look through some papers, Nurse Bloom headed out the door and placed the teapot and small knife from her pocket into her satchel among her personal things in the hall closet.

"I can take care of that when I get home," Nurse Bloom muttered to herself as she returned to the nursery. Passing through, she noticed that Lena's bassinet, like most of the others, was empty of its little occupant.

That's even better, she thought as she went back to the nursery closet, picked up the baby bottle of caul tea still warm and undisturbed on the counter, and headed for Nellie's room. I'll let her mother give it to her. That's the way it should be anyway.

FOUR

ఌ   ఌ

TEA

When the old nurse entered Nellie's room, the new mother was holding Lena in the crook of her arm, which rested on the fluffy white pillow at her shoulder, watching her little girl suck greedily at her breast. While Lena drank, Nellie was doing what every new mother does. She had stripped the infant naked and was checking her over, head to toe. She was fingering Lena's little seashell ears, counting her fingers and toes, pinching her nose to see her breathe through her mouth, bending her arms at the elbow, kissing the tips of her tiny fingernails.

Nurse Bloom starting smiling as soon as she entered the room. "She got everything she supposed to have?"

Nellie just gave a sheepish grin in reply. This room, a vision in pink, was one of the prettiest private rooms in the hospital. Bright morning sunlight poured into the tall window on the east wall and flooded the foot of the new pink hospital bed with dust beams. A large green vase of red roses stood on the bedside table right by the window.

Maybe I'll cut some of those last lavender chrysanthemums from the front yard and bring them in here, Nurse Bloom thought as she looked around the room for some nicety she could add to make Lena's first home even prettier.

She approached Nellie's bed playfully. She was still grinning the way she had in the delivery room. But at that point the caterwauling of some other woman's baby from down the hall began to get on her nerves. She stopped a few feet from the foot of Nellie's bed and said, "I'll be right back." Then she turned on her heels and charged out of the room and down the hall to the women's ward. There a young mother, still in her teens, was sharing the ward with three other women; the teenager hugged her crying child to her breast and eyed the nurse suspiciously.

"If you don't keep that crying youngun quiet, I'm gonna throw him in the trash can," Nurse Bloom barked.

"Oh, please, ma'am, don't throw my baby in the trash can," the mother pleaded as she gripped her bundle of joy tighter in her rail-thin arms.

The old nurse just looked at the woman cringing in her pastel-blue bed a moment and sucked her teeth in exasperation. "Girl," she said finally, "don't you know I wouldn't go around throwing babies in the garbage can?"

The young mother wasn't so sure. She clutched her child tighter, which made the baby cry all the more. Nurse Bloom stormed across the black-and-white linoleum floor of the ward and silently took the child from the mother's grasp.

"Lie back," the nurse ordered as she rocked the baby in her arms, quieting the infant instantly.

The young mother obeyed. The nurse expertly flipped the child over in her hands and gently laid him on his mother's stomach, his face between the girl's pitiful little titties.

"Now, put your hand on your baby's back and pat and soothe him instead of being a frantic Frances," Nurse Bloom instructed as she marched out of the room.

"Young fool girls don't know nothing about babies but how to get them," she muttered venomously as she walked back down the hall to Nellie's room. When she entered, she turned to Lena and her mother with a new face of kindness replacing the face of anger she had worn a second earlier.

"Now, where's that sweet little girl baby who came to us with a veil over her face," the hoary nurse purred. "I got something for that little girl."

The old woman felt as frisky as she had in the delivery room when the child had been born. She waved the bottle of clear tea back and forth before the child's eyes as if it were a toy.

Nellie tried to look interested, but she was still tired from the long, difficult labor and delivery, and she resented this intrusion on the first minutes she and her baby girl had together.

"I'm naming her Lena," Nellie said in an effort to be polite as the nurse lifted a straight-back chair from its place by the wall, brought it over to the side of the bed, and sat down.

"Well now, ain't that a pretty name?" Nurse Bloom said in a singsong voice that cracked in her throat. "I got something for that baby named Lena. In fact I've got two things, one for the baby and one for the mama."

"What's that, Nurse Bloom?" the mother asked.

"Nellie," the nurse said familiarly, lowering her voice as if others were in the room. "I guess you know you got a special child here. You were aware enough to see she came here with a veil over her face?"

"I sure did," Nellie said proudly as Lena began to fret a bit and her mother's nipple slipped out of her mouth. "Oh-oh, did you lose it, sweetheart? Here you go. Now, don't be in such a hurry.

"I sure did," she repeated to the nurse, who sat by the side of the bed smiling down at the feeding baby.

"Well, I don't know you all that well. I never knew your people, 'cept your aunt that ran the barber shop, so I don't know how much you know about things like veils over babies' faces and such." Nurse Bloom let the statement hang in the air like a question.

"To tell you the truth, Nurse Bloom," Nellie said, "not a whole lot."

"Well, there's no reason to worry, 'cause I know all about that kind of thing. Your little girl coming here to this world with a caul over her face means something, Nellie. It means she's a very special child."

"She certainly is, Nurse Bloom. I been hoping and praying for a little girl each time I got pregnant. That's what I always wanted since I was a little girl myself. But I had two boys first, and now it is almost five years since the last one. I was beginning to think I wasn't gonna have me my own baby girl."

"Oh, I know she's special to you, 'specially since you wanted a girl and all. But what I mean is she's special in her own right. That caul she was born with over her face was more than a piece of thin skin, you know. That caul was a sign that your little girl got a link with all kinds of things, all kinds of powers that the rest of us ordinary people don't have."

"Oh, Nurse Bloom, I have to tell you, I've never been one to believe in all those old-timey ideas," Nellie said with a smile. She didn't want to offend the woman who was sounding so sincere. "I guess I'm just not a superstitious type of person."

Nurse Bloom's face fell a little, but she leaned in closer, rested her elbow on Nellie's bed, and continued.

"Oh, this isn't superstitions I'm talking about, dear," she said. "What I'm talking about is what really is. I've been in this world almost sixty years and I know of what I speak."

"Well, Nurse Bloom . . ." Nellie began slowly.

"Now, just listen to me, Nellie," the nurse said, sounding a bit more like her normal stern self. "There's all kinds of things in this world that people call superstitions because they don't understand them or they don't fit neatly into their way of thinking nowadays, but that doesn't mean that these things are just some crazy mumbo-jumbo of ignorant country people."

This was not going anything like the nurse had thought it would. She had been sure the mother would be thrilled that her baby had a nurse right in this hospital who knew so much about her and the veil over her face and what it all meant. Instead Nellie was acting like she didn't appreciate what she had.

Lena whimpered a bit and let her mother's nipple fall out of her mouth again, but her tiny lips continued to make sucking motions in the air.

"Is this baby still hungry?" Nellie asked in a baby voice as she began to heave herself up on the pillow in preparation for turning the infant around to her other breast.

Nurse Bloom stood up quickly and gently took Lena from her mother's arms. "Let me give you a hand there with that pretty little hungry thing," she said as she turned the baby around and laid her with her head against her mother's unnursed breast.

Seeing the old nurse handle her little girl with such care fairly melted Nellie's heart. After she took her nipple and rubbed it against Lena's soft cheek to get her to start nursing there, she looked up at Nurse Bloom with softer eyes.

"I didn't mean to imply that you were country or ignorant, Nurse Bloom," the mother said sincerely. "Everybody knows how much everyone around here looks up to you."

"Well, I *am* country—spent almost all of my life there," the nurse answered, herself softening. "But I sho' ain't ignorant. I brought more babies into this world as a midwife than you can shake a stick at, and I learned a thing or two in the process. When I tell you your child is special, I mean it, and I know what I'm talking about."

Nellie didn't say anything, but she looked interested.

"Nellie, a child born with a veil over its face is an unusual thing. It don't happen every day, or every month for that matter. And believe me when I say it, it means something."

"What's it mean, Nurse Bloom?" Nellie asked.

"It means that little Lena is not like your other children and never will be. She is gonna be very wise and wise in ways we don't always appreciate. Nellie, that veil over her face means she has a link to that other world that most of us just pretend don't exist. Well, it does. I know you've heard tell that a child born with a caul over its face can see ghosts."

"I have heard that," Nellie said slowly.

"Well, it's true. When people talk about ghosts, they usually think of spirits of dead people. It's just not that simple. Of course there are spirits of dead people that still wander the earth. But there are two kinds of ghosts, one is the peaceful and harmless kind that appear before you just the way they were on earth, natural-like, and they can be helpful, too. Then there's the other kind, and they can scare you plenty. Some of them look like death itself, some don't have any heads or any feet, or their heads are turned around on their shoulders."

Nurse Bloom saw Nellie's eyes begin to widen, and she wondered what kind of family this smart-looking young woman came from that she hadn't heard all this at some time in her life. But the old nurse didn't want to scare her now that she had her attention and, seemingly, her respect.

"Oh, don't you worry any about your little girl, now. What I have in this bottle will take care of any problems she would ever have in that area." The nurse waved the bottle again like a rattle before Lena, who was absorbed in her mother's tit.

"You see, I made a little tea for the child that will blind her to any of those scary kinds of ghosts, so she won't be terrorized by those spirits. Now, she was born with a veil over her face, so the child is gonna see some ghosts—you can't get away from that—but at least after she drink this tea, it will just be the harmless kind she'll see. Nothing that'll ever scare her."

The nurse smiled as if she had just accomplished an act of charity. When she reached out and gave the mother the bottle of caul tea, she was beaming. Nellie felt that there was little she could do but accept the bottle with a smile. The woman seemed so proud of what she was doing for Lena, Nellie knew she could never tell the nurse what foolishness she thought all this talk was.

She stood the bottle on the bed, propped up next to her waist, and kept smiling at Nurse Bloom, who acted like she wasn't anywhere near ready to leave. The old woman sat in the straight-backed chair looking at Nellie and Lena with all the self-importance of a grandmother.

"Now, don't let that bottle tip over and drip all that good tea out on the bed there before little Lena gets to drink it," Nurse

Bloom said a little nervously. "It won't do her no good on that sheet."

"Don't worry," Nellie said as she steadied the bottle next to her body. "It'll be fine right where it is."

"You mean, it'll be fine there until you give it to the child," Nurse Bloom prompted.

"Uh-huh," said the mother vaguely, then added quickly, "So my baby being born with a caul over her face really sets her apart, does it?"

"There's all kinds of things connected with being born with a veil over your face," the nurse said, happy to impart her knowledge. "When I was handling this caul of hers downstairs I could feel some mighty power in it. Shoot, Lena may be able to read people, see things, do all kinds of things."

"Handling it? Why would you be handling it at all?" Nellie wanted to know suddenly.

"Well, you don't think I would just dry something like that in a big clump the way it fell, do you?" Nurse Bloom asked. "No-siree. This caul is a special thing. Let me tell you, I sure am glad that you decided to have your baby at this here hospital instead of over at the big county place where them white nurses take their time about getting you in and then rush you out. Shoot, one of the cleaning women up there told me that when a child is born with a veil over its face up there, they just take it and throw it away in the trash." The old nurse clutched her chest in distress at the thought.

"Thank God, there's no such goings-on in this hospital, not as long as I'm here," she continued proudly. "Naw, I gave little Lena's caul the right attention, spread it out on this white paper." She reached in her pocket.

Nellie was repelled by the idea of this woman playing around with the caul she had last seen over her baby girl's face. Nellie had a weak stomach. She would always tell people, "Uh, don't show me that, I've got a weak stomach, always did." Or she'd tell her sons, "Boys, one of you run in the fish house right quick and get me some pretty mullet. You know I can't go in that fish house and smell all those fishy odors. I've got a weak stomach and will throw up in a minute."

She had just in the last year been able to clean chitterlings at the kitchen sink without getting sick to her stomach as she fingered the slimy greasy membranes and picked them clean of dirt and hair and flecks of paper. Now she imagined Lena's veil like the sink full of chitterlings—thirty pounds of them, for the whole family—sloshing and slithering around, sliding away through her fingers when she tried to pick up a piece of the intestines.

At the thought, she had to bring the flat of her fist quickly to her mouth and press it there firmly. She took deep breaths through her nose over her bent index finger.

"Now, don't go getting overexcited, little mother." Nurse Bloom reached for the back of Nellie's head and gently bent it forward onto her chest. "Now, just breathe deeply. Take it slow, now—just in and out. Slow, now—in and out." She massaged the back of the new mother's neck.

The antiseptic smell of Nurse Bloom's uniform snapped Nellie right out of her sick-to-the-stomach spell. She pushed her head back and shoved the nurse away with one motion. Nurse Bloom sat back down and continued talking.

"See, that dizzy spell just passed. Now, like I was saying, I dried the caul all nice and neat on a piece of white paper for your little girl. You understand that you must keep this caul for your child until she is grown. That's important. She may never do anything with it but take it out once in a while and look at it, or she may need it right away, but it has to be kept, just the same. So until she's grown, you're gonna have to keep this in some very safe place. If it's lost or misplaced, it will make the child forgetful."

Nurse Bloom felt as if she were trying to cram a lifetime of common sense into a few minutes. This whole confrontation with the new mother was setting her on edge, ready to jump at the least thing. She didn't know when she had last felt so tense.

"But then I guess I don't have to tell you everything at once, do I?" she asked Nellie, as she tried to fight the nervousness that was overwhelming her. "We all live right here in Mulberry, don't we? Now, if you ever have any questions you know you can just come to me."

She paused. The only reason Nellie could see for pausing was for effect. It seemed a rather dramatic gesture. Then, the old nurse reached in her pocket and pulled out the thick rectangle of white paper.

Lord, I got more gris-gris, as mama's mama used to call it, in this room than Madame Hand out on Highway 17, Nellie thought. But there is no way I am going to go around handling my child's birth veil.

"Oh, Nurse Bloom, I can't believe you went to all this trouble," she said.

"Wasn't no trouble at all, child. It was my pleasure. You have to know that," Nurse Bloom said. "Here. Here's the caul in this paper. Here, take it, it's for you to protect and keep safe."

Nellie lay there a long moment just looking at the thick paper the nurse was offering her. She had the half-sick smile on her face that she used when she couldn't come up with a social lie quickly enough. Now what must I do? she wondered. If I take this piece of skin from this woman, I bet she'll be asking me about it every time I step foot in this place, expecting me to keep up with some old-fashioned foolishness like it made any difference in my baby girl's life. But if I don't take it, I'll hurt her feelings and she'll let me lay up in this bed and rot before she'll answer my buzzer again. What must I do?

Nurse Bloom stood there smiling, with the white rectangle of paper extended toward the new mother. "Go on, Nellie," she insisted, "take it."

Nellie shifted Lena a little bit up on her breast to stall for more time, but she couldn't think of any way out of taking the paper. She bit her lip and took the paper between two fingers and gingerly laid it on the bedside table.

"Now, you just be sure to give her that little bit of water in that bottle for me. Give it her a couple of minutes after she finish feeding. Then she'll take it right along, so don't worry 'bout that—I never seen one child turn it down yet."

Nurse Bloom slapped her chubby knees and stood up as if she were finished, then said, "Now, don't just leave that caul sitting right there."

"Would you put it in my overnight bag for me?" Nellie asked the nurse with a smile. Nellie wanted to touch the thing as little as possible.

Nurse Bloom did as she was asked and smiled in return. Then, reluctantly, she headed toward the door. "Just buzz when you're ready for us to come get that little prize for you. As a matter of fact, I'll come get her myself." And the old nurse disappeared out the door.

Nellie heaved a sigh of relief and held the bottle of nearly clear liquid up to the sunlight. She was surprised to see strains of color floating through the water. "What in the world . . . ?" she muttered to herself as the sunbeam that sparkled through the water disappeared behind a cloud and the colors in the water vanished, too. She shook off the chilled feeling the disappearing sun gave her and kissed her baby girl lightly on the top of the head.

"Nurse Bloom is a sweet woman, going to all this trouble for my baby, yes, she is, for my sweet little Lena." Nellie looked down at the baby at her breast, who seemed to stop sucking and listen. "But if she thinks I'm gonna give my baby girl any of this old-fashioned potion shit—God only knows what's in it—she better think again. Just imagine, Lena, a grown intelligent woman like that believing in ghosts."

As she cooed to Lena, Nellie unscrewed the cap of the glass bottle, lifted off the nippled top, and slowly poured the precious water into the vase of roses her husband had had waiting for her when she awoke after being rolled back in from the delivery room.

"But there's no reason anybody but us needs to know anything about this, not anybody—not Nurse Bloom, not your grandmama, especially not Grandmama, you know how she is about all this old-timey stuff, she's almost as bad as Nurse Bloom. It'll be our little secret, our first secret, my baby girl."

The modern new mother screwed the lid back on the empty bottle and put it on the table next to her bed.

"I'll burn that thing as soon as I get home." Nellie wrinkled her nose as she glanced at the stiff white paper with the baby's caul inside sticking out of her cosmetic case. She brushed her lips across the top of Lena's head. Then mother and daughter fell asleep before Nellie had a chance to buzz for the nurse.

FIVE

❧ ❧

PICTURE

It was a quiet Sunday evening. Lena had been lying on her grandmother's big four-poster oak bed, the one the old lady told her had been her bridal bed forty-eight years before Lena was born, three years before. Her grandmother, a small smooth-skinned snuff-colored woman, did not allow just anybody to enter the private sanctum of her room. But Lena was special, and many nights at her bedtime, the old lady would give Lena her bath, dust her all over with talcum powder, slip on her little cotton gown, and say, "Come on, baby, you been such a good girl today, you can sleep in grandmama's bed."

Walking into Lena's grandmother's room was like stepping back into another century. Lena's own mother was very modern. Nellie had even bought pale blond furniture and angular pastel lamps for the guest room. But there was none of that modern new-fashioned, in-one-year-out-the-next nonsense in her grandmama's room. Besides the old four-poster bed, there was a big overstuffed easy chair pulled up to one of the room's windows and, next to it, a small pine piecrust table and a maroon-shaded floor lamp with gold fringe. Lena's grandmother ignored the large closet in the room and kept her cotton shirtwaist dresses and jersey knits in a red wooden chifforobe. And although she didn't use it, there was even a china basin and pitcher on the old marble-topped pine dresser in her room, as if they didn't have two bathrooms in the house.

"When your granddaddy came to ask my daddy for my hand in marriage, that dresser was sitting in the front bedroom," the old lady told Lena nearly every time they entered the room. "When Daddy turned his nose up at this here diamond ring, Walter strutted straight across the hall into the bedroom and ran this stone over the mirror, leaving this little old scratch right here." Lena and Grandmama would lean close to inspect the scratch. "Mama was so outdone she spoke right up. 'Lizzie?' she asked me, 'you mean to tell me you want to marry this crazy man?' I nodded my head, and she said, 'Well, go on then, and you might as well take that dresser and mirror too.'"

On the highly polished hardwood floors, her grandmother had scattered three bright rag rugs, with colors of red and pink and yellow: one at the door, one by the side of the bed where the old lady swung her feet out in the morning, and one at the foot of the bed near the big easy chair.

The beige walls of the room were bare except for one elaborately framed picture that hung over the bed. It was a sepia photograph of an infant dressed in a frilly white christening gown. The baby's cheeks and lips were dusted pink and her eyes were painted brown.

"Who's that?" Lena asked her grandmama one day as they both sat in the big mauve easy chair facing the large, nearly life-sized portrait.

"That was my baby girl. My firstborn child. She died right after that picture was took. Ain't she precious?"

"Uh-huh," Lena agreed and sat all afternoon staring at the picture of the pretty little girl who would have been her daddy's sister.

Early that Sunday evening after her bath, her grandmother led her into the room by the hand and walked over to the tall bed and folded back the pink chenille bedspread. A perfume, old and sweet, wafted up from her pure white linens and overpowered the smell of talcum powder rising from her own body. It was the smell that Lena inhaled when she nestled her face into her grandmother's thin breasts and drifted off to sleep.

Grandmama lifted Lena up onto the bed, letting go of her grip on the child a little early so she bounced a couple of times on the firm mattress when she landed on her fat little bottom. The bouncing gave Lena the giggles and at the sound of the little girl's lilting laughter, her grandmother giggled, too. Then she pulled the top sheet up over the child's body and kissed her on the forehead.

"Now, you close them pretty brown eyes of yours and drift on off to sleep. Can't nothing touch grandma's little puppy in this bed. Look," she said pointing above Lena's head at the portrait, "you even got grandma's own little girl looking down on you."

Her grandmother's dry kiss reminded Lena of a butterfly fluttering across her face. When the child closed her eyes to quietly enjoy this feeling, her grandmother got up from the bed and silently tiptoed away, pulling the door shut after her.

"She's up there sleeping as peaceful as an angel," her grandmother assured the rest of the family when she returned to the living room.

But back in her grandmother's bedroom, Lena opened her eyes. She expected to see her grandmother still sitting there next to her, and when she found herself alone in the old-fashioned room, she lay there a minute taking in the shapes around her in the early-evening light. But that soon bored her and she wasn't a bit sleepy. Then she remembered the picture hanging over the bed above her head.

This was the perfect time, she decided, to do what she had been wanting to do ever since she had first seen the portrait. Pushing away the sheets that her grandma had so carefully tucked around her, she scooted to the foot of the bed on her behind and turned around with her back resting against the spooled railing there.

When she gazed up at the picture, it looked as if the dead

baby's eyes were looking directly at her. She smiled because her grandmother had already pointed that feature of the picture out to her.

"See how her eyes seem to follow you all around the room, no matter where you stand?" Grandmama had said.

Lena had run all over the room looking into the eyes of the furbelowed little girl to see if her gaze really did follow her into the corner by the big red chifforobe and over to the door and back across the room to the windowsill. Sure enough, the velvet brown eyes seemed to roll around in their painted sockets to follow her progress.

Lena stood on the mattress and walked to the head of the bed as if she were stepping across the floor. When she reached the head of the bed, she pushed the fluffy feather pillows aside and, leaning against the headboard, reached up to touch the child's portrait. What she wanted to do was touch the child's cheeks, to feel the texture they implied, but she couldn't reach past the bottom of the frame.

Determined to take advantage of her solitude and the opportunity to touch the dusty pink cheeks in the picture, Lena stood back from the picture with her hands on her hips and looked the situation over the way she had seen her grandmother do many times when faced with a problem. A voice inside the room or inside her head said, "Pile the pillows up and stand on them, Lena."

"All right," Lena replied and got right to work pulling the two big down-filled pillows together and stacking one on top of the other. The two pillows made nearly a mountain next to where she stood at the head of the old bed.

"That's fine," the voice said. "Now climb up on it."

Again Lena obeyed the voice and, steadying herself with a hand on the dark headboard, began walking up the side of the mountain of pillows. She was determined to get on top of the pillows so her hands could reach the pastel-tinted picture of her baby aunt. With each step up the side of the pillows, her bare feet barely made a dent in the fluffy surface. She weighed only thirty pounds dripping wet.

When she reached the top of her shaky perch, she was so proud of her accomplishment, she beamed like a mountain climber at the top of Everest and leaned her small back against the wall below the picture to enjoy the feeling. And when the voice praised her accomplishment with "Good girl, Lena," the child ducked her head with pride and her cheeks blushed almost the color of the girl's in the frame.

Remembering the object of her climb, she turned around with a smile and stretched both of her arms as far as she could toward the oak-framed portrait, then splayed her fingers to reach farther. Now that she stood on the pillows, she expected to be able to touch the frill lace of the child's christening gown, so she was surprised when her hands met the cold surface of the sheet of glass covering the picture. The glass was so cold that at first it felt hot to Lena's hands. It reminded her of when she had touched the hot potbellied stove at her grandmama's friend's house.

Instinctively she yanked her hands back from the portrait's strange feel, throwing herself off-balance on the pillows. But just as she began to topple backward onto her grandmother's bed, two small hands with yellowed lace at the wrists poked from the picture, grasped Lena's own small hands, and began pulling her arms and head effortlessly through the frame—glass, picture, and all—as if it were an open window.

Lena had never felt anything like this in her life. She let out a scream that she thought would surely burst her throat open, but no sound came out of her mouth. She felt the way her grandmother must have felt when she awoke some mornings sunken-eyed and breathless to say the witches had ridden her all night and no one in the house had harkened to her cries of distress.

Lena's second terrified scream was muffled in the warm soft lap of what seemed like yards of rotting old lace. Lena kept trying to yell as she felt the strong tiny hands that had pulled her in-to the picture move up her forearms, over her elbows, past her upper arms, and take hold of her firmly under her armpits.

Lena gasped for breath, turning her head this way and that, trying to escape the fetid smell of the dingy lace she found her face buried in. She was suffocating in its old, dry, airless scent. But the more she struggled—half her little body still hanging from the picture, her bare legs and feet flailing against the wooden headboard, making a dull thudding noise—the tighter the small warm hands gripped her.

"Come inside, come play with me," said the voice that had told her to climb up on the pillows.

Lena tried to shake herself loose from the baby in the picture, but the baby's grip was like steel, suddenly turning cold, too.

"Mama! Grandmama! Come help me!" she screamed over and over as she kicked the headboard with her feet and fought against the child who was pulling her into the picture frame. But the only noise Lena heard in the room was the sound of her feet crashing against the headboard, which was now shaking the entire bed, causing its bulbous legs to scrape on the hardwood floor.

Just when Lena knew she could stand the deathly grip and the fear in her chest no longer, she heard her entire family—mama, grandmama, her brothers Edward and Raymond, and her daddy—come crashing up the stairs and into the room, nearly breaking the hinges from the door as they entered.

Suddenly the baby in the photograph released her grip on Lena, and she slipped out of the picture. She fell screaming and sobbing onto the hard surface of her grandma's bed, landing on her behind and bouncing the way she had earlier when her grandmother had dropped her there after her bath.

As her family rushed into the room and surrounded her on the bed, taking turns holding her in their arms, kissing her, soothing her, cooing to her that she was all right now, Lena slowly lifted her stinging eyelids and looked at the picture over the bed. The little girl in the portrait sat as always on the royal-blue velvet throw, her little white baptismal dress spread out around her, but her tiny feet and round head were turned backward.

Lena screamed, "The picture, the picture, the girl in the picture, she had me!" Immediately she went into convulsions.

"That's what you get for telling," the voice said as Lena thrashed around on the bed.

After that, Lena refused to go back into her grandmother's room while the portrait still hung over the bed. She never told her family why. She didn't want to ever get as sick as she had the night she told them that the ghost of the little girl lived in the picture. But she dug her heels in and shook her head wildly whenever her grandmother said, "Come on, baby, you can sleep with Grandma tonight."

This stung the old lady to the quick. So, she reluctantly took the treasured picture down and stored it in the attic. After a few weeks Lena's terror subsided, but she always remembered the sickness, the vomiting, the fits that had struck her when she told her family about the ghost. Especially when she awoke in the middle of the night.

SIX

❧ ❧

NIGHT

From the age of three Lena had always woken at 4:00 A.M. to go pee. Her bladder's message and her response to it, even in the depths of a dream, pleased her. It made her feel responsible and older, able to control her water, not a baby who wet the bed each night, having to lie there in the cold wet pissy-smelling sheets until morning.

She wasn't a baby; she was a big girl. She was almost four. Didn't she wake up each night on schedule? Didn't she pad past her grandmother's room, past her brothers' room, down and across the hall all by herself to the bathroom even though she knew what lived in the night? Didn't she remember to wipe herself instead of drip-drying or forgetting altogether and bringing the smell of pee back to bed with her, drying on her inner thigh? Sure, she was a big girl, not a baby.

But her family still left the lights on all along the hall and in the bathroom with the door open for her to see her way.

At night, when the scaries and ghosts stirred up by her memories and the stories her grandmother told her—of old-time hearses pulled by black horses with ebony plumes attached to their heads, and of swarms of flies converging on windowpanes after a death in the house, and of diamond-ring-wearing cats

sticking their paws into open fires, and of haunts of all kinds—
came into her room to scare her, she knew she didn't have to stay
and take it. Lena knew she could jump out of bed and dash down
the lit hallway with her eyes turned away from the big mirror in
the upstairs hall and knock on the door of her parents' room.

They almost always let her in and allowed her to climb onto
their wide firm mattress and snuggle down in the covers between
them. Her brothers Raymond and Edward teased her that she
would probably be found some morning squashed flat under the
weight of her parents, who had rolled together in the night. But
even as a tiny thing, Lena knew this was just jealous talk. Some
nights her father didn't come home after closing The Place at
midnight, and then Lena and her mother slept together, lying
close in the big bed. "Jonah claims he's got business to take care
of tonight," Nellie would mutter as they lay there. "But I know
what kind of business he has this late at night."

But no matter how many times Lena plunged into the darkness
surrounding her bed and made it to safety in the path of light
outside her door, she didn't quite trust the dark. She tried not
to think of it, but she knew that things with their heads turned
backward on their shoulders and some with no heads at all
roamed the world. And she was certain that they lurked in the
dark, because some of them routinely wandered past her bedroom door.

Whenever she remembered the first time she had come face-
to-face with such a creature, she shivered a little, no matter how
warm it was.

But as soon as her eyes opened this night, Lena knew that it
wasn't her bladder or a wispy creature floating through her room
that had woken her. It was a sound. She wasn't sure, but she
thought she had heard crying even before she awoke. She
brought her hand to her face just to make sure it was not she who
had been weeping, but all she felt there was the soft downy hairs
that dusted her cheeks.

It was a small sound that she heard, not steady and even like
a hum, but here and there in small gulps like a busted machine.

And she knew immediately why she had heard it. It came to her ear because she understood it. She knew that sound. It was like her own cries when she was brokenhearted about something she wanted very badly but couldn't have.

The sound drifted up to her on the night air from outside. The uncontrolled hiccupping cries came to her through the open screened window next to her bed, just like the call of the bob-white and her fat little babies who lived in the bushes at the edge of the yard.

"Bob-*white,* bob-*white,*" they called all evening and some mornings.

Lena sat up in bed and listened for a good long time before swinging her legs into the darkness to go look for the source of the noise. She had no wish to go wandering around by herself in the middle of the night, but her desire to find the source of the noise was stronger than her fear of what she might encounter in the dark. The sound clutched at her heart and drew her through the house.

That's grandmama's moonflowers, Lena said to herself as she stood in the lit hall upstairs, sniffing the perfume of the big white night-blooming flowers that her grandmother told her looked like ladies' fancy lacy umbrellas turned inside-out in a sudden storm. They grew on shiny-leaved vines that crawled all over the walls of the old brick house. She didn't know how she knew that the scent emanated from those blooms. She had never seen the flowers fully open, when her grandmother said their scent was strongest. They bloomed after her bedtime. By the time she got up each morning and ran outside to look at the flowers, they were already curled closed and limp, hanging lifeless from their horned seedpod shells with ants crawling all over them.

She made a quick promise to herself to go outside before this night was over to look at the legendary flowers in full bloom and stick her nose in their wide-open mouths and drink the scent she smelled now floating on the air. But as soon as she heard the sound again, the jerking weeping that had woken her, she forgot all about the moonflowers and continued walking down the lit hallway.

She was beginning to get that sick, fluttery morning feeling she got in her stomach whenever her mother or grandmother woke her up before dawn to get ready for an all-day picnic in the country. It was a sensation hard for Lena to describe because it was sort of sickening, like she might throw up any minute, but it wasn't altogether unpleasant because it excited her and told her something interesting was about to happen. Years later, when she first heard a nun in school speak about butterflies in her stomach, Lena screamed right out in class, "That's it!" and had to stand in the corner for the rest of the afternoon for being disruptive.

She stood at the top of the staircase next to the linen closet door a good while, listening to the weeping, waiting for her eyes to become adjusted to the darkness, and getting up her nerve. The staircase was a beautiful open oak structure that had a landing where the stairs turned in two sharp right angles and continued down in the opposite direction to the floor below. Moonlight streamed in through the big multipaned vaulted window, flooding the pale green landing which looked out over the nearby woods and the roof of the simple porch beneath it, splitting the darkness with its soft shafts of light.

A simple carved varnished oak banister ran along the left edge of the steps. Lena always thought the banister should have been shinier than it was, considering the number of times she and her brothers had slid down its length. If it hadn't been the middle of the night, she would have stopped descending the steps one by one and climbed aboard the handrail for one swift ride down to the landing, then another down to the ground floor.

But she didn't want to swoosh down into the arms of some headless thing in the dark at the bottom, so she walked down the steps carefully and slowly, watching her step and the space directly ahead of her. Each time she thought of turning back to the safety of her bed, the sound of the crying pulled her on.

At the bottom of the staircase she instinctively turned to the left and walked toward the sewing-room door. Now that she was downstairs, the sound she was following was muffled behind closed doors, and she couldn't be certain where it was coming from. But she thought it was from the direction of the screened porch that stood under her bedroom window. She opened the door in front of her and entered the sewing room, where it always looked like a small explosion had occurred. Spools of thread, bolts of various materials—solids, plaids, stripes, prints— and dress boxes filled with sewing patterns lay on the narrow twin bed and propped up against the walls and inside the open closet. On one wall two sewing machines sat catercorner to each other under a long overhead light. One was an old Singer in a sturdy, weathered walnut cabinet with a wrought-iron base and a worn foot-pedal, that her grandmother used. The other machine was also a Singer, but it was the newest model they made, in a modern oak cabinet. That's what her mother had asked for when she had taken Lena downtown to the dealership to purchase the machine for herself as a Christmas gift from the family. "I'd like to see your latest model," she had said in that haughty way her mother had of talking down to white salespeople when she was paying in cash, which she almost always did.

Cash was something her mother always seemed to have. Lena had seen her father bring in a brown paper bag full of money one day and throw it on the dining-room table, where her mother was cutting out a pretty little white Sunday dress for her. Without saying a word, her mother had looked in the bag and taken out a handful of bills which she rolled into a wad and stuffed down the front of her dress into her ample bra. Her father had just laughed and peeped down the front of her mother's dress into the well of her titties with a grin on his face. Then he picked up the bag and went on out the door. Her mother, the long sharp black-and-silver scissors in her hand, had gone back to the tiny pattern on the table with the strangest little smile on her face.

Two straight-backed chairs were pulled up to the machines

like soldiers waiting for orders. A pink corduroy cushion was in the seat of one chair; and a red chenille cushion lay on the seat of the other, with another pillow just like it propped up against the back.

Over in a corner stood a dusty model's stand with a wide straw hat thrown on its shoulders where its head should have been. Lena had been told that it was made in the shape of her grandmother's body when she was twenty years younger. But it was only used as decoration in the room now, because her mother and grandmother fitted clothes on each other when they were sewing for themselves. Considering how her grandmother sucked her teeth at Nellie all the time and the way her mother heaved her big breasts in heavy sighs at her grandmother, the two women usually made a pretty good team.

In the sewing room Lena walked especially carefully in her bare feet. She knew that pins and needles, escaped from their paper folders and their pin cushions shaped like plump red tomatoes, lay in wait at every step to prick her feet. Here the sound Lena was searching for was louder and clearer. Now she was sure it was coming from the porch on the other side of the next room. The sound was nearly as strong to her ear as it had been upstairs in her bed near the open window.

Moonlight, glowing through the pines' spiky needles, was streaming in every window like candlelight. Through the opened door to the music room, next to the sewing room, Lena saw that the door leading to the screened porch also stood open. Still stepping carefully for fear of pins and needles, she moved through the sewing room and into the music room past the beautiful dark wood piano. She took the opportunity to glide her hand across the smooth wood on the curved side of the piano as she walked past it.

Without stopping, she walked on to the open door leading to the screened porch, and the sound was right next to her ear.

The air out on the porch was so different from any she had ever smelled before that it stopped the child right in her tracks.

It was as different from morning or evening air as it was from the heat of the day. The scent of the moonflowers—it had to be the moonflowers—was intoxicating. Crickets still rubbed their hind legs together making an evening noise, but a couple of birds also chirped intermittently.

Is it almost morning or still night? Lena wondered to herself.

She half-expected colors to be different from those she had seen earlier in the evening: the wicker furniture red instead of white, the bricks of the house blue instead of red.

In this air, feeling like this, nothing bad could happen to me. I've been a baby to be afraid of the dark, she thought.

But when she looked around the porch and saw the outline of a figure stretched out on the wicker couch, she almost let out a little cry. The child's first thought was of ghosts and she started to dash back into the safety of the house, but something familiar about the shape on the sofa made her stay. As Lena wound her way to the sofa, she saw that it was her mother who lay there, her forehead resting on her folded arms, her shoulders shaking softly.

On such a gentle night it was even more confusing than it would have been at any other time to find her mother crying on the porch sofa. But there was no mistaking the sobs that made her mother's shoulders quiver.

At the sound of the child's footsteps on the shiny green floor, her mother sniffled a few times and turned her head on her arm to see Lena standing right next to her. Nellie's face looked as wretched as the sobs had sounded. All Lena wanted to do was make it better.

Little Lena reached up and patted her mother's face, wet with tears. "This my mama right here," she said.

Her mother looked as if she would burst into tears again. Instead she answered with a catch in her throat, "This my baby right here," and pulled the child up on the wicker sofa to lie snuggled in the curve that her chest, belly, and thighs made.

Satisfied that she had done all she could to comfort the crying woman, Lena fell asleep immediately. Her mother breathed a few convulsive sighs and followed her baby daughter into slumber.

They lay together that way until morning crept through the tall pines surrounding the house, long after Nellie felt the warm little stream of urine trickle through the tail of Lena's nightgown and completely soak the front of her shirt and shorts.

SEVEN

ഉ   ഉ

REAL

Lena was just five when she learned she was real. One day, the summer after she started going to Miss Russell's kindergarten class over on Pringle Street, Lena and her brothers Raymond and Edward were sitting in the light green station wagon with wood paneling on the side, waiting for their mother outside the old Piggly-Wiggly. The supermarket stood across the street from the Sears and Roebuck where the newly installed escalators, Mulberry's first set, had become the number-one attraction in town. There were so many people—children, mothers, adults, teenagers on Saturday-afternoon dates—waiting their turns to ride the moving stairs that one day the manager had been forced to close the store's doors in the middle of the work day to prevent a tragedy. They even wrote a story about it in the Sunday-morning newspaper.

"Threat of Stampede Shuts Sears' Doors," Lena's grandmother had read over her son's shoulder at the breakfast table. Then she chuckled to herself. She had never ridden the moving staircases and she didn't plan to. "Fools," she had muttered, her head an aurora of steam rising from a big serving bowl of buttery grits. "Would have served them right if they'd all been trampled."

Nellie had promised the three children at least four round-trips on the escalator if they sat there quietly in the car while she ran into the Piggly-Wiggly for a bag of rice.

"That's all I need, one little bag of rice. Just for you children, your grandmama, and me. You know your daddy doesn't eat rice, it makes him sick to his stomach, so he says. And damn if he doesn't refuse to buy it either. So will you children please, please sit here and stay in this car till I come out. And you boys, if you could, would you keep your little sister from getting out of this car and running all over the parking lot and darting out in the street and letting a big Mack truck run over her. That's the least you can do," she said in one breath. Then she blew a wisp of auburn-tinted hair out of her face, turned, and headed briskly into the store's wide glass door, her round low butt twisting prettily inside her beige sleeveless linen sheath. The soles of her high-heeled summer mules flapped gently against the smooth heels of her feet as she walked away, and the heel tips made clacking sounds each time they hit the Tarmac of the grocery-store parking lot.

Raymond, twelve then and tall for his age, was sitting in the front seat by himself on the passenger side, his legs stretched out all the way to the front of the floorboard of the big green wagon. Lena stood in back with Edward, who sat directly behind his brother.

Lena was trying to get her lips just right so she could whistle. She was having a hard time learning. Whenever the boys tried to teach her at home, her father would say, "Girl, stop that whistling. A whistling woman and a crowing hen never come to no good end."

The boys talked lazily over the back of the front seat, not bothering to look at one another. They were just swapping loose talk to stir the air further, with Edward stuttering every now and then when he became excited by the prospect of the escalator rides.

"I wish Mama would hurry up," Raymond said. "It's gonna be crowded on those escalators before long." He shifted his position in the front seat and propped his big feet on the car's dashboard. Wide and covered with yellowish-brown leather, the dashboard was a steady and sure pilot house in the huge ship of a station wagon. All the windows were rolled down to catch a breeze from off the muddy Ocawatchee River on the other side of the highway from Sears. But not a breath of wind was stirring, Lena could tell. She was standing in the back on the hump that rose in in the center of the floorboard, so she would have felt a cooling breeze before anyone else.

The hump was a special spot of hers, but her favorite place in the car was the spot in the middle of the front seat, with the seam dividing the backrest going straight down her spine when she sat straight up. That spot was truly special.

For one thing it placed her right in front of the dials of the radio. Even with the sound off, the face of the radio seemed to glow. The volume knob to the left of the dial had tiny ridges in it. And to the right the knob on the tuning stem was missing, leaving the metal prong sticking out alone.

Unlike her two brothers, one of whom had broken the radio knob, she was allowed to play with the radio as much as she liked, punching the buttons and turning the knob until the noise and movement got on her mother's nerves. Then she had to stop immediately. But there weren't too many mechanical things that she was not allowed to touch—for a little while at least—because she had the ability to "put the magic" on stuff. That's what her family had always told her.

Lena couldn't remember the first time she had put the magic on something, or where the idea had originated. It seemed to Lena to have always been part of her family life. Most people would have considered it a family joke, but her family took it seriously. If a stranger was present when Lena put the magic on something, someone in the family would explain casually, "You know Lena was born with a veil over her face."

If the car didn't start after two or three tries, everyone in the car would turn to Lena.

"Come on, baby," her mother would say, "put the magic on this car for us so I can get these boys to school in this rain." Or one of the boys would say, "Let Lena put the magic on the car so we won't be late for church again. I don't want to start tramping in late every Sunday like the Fosters 'cause Sister Mary Margaret Therese will blame us for it Monday in school."

Lena loved this ritual of putting the magic on things. With no very serious realization of what she was doing, she would lean over; rub her little hands, still chubby at the knuckles, on the steering wheel a few times; jingle the ring of keys sticking out from the ignition; then sit back and wait for her mother to start the car, which usually turned over right away.

She could put the magic on just about anything: a radio, the television, a stuck door, a rusty ice-cream churn. Her magic was sometimes only temporary, but it nearly always worked for a time. It was a stopgap method until the TV-repair man came or until dinner was over.

But the real attraction of sitting front and center in the car was the veil of protection that enveloped her there. When she sat up front, she could always count on her mother in the driver's seat reaching over with her arm extended, palm flat against Lena's little chest, fingers spread wide like a web, holding her safely upright whenever she had to bring the big green car to a sudden stop.

"Ho-o-o-ld the baby," her mother would intone.

Lena's family did the "Hold the baby" for her alone and continued to do it long after she was anything like a baby. The ritual, right down to the magic words "Hold the baby" spoken just so, made Lena feel safe and warm and looked-after. Her brothers, who routinely terrorized her, even got into the habit of doing it when one of them sat up front next to her. "Ho-o-o-ld the baby," they would say with the same singsong inflection as their mother and would reach over to save her pretty little face from crashing into the broad dashboard.

While they were parked at the Piggly-Wiggly, Lena settled for standing on the hump in the back floorboard. From here she could see out all the windows, front, back, and sides, without having to strain up on her toes or scramble about. Besides that, in this spot she could also look at her reflection in the rear-view mirror.

She liked the face that she saw in the mirror, its caramel-candy color, its long oval shape. Even though her mother sometimes called Lena "you little horse-faced heifer" when she was exasperated. The insult was lost on her. She liked the sound of the words.

"Horse-faced heifer, horse-faced heifer," Lena would repeat to herself softly, enjoying the feel of the air as it rushed over her lips. Then she'd laugh and make her mother laugh with her. The annoyance would melt from her mother's face like a scoop of ice cream on a hot day.

Her lips were wide, full, and shaped like an arrow's bow turned on its side, with a deep cleft above her top lip that was soft with a faint sun-reddened down. Whenever her chatter got to be too much for her mother's nerves, Nellie would gently lay her finger on the cleft above the child's mouth the way *her* mother said an angel in heaven had done to keep her quiet. Then she would say, "Hush, baby."

Lena's nose was her father's: long from the bridge to the tip and slightly flared. Lena had the ability to flare her nostrils as if she were yawning whenever she wanted to. She performed this fascinating trick for her brothers whenever she had a favor to ask. If she would "bull" her nose, as the boys called it, ten times in a row, they would give her a ride on their bikes or share the brightly colored Sunday funny papers with her.

Whenever she looked into the car's rear-view mirror, she smiled at her reflection. But this time when she caught sight of herself, she was shocked by the image. She saw a person staring back.

For the first time she saw eyes that were obviously connected to a soul, a beating heart, throbbing veins, a growling stomach, a brain. In a flash, as quick as she could blink her eyes a couple of times to be sure that the person in the mirror was her, she saw that she was *REAL!*

The notion struck her speechless for a moment. The childish tune she was la-di-da-ing to herself trailed off to nothing. This was a revelation. It was a thought on a plane she had never probed before. *She was real!*

She could breathe, she realized as she inhaled and exhaled deeply. Uh-*huh.* She could think, she could see, she could move any part of her body just by thinking of it. She wiggled her nose, lifted an index finger to right before her eyes, and spun the finger in small circles from its socket at her knuckle. Then she held her breath until she became dizzy. She was real. She couldn't imagine why she had not thought of it before.

Looking into those eyes, her eyes, almost frightened her. She half-expected some other creature who looked just like her to jump out of the mirror. That wouldn't have surprised her. It had happened before, but it didn't happen this time. She was this living, breathing, exciting person. The revelation was so exhilarating, she never even considered giving in to fear as she usually did when she saw ghosts and other strange things. And somehow she knew it would be okay to tell.

"Edward," she whispered to her brother sitting next to her without taking her eyes off the face in the rear-view mirror. "Edward, I'm real."

Edward and Raymond stopped their boyish chatter, their bragging, topping each other about how many times they would ride the escalators at Sears if given unlimited time there. They both stopped talking at the same time and silently looked at their little sister long and hard.

Her older brother Raymond was the more compassionate one, who didn't harbor Edward's resentment toward her for having been born right after him and taking over his place as the baby of the family. Lena could usually count on Raymond's taking pity on her. He was the one who carried her carefully—not clumsily, as Edward did—upstairs when she fell asleep in front of the television.

"Raymond, I'm really real," she continued with her gaze fixed on the rectangular mirror. "For real, Raymond—look in the glass. I can see me. I'm real."

The three of them sat silently for a few seconds. Raymond turned around all the way in the front seat.

"You real crazy, that's wh-what you are," Edward said, and Raymond laughed.

"Yeah," Raymond added, "you're real crazy, all right."

They both laughed again, but it was an uneasy laughter. It reminded Lena of the evening they were supposed to be watching her for their mother and instead took her, on the back of Raymond's bike, into the graveyard at the top of Pleasant Hill because they wanted to stand on her tiny feet, look over her shoulder, and gaze into the night in search of a ghost. Grandmama had assured them ever since little Lena's birth that this was a certain legacy of her being born with a veil over her face—that others could see ghosts when looking over her shoulder.

The boys hadn't seen any spirits as they gazed over the top of Lena's head and shoulders. But the whole thing—the excursion into the falling darkness, going into the graveyard, her suddenly overexcited brothers leaping from grave marker to grave marker in a half-crazed dance—unnerved Lena. She wished she could tell them that if they wanted to see ghosts they need only go up to the attic at home and touch the baby's portrait turned to the wall.

In the bright noon of the late summer day, the boys got a good look at their sister's face and saw something new there, some new understanding. The look scared them as if they had really seen a ghost.

But Lena was no ghost. And she didn't realize until she saw her spirit look back at her in the mirror that that was just what she had feared: that she was not a real girl but a ghost just like those creatures who haunted her.

"I'm real," she kept whispering, until Raymond called a halt to "all that crazy shit." He tried to distract her with talk of upcoming rides on the Sears escalator. But the Sears escalator could not compete with her new knowledge: she was a real person.

She could hardly wait for her mother to come back to the car so she could tell her about the discovery. As soon as Nellie rushed out of the grocery store carrying a small brown paper sack with one large bag of rice inside, she started repeating her promise of four rides on the escalator so she could avert the whining she anticipated. Nellie always swore she was delicate and couldn't stand too much noise, but when things got busy down at Jonah's bar and grill, Lena had seen her mother swing skillets of hot grease and quarts of beer with a hearty, determined strength while keeping an eye on the cash register. Still, her mother insisted that she was "delicate," easy to wear out, easy to bruise, seeming to enjoy the myth of her delicacy.

When her mother slid into the car, Lena was ready to pounce on her with her news. "Mama, I'm real," she was going to say, so proud of her revelation.

But the boys saw it coming and sat up, ready to deflect their baby sister's prattle. They knew that their mother sometimes took Lena's ravings seriously, and they didn't want their sister's crazy talk to interfere with their upcoming escalator rides—talk about she's real and all that. Their little sister was such a fool sometimes. But they had to be real careful with the things she said, because her crazy talk could sometimes get inside their heads and gnaw away at their thoughts until they gave in and began to think about it.

It happened all the time: Lena would say something crazy like "Look at me in the mirror, I'm real," and by the end of the week the boys would find themselves staring in the bathroom mirror, gazing into their own eyes and thinking that they too were real, a thought that had never occurred to them before.

Lena was like that. She was just five, but already she could read as well as Edward, and when the family sat around listening to homework reading, she asked the strangest questions about the history and geography and catechism that the boys were studying in school at Blessed Martin de Porres.

"How can the President be the leader of all the people in the country when I haven't even seen him and looked at him in person?" Or, "If God made me to know, love, and serve him in this world and be happy with him in the next, why do we have to be in this world at all? Why don't we all get dressed up and go to the next world and be happy?"

Regardless of her moods, their mother responded to each and every one of Lena's questions with a seriousness that sometimes made the boys mad.

"What's that, baby?" her mother asked Lena as she settled in behind the wheel of the station wagon with a paper bag in one hand and her purse in the other.

"I'm real," little Lena said proudly. The boys knew they had to act quickly. Raymond was the first to make his move. He drew his long legs toward his body and lunged for the paper bag his mother was about to place down between them on the seat.

"What'd you get, Mama?" he asked as he tore the bag from her hand and began riffling through it. "You buy anything for us?"

Edward followed his brother's lead.

"Yeah, anyth-th-thing for us?" he asked as he pulled the bag from his brother's hand. The bag tore down the middle, leaving each boy holding half of the brown paper sack and the bag of Uncle Ben's rice lying on the car floor.

"Just look at what the two of you have done!" Nellie yelled at the boys. "Just look!"

"Mama," Lena interrupted, pulling on the shoulder of the woman's dress. "Mama, I'm real."

"Just a minute, baby. Now, how many goddamn times do I have to tell you not to go grabbing at my packages the minute I get in the car. You know how I hate that, you know it!"

Lena tried again. "Mama, listen, I just found out. I'm real."

Her mother was angry now and would not be stopped. "But the second you see me with a bag in my hand, you go to grabbing and snatching it like you ain't never had nothing in your lives. You'd think you were born in Switchblade Alley."

The boys had noticed that their mother got the prettiest red glow to her golden brown skin when she became slightly enraged, as she usually did at least once a day. The glow was beginning to light up her sweaty face now as she lectured them about being so damn wild. Lena, who was standing at her mother's shoulder, shaking the fleshy part of her mother's arm to gain her attention, could almost smell Nellie's exasperation with the boys. In the adventure stories Lena read in the magazines her father left lying by the toilet, the women all had flashing black eyes. Even though Nellie's eyes were a deep rich brown, they too flashed with anger.

"Mama, I'm trying to tell you something, Mama, listen to me, Mama." Lena kept trying to chip away at her mother's distraction. She shook the woman's arm rhythmically and insistently at each word.

"Lena, stop that," her mother said as she lightly slapped the girl's hand away from her shoulder and continued blessing the boys out. The child snatched her hand away before the lick landed, and flopped back into the seat, with its prickly straw covers, a hurt expression on her face.

"You boys act just like some little wild younguns raised in the woods sometimes. Raymond, you're almost thirteen now, and you're still as big a damn fool as your brother."

Both boys ducked their heads and looked offended at the double insult. It didn't stop their mother. She was on a roll.

"Neither one of you little fanatical fools ever worked a day in your lives, never even hit a lick at a snake in the things you supposed to do around the house every day. And here you come every damn time I go in a store yelling 'What's for me? What you got for me?' What the hell you think I got for you? Not a damn thing, that's what I got for you. Did you give me any money to buy some damn thing? No, you never hit a lick at a snake to earn any little pocket money, but the first ones to go tearing open my packages as soon as I step my foot in . . ."

Lena could take it no more. She had something important to say and she was going to say it. As her mother continued to fuss, she stood up on the hump in the back floorboard and screamed at the top of her lungs, *"I am REAL!"*

It worked. All other sound in the car stopped as her mother and brothers spun around to look at her. The sound of her voice seemed to echo inside the cavernous car, then roll out the windows in the direction of the slow-moving Ocawatchee to be lost in the noise of the traffic passing on the street.

"Shit," Edward hissed under his breath and fell back in his seat with a resigned sigh. Raymond mimicked his brother and slumped back in his seat, too.

The sound of Lena's scream seemed to hit Nellie in the face and relax nearly all the muscles that had tightened up there. The only muscle left flexed was the one controlling the furrows that were raised quizzically between her thin eyebrows. And she kept that one tight as she sat looking at her little girl standing in the back of the car. Now that Lena had said what she meant to, she felt so relieved and unburdened she just looked back at her mother with a pleasant smile on her face.

"Lena," Nellie said, lowering her own voice, "there's no need for you to yell like that in this car. What's gotten into you?"

"Mama, I told you, I'm real," Lena said matter-of-factly.

Nellie turned her head to one side, trying to figure out her youngest child. She had always known that Lena was going to be different from her boys—ever since her birth and all that hocus-pocus old Nurse Bloom had been talking about—Nellie had known that. But the child unnerved her sometimes with the things she said and did. So often her thoughts and actions left no room for Nellie to respond in a sensible way.

"Now, what am I supposed to say to a five-year-old who screams that she's real?" Nellie asked herself.

She just sighed and turned back to the steering wheel. As she started up the car, she said, "Well, of course, you're real, baby. You're our Lena. Now, let's get on over to Sears before the escalators get all filled up."

As Nellie slammed the car in reverse and sped over to the Sears and Roebuck, she considered taking Lena by the hospital to see if Nurse Bloom could tell her something about the girl's strange ways. But when she looked in the rear-view mirror and caught a glimpse of Lena smiling to herself unselfconsciously, she dismissed the idea.

Lena wasn't too disturbed that no one in her family seemed as impressed as she was with her discovery. She assumed it was just another thing she had said or thought that made her household uncomfortable. Like the time she described her grand-mama's wedding dress right down to the ripped hem that the bride had gotten caught on her white shoe back in 1901. "Musta seen the pictures," Grandmama had muttered nervously and changed the subject.

Sometimes she could see her brothers, mother, and grand-mother pull away, almost recoil from her, when she said or did something they weren't expecting, which could be just about anything. It didn't really hurt her feelings. It was always just a fleeting look or feeling, anyway, and she never doubted the love her family felt for her—even when she was mad with all of them. She just figured that their reactions were part of the way life was, like her seeing ghosts and knowing not to tell anyone about it.

Anyhow, when she made the people in her household too edgy, she knew she could always scoot across the street to the house where nothing she said or did seemed to disturb anyone.

EIGHT

❦   ❦

HOUSES

Lena's house was bigger than was needed for a family of six. There were rooms that they didn't even use regularly and rooms that she never saw in other people's houses.

Besides a living room, dining room, kitchen, and six bedrooms, there was a breakfast room, a music room, a sewing room, and a walk-in pantry. There was a long, narrow linen closet big enough to play in, which was lined with shelves loaded down with packs of freshly laundered sheets and tablecloths always neatly wrapped in heavy green paper from the cleaners. And some of the hallways were as big as rooms. Even the basement, with its huge steam furnace and cold damp concrete floor, was partitioned into rooms, which were used for the laundry and storage. And there was still enough space left for the heavy pool table with its pretty green felt cover, which her father had had men move into the basement during the night.

The little girl loved the big solid brick house with its porches on every side and its attic making it look like a three-story building. Its size and structure, the way it seemed set in the ground firmly—not up on legs of brick and cement the way some houses on her street were—pleased her. She was sure no wind could

62

ever move her house, no catastrophe could be so bad that it would shake its foundations.

The house was originally built as a residence for teachers of a black private school located in front of it on the street. But the school, which both of her parents had attended, had been razed years before Lena's birth. Kudzu and small pine saplings, their seeds blown from the adjoining woods, had taken over the vacant land where the huge school had stood, making the house barely visible from the street.

The house didn't even look as if it belonged to the neighborhood, because it sat so far back from the street and was surrounded by tall Georgia pines. The trees kept a soft blanket of pine needles on the ground summer and winter.

As though the house were a community unto itself with a mind of its own, its real front porch didn't face the street. At the official front of the house, the entrance they rarely used because it was so inconveniently situated, there was a small open porch with two plain painted wooden posts supporting the roof. The floor was made of cement edged in the same old red brick that the house was made of, and two wide brick steps led to the porch.

Her mother always kept two Boston ferns hanging from the eaves inside the pillars, where people who didn't have enough sense to see that this wasn't the right entrance to use bumped their heads when they came to ring the bell there. In winter, when the ferns withered and died, she just left the pots of rich Georgia dirt hanging in their places.

Another porch extended from the kitchen. It was enclosed and sat at the top of twelve smooth cement steps. Here Lena's family stacked crates of Coca-Colas and empty bottles, mops, buckets, rags, brooms, the ice-cream churn, garden tools, moldy umbrellas and shoes, and an earthenware crock jar.

Down an embankment from the porch, the land sloped gently to a narrow strip of a brook that meandered past the house from the top of Pleasant Hill and vanished into the woods. Although Lena herself had never been allowed to follow the stream to its destination, her brothers Raymond and Edward told her stories of a small waterfall and a glassy smooth pond surrounded by luscious blooming plants that the stream fed. Her grandmama would send the boys into the woods with shovels, buckets, and instructions. They would return hours later with white and pink dogwood trees already in bloom, ready to be transplanted into the yard around the house.

Lena would have given anything to see the pond herself, but she didn't have enough anything—possessions, tricks, charms, information for blackmail—not enough anything to force the boys to take her into the woods. They knew if anything happened to Lena while she was in their care, their grandmama would skin 'em alive, their father would beat them until he was breathless, and their mother would promise to beat their butts till they roped like okra, even if they knew for certain she would wear herself out trying to hit them with whatever was handy, long before they had been properly whipped. Often their mother would throw her hands up to heaven in exasperation and declare, "I just can't take this aggravation anymore. I'm going out in the woods and live and eat with the animals. Ya'll can just have this house. I'll just live with the animals in the woods."

The first and only time the boys had tried to help Lena cross the stream to the wooded side, she had slipped on a mossy rock and fallen into the icy water, getting her thick nappy hair soaked and splitting the skin on her left kneecap. Her wails brought her mother and grandmother running down the embankment with swift punishment for the boys right then, and even more when their father came home for dinner.

"Go get the belt," Jonah had barked at the boys even before their mother had finished explaining the bandaged cut on Lena's knee. Then, for three days in a row, their father had repeated his order and the whippings each time he looked at Lena's little scarred knee and her big brown eyes.

"You gonna ever do that again?" their father had said, slightly out of breath from flailing Raymond with one of his big heavy leather belts.

"No, no, no!" Raymond screamed as he dangled from his father's tight grasp on his left forearm. "I won't never do it again!"

"Are you gonna do it again? Are you gonna let your baby sister go down to that stream, let her go into the woods and hurt herself?"

"No, Daddy, no, I ain't gonna do it no more!" Raymond swore as he danced in a perfect circle around his father.

"Are you gonna do that again? Be that careless?"

"No, I cross my heart, I promise, I swear!" Raymond had screamed.

His father wasn't satisfied. "Yes, you will," he said, and continued beating the boy, forgetting to save some strength for Edward's whipping.

After that, if she even looked like she was thinking of going to the woods on the other side of the brook, Raymond and Edward went running to the house screaming, "Lena's headed for the woods! Lena's headed for the woods!"

The porch on another side of the house was directly opposite the formal front porch. It was really more of a small covered patio than a porch. At Christmastime her mother got the boys to climb up on the roof's flat surface and string colored lights and pine garland from the woods around the outside of the big vaulted window at the landing of the staircase inside.

The doors at all the entrances to the house were oversized to Lena, but the one at this entrance seemed to take over the tiny foyer. At the top of the door was a big glass window with beveled edges. Lena understood why her mother had never put a curtain at that window. The girl too loved the unobstructed view of the woods from that clear glass. The only drawback to the glass was that unwanted visitors, like Father O'Donnell, the priest from church, could look in and see who was home when no one felt like answering the door.

Whenever her mother or grandmother walked around the house in her bra and panties, trying to relax after an especially hot and frustrating day of shopping or working in confining rubber girdles and hot nylon hose, Lena made sure she stayed nearby in the house because she knew Father O'Donnell would show up soon.

The Irish priest's pockmarked red face would appear magically at the door's wide window, his thinning red hair standing up all over his head, his green eyes darting from side to side as he tried to glimpse a bit of movement anywhere within his view. Once he had seen someone, he had her—no matter how quickly she darted out of his line of vision and hid behind a door.

"Oh, good woman, good woman, open the door, open the door. It's only I, your parish priest, come to visit your lovely family, lovely family."

And if the door had been left unlocked, he would turn the knob and come on in as if he were a welcome neighbor. Lena's mother and grandmother would squeal and run for cover as the priest, his dusty black suit wrinkled and damp with perspiration, followed the screams of his retreating prey on upstairs or into the kitchen or out on the side screened porch.

"No, no, Father, wait! Stay right there, no, don't come up here, Father. Go on in the living room, go on, Father. We'll be down in just a minute," Lena's mother would yell over her shoulder.

"Lena, go on down there and keep that crazy priest company till we can get some clothes on," her mother would say.

Lena knew just what to do. She would run down the stairs to head the priest off at the landing and start talking as loudly as she could to try to drown out her grandmother.

"That damn fool was gonna come right on up here. I don't care if he is a priest, somebody is gonna shoot him dead one day," her grandmother's voice would float down the stairs behind Lena. "I can see the headline now: 'Irate Mate Shoots Intruding Paddy Priest.'"

"Hello, Father," Lena would shout, taking the priest's soft dry hand, which felt as if he had just dusted it with talcum powder, in her own and leading him back downstairs toward the living room. "Mama and Grandma getting dressed. They want you to wait for them in here."

"Oh, yes, child, what a lovely child, lovely child. And your name is . . ."

"I'm Lena, Father," she said with a giggle.

"Yes, that's right, Lena. Would you like to hear a poem, a poem for the lovely child?"

Lena knew she need not answer. She would hear a poem whether she liked it or not.

" 'The wise old owl sat on an oak,' " the priest began.

Lena left him in the living room reciting and headed across the hall to the dining room.

" 'The more he heard, the less he spoke,' " he continued without her.

She was barely tall enough to reach the handles of the metal liquor caddy that stood in the corner by the window. She gave it a push and began rolling it back across the hall toward the living room.

" 'The less he spoke, the more he heard,' " Father O'Donnell continued.

The bottles of Old Forester and Beefeater and Chivas Regal and Courvoisier and tall and short glasses on the caddy rattled a tune like a one-man band as she hit the door jamb, pushed the service cart into the living room, and pulled it to a stop right next to the parish priest sitting on the sofa.

" 'Now, wasn't he a wise old bird?' " the priest finished.

By the time her mother and grandmother joined them, the good father was well into his fifth poem and second rye, straight up.

The porch on the last side of the house was everyone's favorite. It ran the length of the house and was enclosed by a dusty-smelling screen and high hedges all around that made it a cool and private retreat. The living room's French doors and the music room's heavy door opened onto this porch. The porch's screen door was the entrance that most people who had good sense used.

It was on this porch that the family sat and shelled peas in the summertime, and it was here they all sprawled after a heavy Sunday dinner.

The porch was furnished just like a room, with heavy wicker furniture painted shiny white and high-backed cane-bottom rocking chairs painted forest green. The long wicker sofa and wingback wicker chairs were piled with forest-green cushions of polished cotton that her mother and grandmother had made and stuffed themselves.

Forest green was one of her mother's favorite colors. "It's so cool," she said. She had Whit, the man who did all their repairs and odd jobs, paint all the wooden trim on the house in the same green. Even the wooden floor and ceiling of the porch were painted a glossy forest green. The color scratched easily with all the traffic that passed over it. But her mother didn't care and said she loved the way the color looked in summer.

The white wicker sofa was placed between the living-room and music-room doors, along the brick wall of the porch that was the side of the house. A long white wooden table with wicker legs was set in front of it with big ashtrays on top. Chairs were scattered around the edge of the porch near the other three screened walls, with small round metal white-lacquered tables beside them. Boston and maidenhair ferns cascaded around the porch from hooks in the ceiling and from old-fashioned wicker stands in the corners.

In the spring and summertime, this porch was where her parents had their parties. The women in bright halter-topped dresses and pedal-pushers and sleeveless blouses; the men in big short-sleeved cotton shirts splashed with wild colors and roomy beige slacks gathered at the waist with tan leather belts.

Lena loved these times out on the wide cool porch with highballs and cigarette smoke and men's loud talk and women's soft perfume. She and the boys were only allowed to stay a little while at their parents' parties, just long enough to speak to everybody and ask about the visitors' children. Even though she was the youngest, Lena usually stayed the longest, because the boys, five and seven years older than she, soon tired of the attention and noise and sneaked off to watch television upstairs in their parents' room. But Lena never tired of it. Besides, she had to stick around long enough to drink the first sip—Jonah called it "the poison"—off her father's first bourbon and Coke with a wedge of lemon in it. She had to walk around the dining-room table and sample some of the beautifully arranged food her mother and grandmother had worked on all day. And she had to go sit awhile with her mother's childhood friend Mary, who wore hats so stylishly that she had a whole closet full of them. Lena's "Aunt Mary" would ask her about her day and listen to the answer with such wide-eyed interest that Lena never doubted her curiosity about mud pies and skinned knees.

But then, just when Lena was beginning to enjoy herself, her father would announce, "Isn't it about your bedtime, young lady?" Her face would fall, her brown eyes would fill with tears, and for Lena the party would be over. She'd run off to her grandmother, her heart broken anew as if, instead of a family ritual, it were happening for the first time.

Lena usually played in her own yard, but one afternoon after Miss Russell's kindergarten class she wandered away from her house down the long dirt drive to the street and discovered a treasure. Even though Lena had a feeling she had already broken some basic rule of the house by leaving her yard by herself, she knew better than to make matters worse by crossing the street by herself. Even if Mrs. Willback's big white wooden house was very tempting with its red brick porch and steps that stood next to a garden that was so big it looked like a small farm. Instead she satisfied her yen for exploration by walking up the road a bit on her side of the street.

She walked past the blackberry patch where in summer her brothers, dressed in long pants to protect their legs, scrambled through the briar and brambles in search of the dark juicy fruit her grandmother and Nellie made into the rich buttery cobblers the family ate after dinner.

Nellie would be amazed at Raymond's and Edward's bravery. She warned them that "snake's grandmammy" lived among that tangle of seductive growth. But the boys just waved aside their mother's protestations with the big tin pans they carried and waded into the bush. They weren't a bit afraid of snakes. In fact they liked them. Once Lena had sneaked into Edward's room when he was away and found a shoebox under his bed with tiny eggs inside lying on a mat of dried grass. Inside one of the cracked eggs was the shriveled body of a baby snake. But she never told her mother.

Everyone knew that nothing exceeded Nellie's fear of snakes. Once, when Lena was at home alone with her mother, Nellie killed a small snake she had found behind the freezer with nothing but a hammer, banging away at the wiggling, writhing reptile and calling on Jesus the whole time. "I always will believe one of Jonah's women put that snake there," she said later as she stood at the liquor caddy drinking straight from the bottle, trying to settle her nerves.

The trees and brush that grew on the other side of the berry patch had been thinned near the stream, which ran parallel to the street. And although it wasn't really the woods, the real woods, where her brothers disappeared for hours, Lena still approached it as an adventure. She picked her way steadily along the edge of the brush by the side of the road until she came to a patch of weeds in flower with soft yellow blooms.

"Oooohhh," she said in surprise at the sudden bright buttercup color among the browns and greens.

As much as her grandmother worked, raked, fertilized, and watered her garden, few of her flowers were still in bloom so late in the fall. Yet the flowers growing along the side of the road made it look as if it were the middle of summer. They stood there, bending in the wind as if they had been waiting all day for Lena to come along. But when she stooped beside the flowers and reached out to pluck one of the saffron heads bobbing in the breeze, a low-pitched voice stopped her.

"Uh-uhn. Don't touch that thing, it smell like do-do," the voice cautioned.

Lena jumped to her feet like a skittish cat and looked around with widened eyes.

Across the street from her a little girl with dark glassy eyes was standing under a wide, low-hanging tree with half a piece of fruit resembling a big red jeweled brooch in her hand.

Lena's first inclination was to greet the little girl with glee. Then she remembered the child in the picture that used to hang over her grandmother's bed and decided to hold her delight in check. Lena knew that with no one here to protect her, this other child could very easily rise from the dusty ground where she stood and soar into the treetops. For a while Lena had thought that ghosts appeared to her at or around first dark. Her grandmother, when she told ghost stories, always said they came out at midnight. But now that Lena was going on six, she knew that they could appear at any time they wanted to appear.

The two girls stood for a while on opposite sides of the street, surveying each other from head to toe. Lena saw a dark brown girl a little larger than she, whose shiny black eyes were almost level with hers. The girl was slightly swaybacked, or perhaps just looked that way because her stomach was a bit protrudent. At one time her thick short hair had been combed into a neat pattern of six plaits braided into one another from her high broad forehead down the back of her head. But the short edges of her hair had worked themselves away from the braids and formed a roll like a diadem around her face.

She wore a green plaid dress in a style something like the red one Lena wore. But Lena's dress, made with love and care by her grandmother with white smocking across the chest and around the tail of the full skirt, was clean and lightly starched. The dress the little girl across the street wore was not only stained down the front and soiled in the back where she had sat down in the dirt, but it was also torn at the waist and ripped under the left arm of the short, puffed sleeve. And the left sleeve itself was no longer puffed like the right one because the elastic in its hem had broken and the material hung limply on the child's arm.

Lena wondered how long it had been since the girl had rubbed any Jergens lotion or Vaseline on her body after she got out of the bathtub. Her arms, legs, elbows, and feet were nearly gray with dry scaly ash. If Grandmama got hold of her, she'd have her shining, Lena said to herself.

"This damn ash," the old lady would grumble as she coated Lena's legs with globs of Vaseline she had rubbed between her hands until it was warm and nearly liquid. "It's like a plague visited on the children—the female children—of Africa." Then she would rub the excess Vaseline off Lena's legs with a damp towel. "Even Lena Horne and Dorothy Dandridge have to put up with it. Good-looking Lena leaning up against one of those big white pillars singing her heart out musta been thinking, I hope my elbows ain't ashy."

Lena hugged the red cardigan her mother had bought for her at Joy's Children's Shop in the nearby white neighborhood close to her body as she examined the other girl's bare arms and naked rusty feet stuck down in a pair of stiff-looking brown oxfords. Just the sight of the girl standing there in the crisp fall air without anything on her arms and legs made Lena shiver a bit.

Finally Lena swallowed hard and broke the silence as they continued to eye each other. "Are you really a little girl?" Lena asked the child in a voice barely loud enough for the girl to hear across the distance of the street.

The girl's eyes crinkled up at the corners and sparkled brighter as she threw her head back slightly and let out a deep laugh. Then, without looking either way, she dashed across the street to Lena.

"You so crazy," the little girl said merrily as she landed on Lena's side of the street. "What you mean, am I real? I'm as real as you is. Here, feel my hand. What's that feel like to you? You want a piece of pomegranate? It's one of the last ones we got last month. Be careful, don't swallow the seeds. A tree'll grow up in you. How old you is? I'm gonna be seven soon, but I ain't in school yet. Mama ain't got a chance to 'roll me yet. Let's play in the stream. You wanna be friends?"

Lena simply nodded yes to all the girl's questions and followed her to the edge of the icy water and squatted down next to her. She was pleased to have someone other than family to play with, especially after she was certain that her new friend was indeed a little girl just like her, not a creature sent from another world to Forest Avenue to torment her and then disappear.

They played there in silence at the stream's edge for some time, collecting small rocks worn smooth and shiny under the water's flow and building them into shapes and dams beside the shoals of the water before Lena thought to turn to her new playmate and ask, "What's your name?"

Without looking up from the patty of wet sand she was molding in her hands, the little girl said, "Puddin' Tame. Ask me again, I'll tell you the same." Then she looked at Lena out of the side of her dark eyes and laughed slyly at the quizzical look on Lena's face.

"Girl," she said, "don't you know nothing? That's what everybody says when you ask them something. Come on now, you do it. What's your name?"

"My name's Lena," Lena said proudly.

The girl nearly fell into the water laughing. "No, no, no," she screamed and laughed. Then she grabbed Lena's shoulders with her wet sandy hands and hugged her to her smelly little body in delight.

"Girl, you sho' mo' is funny," she said and her eyes crinkled up again.

Lena didn't know what to do with this cloak of teasing affection that her new friend was embracing her with. She didn't think she had said anything funny. It all made her a bit confused, and it showed on her face. The girl looked at Lena and dropped her teasing tone quickly. "My name is Sarah," she said seriously and stuck out her hand politely the way Lena had seen grown men do to each other on the street.

The two little girls shook hands solemnly, then giggled.

Lena loved the girl immediately. She wanted to take Sarah home with her right then to show her off to her mama and grandmama, but Sarah said, "I got to go home myself. I'm watching my sisters and brother." And she pointed back across the street to the cluster of four wooden shotgun houses built up on legs of cinder blocks. Each house was surrounded with a patch of fine gray dust for front and back yards, and had clotheslines in back crisscrossing each other and a bunch of young children on the porch.

The four were almost identical—peeling gray paint, unscreened front porches with parts of the railings missing, curtains at only a few of the windows—but they looked nothing like any of the other houses on the steep street. Although most of the other houses were smaller than Lena's, they were palaces compared to the four sad sisters across from where Lena and Sarah played.

The trees that grew between Sarah's row of houses and the Willbacks' big white one were still full of orange and red leaves, which helped the houses not look so shabby. But the brown house trimmed in cream on the other side of the houses, where the old man lived, showed them all up to hell. The old man's neatly kept lawn and the bucket plants on his front porch made his neighbors' dusty yards and bare porches look thrown away.

"Which one is yours?" Lena wanted to know.

"That one on the end, next to the big chinaberry tree," Sarah answered. "Where do you live?"

Lena turned around and saw that she could barely make out the green roof of her own place through the trees of the woods and pointed in the general direction of the big brick house.

Sarah drew in her breath and her eyes widened with excitement.

"I'll come visit you first thing in the morning," Sarah promised right away. "I always wanted to see inside that house." Then she darted back across the street right in front of a passing car without giving it a glance. The car, a large green Oldsmobile, blew its horn and swerved crazily to miss her.

They waved to each other one last time, then Lena turned and ran all the way back home, only slowing up to skip down the long driveway and admire her house.

NINE

❧   ❧

SARAH

When Lena ran onto the side screen porch she was too excited about her new friend Sarah to remember not to let the screen door slam. But her grandmother only smiled absentmindedly when she ran into the sewing room chattering away about the little girl across the street.

"Lena, baby, be careful 'round that hot iron," she said as Lena nearly collided with the ironing board that was always set up in the room while her grandmother and mother sewed. Then she made the girl stand straight and still while she held a green-and-red plaid pleated skirt with matching suspenders up to the child's waist. The entire woolen skirt was only about half a foot long.

"Hmmm-huh," the old lady muttered with a few straight pins still in her mouth as Lena wove the story about magic fruit made out of red jewels and a little girl named Puddin'.

Her mother, when Lena found her sitting in the living room in her favorite rose-colored chair reading a thick book without any pictures in it, was no more receptive.

"Lena, baby, sit still for just a minute so Mama can finish this one last page. You've been such a good girl all afternoon. As soon as I finish this one last page, I'll put on some music for you. Some Billie Holiday or some Sarah Vaughan, how about that?

Then you can help me bake a cake. What kind do you want? A chocolate or a coconut?"

Nellie's voice was as seductive as the thought of a homemade cake.

"Chocolate, chocolate, chocolate," Lena screamed as she jumped down from the arm of her mother's chair and ran over to the sofa to sit quietly until her mother finished her reading. The thought of a moist yellow cake covered with warm smooth brown icing pushed the image of Sarah right out of her head.

But the next morning, with the sun barely breaking through the trees and the boys still stumbling into each other half-asleep in the bathroom as they got ready for school, the household seemed to rock with the sound of banging at the front door.

At first everyone but Nellie, who knew she had left him snoring in the bed next to her, thought it was Jonah again firing off shots from the pistol he always carried with him—*bam, bam, bam, bam, bam*—the way he had done late one night when he came home and found that Nellie had locked and barred all the doors against him. Weary from a long night of poker and carousing, he hadn't yelled and he hadn't cussed. He had just pulled the gun out of his back pocket and fired into the roof of the side porch, and the doors of the house had magically opened to him.

The five small holes that the gunshots made were still in the porch's forest-green ceiling. Lena giggled whenever she looked up and saw them. Her father's brashness frightened most people, but it didn't scare her one bit. She knew she was immune.

The gunshots had not only opened the locked door for her father, they also had held in check all the talk Nellie had said she had for him about him staying out as late as he wanted and not expecting anybody to say anything about it. About what did he think she was, anyway? About how sick and tired she was of him and his whores.

Overhearing Nellie's mutterings, Lena, sitting on the toilet, had wondered what a whore was, since it didn't exactly sound like the thing her grandmama used to turn the dirt over in her garden. A simple garden tool couldn't have made her mother as mad as this whore seemed to. And Lena didn't think anything that sounded as bad as her mama made the word sound could be so harmless. The way her mama said it, "whore" sounded like it was covered with spikes and prickly barbs.

So, as she pulled up her panties, she asked her mother for a definition. Nellie just snapped, "Go back to bed, Lena."

The early-morning banging at the door was loud and insistent. Lena's grandmother strode down the stairs with Lena beside her. Lena was walking so close to her grandmother that she almost got tangled up in the length of chenille robe flapping between the old lady's legs and tumbled down the steps head over heels. Grandmama scratched the side of her nose again and marched down the downstairs hall on her way to the front door muttering to herself, "Who the hell is this come to our door this time of morning banging like the goddamn police? If it's one of Jonah's half-witted flunkies, they'll be sorry they were ever born. Yes, if it's one of those fanatical fools from The Place come here this time of morning to borrow a couple of dollars to throw away on some foolishness, they'll be sorry they ever learned how to count pennies when I finish with 'em. Knocking on this door like they the damn police or something."

Lena had to walk fast to keep up with her grandmother. Despite the threatening banging at the door, she wasn't a bit afraid. She thought nothing could befall her as long as the older lady stood between her and the world.

Grandmama was out of breath and still cussing out "that fool out there" when they reached the door. She didn't even peep out of one of the panes of glass that edged the big door first. She just flung it open and stood there with her arms folded over her flat breasts as Lena peered around her legs.

At first all Grandmama and Lena could see in the breaking morning light was a wide smile and a pink blouse. Then Lena recognized her friend.

"Sarah!" Lena screamed as she dashed past her grandmother's legs and ran up to the door, pressing her face against the screen.

Grandmama, still annoyed at the early-morning visit, looked down at Lena with a confused expression.

"It's Sarah, Grandmama, Puddin' Tame. I told you all 'bout her yesterday. She's my friend. Don't you remember?"

Grandmama was still puzzled. It had never occurred to her that Lena could have anything to do with this early-morning commotion at their front door. On top of that she was having a hard time believing that Lena, her baby, had made a friend without her grandmama knowing about it. And what a friend!

The dark little girl who stood on the front porch smiling for all she was worth looked to Grandmama like a little piece of street trash who had tried to doll herself up.

Grandmama was halfway right. Sarah had stayed up nearly all night preparing for her first visit to Lena's big house. It felt like the most important event of her short life, and she knew if she didn't prepare for it, nobody would.

Everyone in Sarah's family was used to her doing things on her own. So the night before, when her mother had heard her bumping around in the nearly darkened house, the woman had just smacked her lips a couple of times sleepily, turned over against the warm body of her husband, and gone back to sleep.

Sarah had stopped rummaging through a cluttered drawer and stood perfectly still when she heard her mother stir. She knew she had her work cut out for her, and she didn't need anybody asking a lot of questions and getting in the way while she tried her best to piece together some kind of outfit.

Sarah wanted so much to look nice when she met Lena's people. But she had so little to work with. When she thought she couldn't find a decent pair of matching socks in the whole house, Sarah sat in the middle of the cold bathroom floor and wept.

The only matching set was the tiny pair of faded lacy pink baby socks she found stuck in the back of a drawer, which her mother had bought for one of the children but had never had a fancy enough occasion to use. Sarah brightened when she found a dark blue sock and a dark brown one that belonged to her younger brother. If she didn't fold down the cuffs of the socks, they almost looked like they were bought for her. And in the light thrown off by the lone lamp with the broken shade in the front room, the brown and blue socks looked like a perfect match. Sarah didn't realize until she was standing in Lena's mama's big bright kitchen that she was wearing mismatched socks. By then she was too happy to care.

There was no shoe polish of any color in the house, so Sarah just took a damp rag and wiped the red dust from her lace-up brown oxfords. They looked fine as long as the leather remained wet, but as soon as the shoes began to dry, they reverted to the smoky hue they had been for months.

At least, Sarah thought, I don't have to worry that much about my underwear. If I keep my dress down and don't flounce around too much, it won't matter if I got holes in my drawers or not. As luck would have it, she found a pair of her own panties that were still white and didn't even have a pin hole in them in a pile of clean laundry someone had taken off the line and left on the swayback chair in the kitchen.

Then her main concern became finding a dress without a hole in it. Because she was usually as raggedy or neat as anyone else in her house, Sarah rarely gave any thought to her attire. She woke in the morning, put on something to cover her body, and went on with her day. But the way Lena had been dressed that day, and the size of the house Lena lived in, had made Sarah look at herself for a long time in the wavy mirror of the old hall dresser and decide she wanted to wear something special to her new friend's house.

With tiny lines of concentration creasing her forehead, she picked up and discarded nearly every piece of clothing she found in two chests of drawers, stuck down between the frayed cushions of the couch, or lying under the cot where she and two of her sisters slept. She had long ago outgrown the only "nice" Easter dress she had ever owned. It had been passed down to her next sister, who despoiled it right away by putting it on and playing in the mud.

The search seemed hopeless. Then she remembered the cardboard box full of old clothes that a white woman her mother had once worked for had dropped off at their house the Christmas before instead of coming up with the five dollars she owed for almost a week's work. Her mother was so disgusted that she had thrown the box into a corner of the porch and dared anybody to go near it.

At the time, Sarah had shared her mother's anger and disappointment and wouldn't touch the box of old clothes for anything in the world. She had even stopped her sisters and brother from messing with it. But that was then. Now Sarah needed something that wasn't ripped and torn and soiled beyond repair, so she broke down and dragged the box into the kitchen from the back porch.

She pulled out dozens of old men's shirts and plaid housedresses and faded pastel dusters before she came to anything that looked like it might fit her. At the bottom of the box, under a piece of a yellowed sheet, she found a layer of children's clothes. She lifted them all out and laid them on the kitchen table. Then she threw everything else back into the box.

The bare light bulb hanging from the cord in the ceiling was one of the brightest ones in the house, so Sarah stayed in the kitchen to examine her discovery.

"Too little, too little, too big, too little, too big," Sarah muttered to herself as she held up each piece to examine it briefly and then dropped it into one of two piles on the table. When she had gone through all the children's clothes on the table, she realized she hadn't once said "My size." So she picked up the small pile of "too little" clothes, dropped them back into the cardboard box, and pushed it back onto the porch. Then she returned to the "too big" pile on the table to see what she could use.

First Sarah went through the pile to check for pants and dresses and blouses that had no holes or rips in them. Earlier, while Lena had been engrossed in the piles of rocks and sand they had been building to dam up the flow of the stream cascading beside the street, Sarah had examined her new friend close up. She had been struck with the vivid red of Lena's frock, which was unlike anything she owned.

But later, going over the afternoon meeting in her mind, the thing that stood out about Lena's dress was not only its bright color but also its neatness. No rips or tears at the seams, no threads hanging down—none of the hem of the wide skirt dipping like a shelf below the rest of the dress. Sarah was sharp enough to see that the collar was hand sewn and the sleeves were eased into the armholes so they didn't pucker. And she just somehow felt that the hem of the skirt had been turned under, ironed flat, and stitched before the final edge was expertly measured and hemmed. That's the kind of dress she was looking for in the pile of "too big" items on the kitchen table.

In what was left of her childish hopes, Sarah fully expected to find it there. But there was no hand-made red dress to fit her in the pile of children's apparel on the kitchen table. The closest she came to it was a long-sleeved pink blouse with stitching on the cuff and around the buttonholes that was only slightly frayed at the collar, and a navy-blue pleated skirt with elastic at the waist that some little girl had worn as part of her school uniform.

The blouse's long sleeves hung below her knuckles and the armholes sagged beneath her shoulders, but when she tucked the hem of the blouse down into the elastic waistband of the blue skirt, it settled into neat little pleats all around her rib cage and looked kind of cute, Sarah thought. The skirt was longer than she would have liked, but it made a pretty unbrella-like display when she twirled around, and since she had a clean white pair of panties to wear that weren't holey, she figured she could twirl around a few times and remind everyone who thought the skirt was a sad little sack that it was really quite attractive on her.

She planned to hit the skirt and blouse a few times with the ancient iron her mama kept on a kitchen shelf under the sink. But when she plugged it in, the iron shot golden sparks from the raw copper coils exposed beneath the ragged black covering on the cord. Sarah jumped back and yanked the plug from the wall socket for fear of going up in flames before she got the chance to see inside Lena's house. She spread the outfit on the kitchen table and tried to press out the wrinkles by running the palm of her hand over and over the material. But she gave up after a few tries.

"I'll just walk fast and whip them wrinkles out, like Mama say to do," Sarah told herself as she went into the bathroom and started running warm water into the sink.

It was much too cold in the small bathroom for Sarah to think about stripping naked and getting into a tub full of tepid water— the only kind that came out of their hot-water faucets. And besides, if she had run water into the tub, everybody in the house would have awakened to find out what was going on that deserved a full bath. Instead, Sarah took the bar of rough gray soap from the wire dish above the sink, held it under the warm running water, and rubbed up enough suds on a rag she took from hanging on the side of the tub to run over the trunk of her body and leave a light trail of suds behind on her skin. It was the type of bath her mother took when she was late running out to work or going downtown to a juke joint. "I don't have time to bathe," she'd mutter to herself as she undressed. "I'll just take a wipe-off."

The toilette was what most women in Pleasant Hill, regardless of where they lived, called a "whore's bath," but Sarah didn't know what a whore was any more than Lena did.

After she rinsed the suds off with the wet rag, she dried off with a stiff towel hanging on a nail behind the door and quickly slipped into the pair of panties and undershirt she had found in the laundry. As she walked around the house in her bare feet turning off lights, she shivered a bit as the air seeping though gaps in the thin walls hit her damp skin. When she finally settled in for the night, she was grateful for the warm spots her sisters, asleep in their narrow cot, made for her to snuggle into.

The walls of her house were so thin and holey that in winter the wind whistled through the small rooms like a prairie storm through a log cabin. The floors, buckled and rough in unexpected places, creaked each time someone in the house shifted, let alone walked across them. And the whole place smelled of dried and fresh urine that seemed to have soaked into the very wood of the structure so long ago that its residents no longer even noticed the scent.

When Sarah awoke the next morning, she didn't feel as if she had slept a bit that night. She had dozed off a little, but the excitement of her visit to her new friend's house woke her before daylight and before anyone else got up. She put on her socks and shoes in the dark room, turned on the light in the bathroom only long enough to find the hair brush and rake it over her head one time, then switched the light off and headed for the kitchen.

Her new pink blouse and blue skirt were still lying on the table, wrinkled as they had been the night before, but Sarah didn't pay the wrinkles any attention as she quickly buttoned up the blouse and pulled the skirt over her head.

She twirled one time to make sure the skirt still ballooned prettily the way it had the night before and headed out the door to Lena's house without waking anyone—not even her father who woke early to get a spot on the day-worker's truck that drove through the neighborhood. By the time she got halfway down the driveway leading to Lena's house, she couldn't keep from grinning.

Before Sarah knew anything, she and Lena were standing on opposite sides of the screen door beaming at each other in the glow of their new friendship. But Lena soon grew impatient with her grandmama's dazed gaping from one to the other of the two little girls and pulled a handful of chenille robe.

"Grandmama, open the door. Let Sarah in. She came to visit me."

"Okay, baby," her grandmother answered vaguely as she flipped the metal hook from its eye and pushed the door just wide enough for Sarah to squeeze through.

Sarah bounded into the hall and stood beneath the overhead light, excitement and awe written all over her ashy face. It was like a palace to Sarah: the highly polished hardwood floors, the pictures hanging on the wall near the door, the simple chandelier over the dining-room table in the next room, the dining room itself with its big oval table and six high-backed matching chairs pulled up to it, the mouth-watering bowl of fruit sitting in the middle of the table were like something in her dreams.

Grandmama thought just what Lena knew she would when she got a good look at Sarah: I sure would like to scrub that little rusty neck and grease her down with Vaseline. And when the old woman got a whiff of Sarah's mildewed clothes, she thought, I bet she hasn't ever had a real good hot soapy bath in a tub in her life.

"So you're our baby's new friend?" Grandmama said out loud.

"Yeah," Sarah answered, her voice gravelly from getting up so early but so respectful that her short answer didn't imply rudeness, even to Grandmama.

"Say, 'yes, ma'am,'" Grandmama instructed Sarah gently.

"Yes, ma'am," Sarah said carefully, repeating Grandmama's gentle inflection.

"Well, next time wait till the sun has come up good before you come visiting," Grandmama said pointedly. Then, "I guess ya'll want something to eat. You had breakfast yet, Sarah?"

"Bre'fast?" Sarah was puzzled.

"Have you eaten this morning?" the old lady rephrased her question as she headed for the kitchen.

"Oh, no," Sarah answered with her eyes caressing the fruit on the dining-room table as they passed by.

All three of them had to blink a few times as they entered the black-and-white kitchen situated at the eastern corner of the house. The early-morning sun flooded the spacious room with shafts of startlingly bright light that hadn't reached the other parts of the house yet. Sarah felt as though she were walking out onto a stage: it didn't seem real. She had seen kitchens similar to Lena's when she accompanied her mother to her occasional daywork jobs in the white neighborhood behind their house. But those kitchens didn't smell like Lena's. In fact there had been no smell at all except the ones she and her mother brought there.

But even first thing in the morning, Lena's kitchen smelled wonderful. And it wasn't just the fresh aroma of coffee brewing on the stove and buttery grits and sausage grease and cinnamon and sugar dusted lightly on buttered slices of toast. It was the layers of smells that had settled on the walls and floor and worked their way into the fiber of the room that made Sarah come to a halt near the threshold. Sarah could smell the vegetable soup Nellie had made the week before when the weather first turned chilly. She smelled the fish dinner they had had that Friday. She smelled the chocolate layer cake even before she saw it sitting in a glass-covered cake dish on the top of the refrigerator. She came close to bursting into tears with the yearning that the room called up in her swelling heart.

Lena grabbed her friend's dry hand and pulled her into the kitchen and over to the white enamel table to sit down.

"Nellie," Grandmama said to Lena's mother who stood by the sink looking out the window in the direction of the woods. "Look who was making all that noise at our front door this time of morning."

Nellie turned around with her thin eyebrows raised. They shot up even higher when she saw Sarah.

"Well, I be damned," she said. "Now, who is this?"

Lena giggled and so did Sarah.

"This is a new friend of Lena's," Grandmama said with a strange lilt to her voice on the word "friend" that made both little girls stop laughing and look into the old woman's face.

Lena kicked Sarah under the table to encourage her to speak.

"Girl, what you kicked me for?" Sarah asked in her gruff, raspy voice.

"This my mama, Sarah," Lena said as she reached under the table and patted the spot on Sarah's leg that she had kicked.

"Where do you live?" Grandmama asked Sarah as she placed a small glass decorated with circus animals and filled full with orange juice in front of each girl.

"She lives across the street in those houses next to Mrs. Willback's house. Next to that big tree. What kind of tree is that?" Lena asked Sarah.

Sarah couldn't answer at first because she had picked up her glass of juice and was drinking down the fresh tart drink in small continuous swallows, allowing the citrus tang to coat the inside of her mouth and throat. With one last gulp and a loud smack of her lips, she put the glass back on the table and answered.

"Chinaberry."

"And just how did the two of you get together?" Grandmama asked as she walked over to the table with more orange juice and poured another stream into Sarah's glass that made the child's eyes light up even more.

But before Sarah had a chance to answer, Nellie jumped in and said nervously, "Oh, with our little girl, it's no telling, but I assume that you didn't cross that street out there, Lena."

"No, Mama, Sarah did. You ought to see her dodge those cars," Lena said proudly.

Nellie laughed softly. "I bet she can."

After that, Sarah would show up on their doorstep regularly to join Lena and the boys for breakfast. Some days she had to run home after eating to "do something." Other times she stayed all day until Grandmama made her go home. When anyone asked her why she didn't go to school, she'd say, "We going up there any day now, soon as mama gets a chance to 'roll me." But for more than a year she never attended any school other than the one she found in her own backyard.

"Lena, what are you and old Rough-and-Ready doing today?" Grandmama would ask as the two girls came into the kitchen and took seats next to where she sat making peach puffs or carefully cutting the seams away from a pile of pole beans covering the table. Lena's father said he had gagged and nearly choked on strings Nellie had left on the beans soon after they got married. From that time on, Grandmama always prepared the pole beans in their house.

"Don't know yet," Sarah would answer for both of them, not minding the old lady's all too appropriate nickname for her. Grandmama made a point of always having something healthful for Sarah whenever she came into the kitchen—a piece of fruit, a sandwich with extra slices of tomato, a pile of raisins—and she always gave the bigger portion to Sarah.

But whatever their plans were, everyone knew that they would involve pretend. It was their favorite game. Everything they played hinged on the basic unit of Let's Pretend. These games sometimes involved props and background and sometimes they didn't, and that was fine, too. At Lena's house, where her attic, filled to bursting, yielded all kinds of costumes and paraphernalia to fill in the chinks of the stories, their games were elaborate and staged. But Grandmama or Nellie or one of the boys always had to go up the steps and drag down boxes or armloads of stuff because Lena still refused to go into the attic as long as she knew the portrait of her dead infant aunt was stored up there.

For the few days each winter when it was too cold to play out-of-doors, Sarah came to Lena's house and they played and danced in the big upstairs hall in front of the wide floor-length mirror so they could see every movement they made. In the daytime, with her friend by her side, Lena was never frightened of the big mirror, as she was during the nights on her bathroom runs.

At Sarah's it was bare-bones pretending under the chinaberry tree, which was the only place they were allowed to play at her house year-round, but that didn't bother the girls. Despite the house's deficiencies—glaringly obvious to the adults in the neighborhood—Sarah had two things in her yard that Lena and every other child in Pleasant Hill envied her for: a mature and flourishing pomegranate tree and the ancient chinaberry whose broad sturdy limbs swooped down to the ground and back to the sky to form natural nooks and dens. Lena and Sarah called it their "house."

The year Sarah and Lena discovered each other, the two of

them planned all winter that, when the warm weather came, they would both move into the chinaberry tree by themselves and live off the fruits of the pomegranate.

"You'll have a room, and I'll have a room," Lena assured Sarah. Sarah's two sisters still wet the cot she shared with them in the front room of her house. "We'll make two beds out of pine straw and Grandmama's flowers, and it'll smell so good in our house, we won't never have to clean up." It was hard for Lena to believe, considering the number of babies and toddlers that roamed the house and yard all day long, but Sarah was the eldest child in the Stanley household. She had responsibilities that Lena never knew about.

They were best friends, sharing games and secrets, special words and questions. But the first time Lena remembered seeing Sarah's world clearly, it was winter and raining very hard, too hard for Lena to head out the door into the cold sheets of water. Lena was stuck at Sarah's for dinner, even though her mother had told her not to accept dinner invitations because Sarah's family had enough trouble feeding their own members without having guests' mouths as well.

"Just say, 'No thank you, I already ate' or 'I'm going to eat when I get home,' " Nellie instructed Lena.

By the time Raymond came running up on the porch with her yellow raincoat and an umbrella, Lena had seen Sarah's family at home for dinner. It was a revelation.

Sarah's mother stood in the tiny kitchen, moving quickly from the sink to the tiny white stove, opening cans, stirring, and chopping. She worked quietly, not saying a word to Lena and the other children assembled on the floor and sitting in the room's one swaybacked chair. When she was finished, Sarah's mother laid down the big metal spoon with holes in it, turned to the children, and announced, "Catch as catch can." Then she walked out onto the lean-to porch to light up a cigarette, blowing long furls of white smoke out into the driving rain.

The other children rose quickly and lined up behind Sarah with small plates and bowls in their hands. Lena could tell what was cooking in the big blue pot even before Sarah lifted the lid off and steam roiled up to the cracking ceiling.

It was neckbones. The distinctive pork scent mixed with tomatoes from the two big yellow-labeled cans sitting on the kitchen table had wrapped itself around the very hairs in Lena's nose. She didn't dare look in the pot for fear of going against her mother's orders and succumbing to the temptation to share the meal, but she guessed that Sarah's mother had put in lots of onions and pungent bell peppers and fistfuls of spaghetti that she broke in half first. Neckbones was one of Lena's favorite dinners. They had them two ways at her house. If her mother cooked, they were made the way Sarah's mother did, with tomatoes and spaghetti. If her grandmother was in charge of cooking the meal, the bony meat was always prepared with potatoes and thick brown gravy.

Although Lena knew both her mother and grandmama wanted her to lean one way or the other in her preference for neckbones, prepared red or brown, she never made a choice. She could never bear the thought of life without neckbones both ways.

When Sarah had filled all the children's bowls and plates, she filled her own plate, broke off a piece of bread from the charred hoecake in the black skillet, and sat on the floor with the others who were already wolfing down their food. Not a word was said until every plate was clean. When Lena asked why everybody was so quiet while they ate, Sarah looked at her as if she had just pointed out the holes in her sisters' drawers, and Lena was sorry she had said anything.

One warm murky day in their second summer, Lena found her friend sitting beneath the protected wings of the chinaberry tree, playing with mounds of dirt between her opened legs. Sarah's house seemed strangely quiet, free of the noises and traffic that usually encircled the house.

The dirt in Sarah's yard was gray and dusty and didn't look as tempting to Lena as the rich brown loam under the pine trees in her own yard. But she had to fight the urge to reach down and put a handful of it into her mouth anyway. Lena understood perfectly why Estelle, who came from time to time to help clean the house, kept chunks of stark white laundry starch in her apron pockets and munched on it throughout the day.

But Lena had promised her mother that she would stop eating dirt. And it seemed no matter how hard she wiped her mouth, Nellie could always tell when she had been eating the stuff. So, instead of picking up a palmful, holding her head back, and letting the grains of dirt trickle into her open mouth from the fist of her hand, she just sat down next to Sarah and started building her own pile of earth into a hill.

"What's your name?" Lena asked playfully, in their customary greeting.

Sarah looked up from the sandhill of earth at her knees and smiled at Lena. "Puddin' Tame," she answered.

"What do you want to play?" she asked Sarah after a while.

"Let's play like we married," Sarah said without hesitation.

"Okay," Lena agreed.

"I'll be the man and you be the woman," Sarah said as she pushed aside the top of the pile of dirt.

"You sit at the table and I'll cook us some breakfast," suggested Lena as she looked around the yard for the few pieces of plastic and china plates and cups they used for serving pieces and sticks for bread; rocks for meat; mounds of dirt for rice, mashed potatoes, and grits; and dark green leaves from the trees around them for collard and turnip greens.

It was a careful game of pretend eating they played. Lena treated it with as much reverence as the real thing was accorded in her own household. She always got a pan of water and washed the rock of "meat" well before putting it in an old dented pot or shoebox "oven" to cook. And she washed and fingered the chinaberry leaves carefully and tenderly, just the way her mother and grandmother did before shredding them and putting them in a pot with a rock for seasoning.

She had been in the kitchen once and seen her grandmother stand at the sink for the longest time examining each leaf in a pile of collards she had just picked from her garden, where they grew year-round. Lena had thought at first that the old lady was looking for worms until she beckoned her over to stand on a chair at the drain beside her.

"Look at this, baby, all these little roads in a single leaf," Grandmama said softly as she traced the separate pale veins in the dark verdant leaf with her wrinkled index finger. "And listen, just listen to this music." Then she had run the soft pad of her thumb over the dark green surface of a leaf, and the thing let out a little baby squeak. They both just smiled in wonder.

Sarah sat near her pile of dirt and thought awhile. Then she shook her head as she watched Lena begin to gather the plates. "No, not like that. You want me to show you how to really play house? I know. I seen it plenty of times."

"Okay," Lena agreed easily, even though she knew she had watched her family all her life and knew how to play house just as well as Sarah. But she figured she and her friend enjoyed each other too much to waste time disagreeing over something that didn't matter all that much.

"We just need one thing," Sarah said. "I'll go get it."

And she hurried off to the empty front porch of her house and returned right away with a copy of the *Mulberry Clarion* in her hand. It looked so stiff and clean, Lena knew it had to be that day's copy of the newspaper. Besides, it was Friday and Lena knew that most people in Pleasant Hill, even those who didn't read the newspaper every day, took the *Clarion* on Fridays because that was the day the paper included the page that Rowana Jordan wrote and edited. Stretched across the top of that inside page, just before the want ads, was the standard heading "News of Our Colored Community."

When Mulberry's one colored newspaper had gone out of business at the beginning of the fifties, Miss Rowana, as everyone called her, persuaded the *Clarion* to insert black folks' news once a week by promising to sell ads, take photographs, and write all the stories herself. And she was true to her word, rushing all over town in her too-fancy dresses and outrageous hats collecting news, church notices, wedding and birth announcements, and gossip, along with receipts and ads from funeral homes, barbershops, grocery stores, and the Burghart Theatre. She already had a tiny storefront office on Cherry Street, far enough away from the newspaper's building to please both her and her employers. So she just changed the sign from the *Mulberry Crier* to the *Mulberry Clarion* and continued working.

The newspaper Sarah carried was still rolled up the way it had been thrown. And the little girl held it out in front of her like a magic wand. As soon as she got back to their spot under the tree, she plopped down in the dust and began unrolling the paper.

"Sarah," Lena said, "your daddy read that paper yet?"

"Uh-uh," Sarah answered as she continued to spread the paper out in her hands.

"Then you better leave it alone till they do read it. Nothing makes my daddy madder than for somebody to come and tear up the paper before he gets a chance to read it. He says it shows a goddamn lack of consideration."

Sarah sucked her teeth derisively as she separated one big broadsheet from the others and laid it up on the elbow of a limb of the chinaberry tree they sat under. "Shoot, nobody'll even notice it's gone. If I didn't move it, it woulda sat there forever."

Lena still wasn't convinced, but she was too intrigued with what Sarah was going to do with the paper to press her argument.

When Sarah had all the sheets separated from one another, she divided them evenly, giving Lena four double wide sheets and keeping the others for herself.

"What we gonna do with these?" Lena wanted to know.

Sarah looked around the base of the tree that was their "house" and picked a corner where the limbs touched the ground.

"We need to go over to our bedroom. It's nighttime," Sarah said as she picked up her sheets of newsprint and stepped into another part of the "house."

Lena followed her.

Sarah sat down and pointed to the spot next to her for Lena to join her in the dust. Lena sat down. She was beginning to realize that this was a private, ritualized game they were about to play. And when Sarah said, "Our children 'sleep so we gotta be quiet," Lena knew she had been right, and she was excited. As many times as she had been frightened by some apparition or discovery, she couldn't keep herself from loving a mystery, especially when she was with someone in her family or Sarah and felt safe.

"This what you got to do," Sarah explained as she crumpled a sheet of the newspaper up into a ball, lifted up her skirts, and stuck the paper down into the front of her panties. She leaned back against the stump of the tree and looked down at her crotch, appraising the difference the addition made. Lena sat next to her staring at it, too.

Lena couldn't take her eyes off Sarah's dingy panties, now bulging at the crotch as Sarah added another ball of newspaper, then another. The newspaper balled up like it was and nestled inside Sarah's drawers didn't look like anything other than what it was. But Sarah continued to fool with it, arranging the rounded part against her body and making one end of the clump of paper into a pointed edge, which she aimed at the pad of her panties.

Lena knew she was supposed to keep quiet because the ritual had begun, but she just had to ask. "Sarah," she whispered, "what's that supposed to be?"

"I'm the man," Sarah said authoritatively. "That's my thing, my johnson. I'm supposed to have it."

She patted her newspaper growth one last time, then grabbed one of Lena's sheets of paper and scooted over to her spot in the dust.

"Here," Sarah said as she handed Lena a ball of the newspaper. "You do the same thing. That'll be your thing, you a grown 'oman, so that'll be your pussy."

"I already got one," Lena said as she started to pull down her panties to show Sarah. "We call it a matchbox at our house. It just ain't as big as a grown woman."

"I know you got a thing," Sarah said, with a touch of exasperation creeping into her voice. "All girls do, but you right, it ain't big enough. So, go on, put the paper down in your panties like me."

And Lena complied, shoving the stiff paper into the front of her white panties, now rapidly turning gray in the dust. "Ouch, that's scratchy," she complained as she moved the paper around trying to find a more comfortable place against her skin.

"That's okay," Sarah said as she scooted over to Lena to sit facing her between her opened legs. "I think it's supposed to hurt some. That's what my daddy make it sound like. He say, 'Oooo, baby, yeah, that hurt so good, do it some more, uh, yeah, that hurt just right.'"

Sarah had moved in so close to Lena that their two panty fronts, both bulging out in front of them, were now touching. Without any further explanation. She started moving her body around, rubbing her paper penis against Lena's panties and making short sucking sounds as she pulled air between her clenched teeth. She threw her head back and closed her eyes, imitating her father, the whole time repeating, "Uh, yeah, uh, yeah, right there, uh-huh."

Lena watched in fascination as her friend continued to rub up against her in the dust and to suck her teeth as if she were in pain.

Sarah's face was a picture of pleasure glazed over with a thin icing of pain, like the faces of women at The Place who danced and ground their hips to the beat of a saxophone solo played on the jukebox. She seemed to pay Lena no attention, so Lena figured she was supposed to imitate her friend.

She threw her own head back and closed her eyes like Sarah and began rotating the bottom of her body, the part in her panties stuffed with stiff newspaper, up against Sarah. Lena felt a little silly at first and couldn't stop thinking about how dirty the seat of her panties was getting from being ground into the fine gray dust under the big chinaberry tree. But since Sarah, with her eyes still closed and her raspy voice still spitting out the litany of "Yeah, ooh, yeah, ooh, yeah, do it," seemed intent on playing this game, she closed her eyes and gave herself over to the pretending.

"Oh, baby," Lena mimicked her friend in earnest and scooted her bottom a little closer to Sarah's. The movement forward suddenly pressed an edge of the newspaper in her panties into the split of her vagina and across her clitoris. "Uh," she yiped in surprise, and the prick of pleasure shot through her pelvis and slowly melted in her stomach.

Her elbows, resting on the crook of a low limb of the chinaberry behind her to prop her back up off the ground, suddenly lost their gristle and slipped off the edge. Her shoulders landed on the ground with a dull plop, raising a dry dust storm around her ears. But Lena didn't stop to give the fall a thought. She was lost in the exquisite wet feeling that was spreading through her hips and rolling down her thighs. Letting the ball of newspaper lead her, she rose up on her elbows and pushed her bottom back toward Sarah, brushing her stuffed panties back up against her friend in search of more of that quick warm feeling.

She opened her eyes briefly to stare into Sarah's face to see if it mirrored what she imagined her own must look like. Satisfied that it did, she closed her eyes again and continued gyrating her little body against her friend's, sucking air between her teeth the way she had done automatically when the quick warm thing inside her had melted before.

Suddenly she felt the large strong grasp of a fist clutch her upper arm just below the sleeve of her dress and pull her roughly away from Sarah. At first Lena thought it was the strong arms of the chinaberry tree come to life to grab her. Her eyes flew open.

Sarah's mama's face was a mask of rage. She had just been weary when she came looking for Sarah, calling her name over and over to ask what had happened to the newspaper, but when she found her with Lena pressed together, rubbing against each other in the dust, their panties protruding with the turgescence of her Friday newspaper, she turned furious.

"What are ya'll doing!" she screamed as she loomed over the two girls. "What are ya'll doing over here?"

But she didn't wait for an answer. She just screamed at Lena. "Don't be trying to hide from me. I see you. I see what you doing. You little nasty girl. I shoulda known better than to let Sarah play with you."

Sarah and Lena didn't know what to say. Sarah's mama still had Lena's arm in her grasp and lifted her away from her daughter like a rag doll. "Think you so damn fine with your little red dresses and your hair ribbons and your big house. Well, you ain't so fine, is you? Just another dirty little girl, trying to do nasty when you think ain't nobody looking."

Sarah, seeing the attack on her friend, tried to jump in with an explanation.

"It was me, Mama, it wasn't Lena. It was my game."

But the woman didn't want to hear any of that. "Shut up, Sarah. I know what I see with my own eyes. You go on up to the house. I'll deal with your butt later. You know better than this." But Sarah didn't move.

Then, turning back to Lena, who was trying to wrench herself away from the woman's grasp, "I got a good mind to go across the street and tell your fine-ass ma just what I caught her precious baby doing. Yeah, I oughta go tell her what her precious daughter was doing with my little girl."

Then she turned on Sarah again. "Sarah, if you don't get your ass in that house, you better, girl."

With her attention wandering from Lena, her grasp on the child loosened too, and Lena, suddenly free, started to dash away from the screaming woman. But Sarah's mama looked back in time and caught Lena's skirt tail in her fist.

"Yeah, but she probably wouldn't believe me. Yeah, probably put it off on Sarah. That's right, little girl, you better run on home, get on out my yard. You don't own everything, you know." Sarah's mother was about to release her grip on Lena's skirt. Then she had a thought. She flipped the girl's skirt tail and grabbed the elastic band of Lena's panties and reached inside.

"And gimme back my newspaper," she said with a snarl as she

yanked the crumpled paper from Lena's drawers. "I ain't read it yet."

Lena ran all the way home and sat quietly on the side porch steps getting her breath until her mama called her in to dinner.

The last thing Lena thought before she fell into a dreamless sleep that night was that she and Sarah would be friends forever, no matter how her mama had acted earlier that day. Nothing could change that. Despite the strange thoughts and ghosts that had popped up unexpected all her short life, Lena still hoped there were some things she could count on.

Sarah had always been there when Lena called her. Usually, when Lena's household got busy midmorning, she would just go to the end of her driveway and yell for Sarah, and Sarah would emerge from her house or the chinaberry tree and lead Lena safely across the street or just come over to Lena's house to play. Lena could count on Sarah's consistency. Consistency of any kind pleased and reassured Lena in her world of apparitions and uncertainties.

So she couldn't understand it when, late in the afternoon, three days after Sarah's mother had found them rubbing their bodies together, she went to the end of her driveway as usual and shouted for her friend and no one appeared in the yard across the street. No one. Lena didn't think she had ever seen Sarah's house when there wasn't someone playing in the yard or sitting on the porch or standing in the doorway. Whenever she and her family drove past, she always threw up her hand in greeting before she even looked over that way good, as her grandmother said, because she was so sure there would be someone there to return her greeting.

Lena called for Sarah a couple more times, and when she still didn't get a response, she looked both ways up and down Forest Avenue then dashed across the street by herself. She giggled with pride at having made it safely across the street, but as soon as she stepped into Sarah's yard she felt something was different. It was so quiet and still.

Not only was no member of Sarah's family visible, there was no sign that any of them were even there. The front door, usually standing wide open except on the few bitterly cold winter days, was shut tight. No light burned in the front room or the kitchen window on the side. The radio that was turned on every time Lena had ever been there was gone from its spot on the front-room windowsill and the window itself was tightly shut.

"Sarah! Sarah!" She called as she headed around the side of the house past the low limbs of the chinaberry tree that looked as deserted as the house did. But there was no answer. When Lena got around to the back of the house she saw that even the raggedy curtains that had hung at the kitchen window in back were no longer there.

Maybe they're doing spring cleaning like at my house, Lena said to herself. She headed up the plank steps leading to the back porch with the idea in mind of looking through the low kitchen window and rapping on it to stir someone inside. With each step she took, the tiny porch made a mournful squeak that sent small shivers up her legs. But even before she made it to the window, Lena had a strong feeling that she wouldn't like what she saw. So the kitchen with its dirty linoleum floor bare of its few pieces of furniture and the hall without its old dresser and mirror and what she could see of the empty front room didn't surprise her. It just left her very sad. As if she had lost the delicate pearl necklace her grandmama had given her.

At first Lena tried to tell herself that Sarah would probably show up soon, laughing in her familiar raspy way, her brother and sisters in tow. But even as she thought of her friend, Lena realized with a start that she couldn't even remember what her friend's voice sounded like, and her sadness turned to fear.

A sudden cool breeze raised goose bumps on her arms and she looked up and noticed that dark clouds were gathering in the western sky. When the smell of rain blew in on the next gust of wind, Lena knew it was time to go back home. There didn't seem to be anything else to do. She couldn't wait any longer.

As she hurried back through the empty yard in front of Sarah's house, big drops of rain began hitting the ground, raising tiny clouds of gray dust like puffs of smoke. Suddenly, going through Sarah's yard felt like a walk through a graveyard. As a sense of loss enveloped her, Lena began to feel as if her friend Sarah were dead.

Not bothering to look either way, Lena dashed across the street toward her house as the rain started coming down in pellets. She didn't stop running until she had reached the kitchen, where she found her mama and grandmama cleaning out the pantry.

"Mama, Mama," she cried as she ran into the first pair of arms she came to, knocking her mother to the floor. "Sarah's gone, Sarah's gone!"

"What, baby? What in God's name is wrong?" Nellie asked, becoming frantic at the sight of Lena's tears.

"Sarah, she's gone—nothing there. I think she's dead!" Lena sobbed.

"Oh, sugar," Grandmama said as she stooped beside Lena and Nellie sitting on the floor. "I forgot all about it. I shoulda told you, baby."

"Told her what, Miss Lizzie?" Nellie demanded.

"It's Rough and Ready, Lena's little friend Sarah. She and her family moved away. Moved on the other side of town, to East Mulberry. You know, Nellie, Yamacraw, you know that neighborhood. Miss Willback 'cross the street told me. Sarah and her people got put out over there. Miss Willback saw their pitiful little few sticks of furniture out in the yard yesterday."

"Sarah's gone, Sarah's gone," was all Lena could say.

"Oh, don't worry, baby, you and your friend can still visit each other," Grandmama tried to reassure her. She would say anything to make Lena feel better.

"Oh no she won't, not in that neighborhood she won't," Nellie said.

"See, I told you Sarah was gone, she's gone for good," Lena cried, her sobs turning into hiccups.

"Lord," Nellie said to Miss Lizzie as she kissed the top of

Lena's head and rocked her in the salty, sweaty valley between her breasts. "My baby is getting to be so high-strung. Just like I was when I was her age."

Nellie's ministration finally calmed Lena down, but it did nothing to ease the knot of pain Lena felt at the loss of her friend. The following fall when she went to grade school for the first time, she stood around in the yard searching for a little girl who looked like Sarah. There was none. All these girls were shined, polished, and pressed, their hair neatly snatched back into braids and barrettes. None had Sarah's rusty beauty. Then one of her first-grade classmates, a chubby girl who stood alone with her blouse already creeping out of her skirt first thing in the morning, caught Lena's attention. Her eyes didn't sparkle like Sarah's, but they did seem to be full of as much mischief. And when Lena sidled up to her, she smiled and slipped her hand into Lena's.

The gesture reminded Lena of Sarah.

When the first bell clanged, Lena and her new friend Gwen marched bravely into the strange schoolhouse side by side.

Still, on her way home from school that day, Lena felt a tug at her heart when she passed her first friend Sarah's house and missed her all over again. From time to time down at The Place, Lena saw Sarah's mother, but when the girl tried to speak and ask about Sarah, the woman pretended she hadn't heard and kept walking from the back door on out the front.

For years afterward Lena couldn't understand why, in a town as small as Mulberry, she never ran into Sarah, not once since she was six years old. Sarah had disappeared from her life.

TEN

❧ ❧

TABLE

The McPherson family at the dinner table reminded Lena of the priest, altar boys, and communicants at Mass. Jonah, at the head of the table, sat in the largest chair, with arms. Nellie sat opposite him, facing the kitchen door. Lena was on Jonah's left, Edward on his right. Grandmama was on Nellie's right, Raymond on her left. Even the fabric her mother had chosen to cover the chairs' seat cushions—alternating strips of maroon satin and beige satin separated by ridges of gold—reminded Lena of the priest's vestments of gold, purple, green, red, and white.

Although there was a huge red brick fireplace in the dining room—identical to the one in the living room—behind where Lena and Grandmama sat, it was never filled with logs and lit. Years before, Grandmama had placed pieces of a set of fine bone china that she had received as wedding presents after the turn of the century over the fireplace on the dining room mantelpiece. Much of the set had been broken while her children were growing up, and Grandmama had vowed to keep the remaining pieces intact. There was a soup tureen and ladle, a huge turkey platter, and a gravy boat and saucer.

By the time Lena was six, even the boys had learned, "No one runs in this room."

The rule was as much because of the small brass urn on the room's mantelpiece as the fine china beside it.

The urn, which Lena liked to think of as made of gold, contained the ashes of Miss Lizzie's husband, Lena's grandfather, who died the year Lena was born. Like Lena he had been born in November and, according to Grandmama, whenever a person born in that month dies, another birth takes place in the family the following November.

Lena liked the sound of that story. Instead of feeling responsible for Granddaddy's death, as the boys sometimes taunted her, she felt a product of his death—a seed from the lips of a dying flower.

"That's your granddaddy there," Miss Lizzie would sometimes tell the children, matter-of-factly pointing a wet iced-tea spoon toward the mantelpiece as she helped them clear off the dishes after a meal. "By rights, he's not supposed to be up there. He always said that I was to sprinkle his ashes on the railroad tracks on Montpelier Avenue right before the seven-ten southbound Silver Crescent headed for New Orleans came through. Your granddaddy worked for the railroad all his life, first as a laborer, then as a boiler washer, finally as a switchman. Lord knows, he loved a train. That's where your daddy gets it from.

"But your granddaddy, he always wanted to be headed for New Orleans, headed for New Orleans. You know, that's where we went on our wedding trip. Went down on the train, stayed a week.

"All you had to do was mention New Orleans to get him to grinning. And it wasn't just that wedding trip, either. It was those porters who put those ideas into that man's head. He always said that that city meant good times to him. People dancing in the street, even after a funeral. Second line, they called it. Playing music when the mood hit 'em. He even liked the idea of Marie Leveau and all her voodoo stuff. Tried to get me to go to one of those all-night rituals while we were there. But I said no thank you. I got enough sense to know not to be messing around with the spirit world, 'specially when I was happy as could be and didn't need no potion to keep my man.''

Raymond and Edward would nudge each other and giggle at Grandmama's confidence, and she'd notice for the first time that all three of the children had stopped clearing the table and were standing around with plates and silver in their hands. She'd motion for them to keep working and caution Edward, ''Boy, don't be shaking that tablecloth out the door after dark. You know that's bad luck.'' Then she'd continue.

''But your granddaddy, he made me swear I'd toss his ashes on those railroad tracks before the Crescent came through. 'Southbound,' he said. 'Make sure it's southbound, Lizzie. Please, ma'am, don't send my ashes north.'

''But after he died, I couldn't do it, couldn't bring myself to let what was left of him be thrown on some cold steel tracks, even though Jonah was perfectly willing to climb up that trellis and do his duty. Shit, it was bad enough that he went and had already arranged to get himself cremated in Atlanta. I figured Walter's soul wouldn't ever find no rest, as it was with his body all burned up like that.

''At the last minute,'' she'd say wearily as she slumped down in one of the dining-room chairs, ''I just couldn't bear to part with his remains.''

Then Lena and the boys would stop their dish-scraping and silver-collecting and come sit down near the old lady and join her in staring at the urn on the mantelpiece as if it were ''The Ed Sullivan Show.'' Lena, leaning against her grandmama, would nuzzle her face into the woman's armpit.

''Hope he forgave me,'' Grandmama would say after a while. ''Walter swore he would haunt me every day of my life if I didn't follow his wishes. But he never did. Sometimes I waited for him to come haunt me.''

''Well, of course he didn't,'' Nellie would say from her reading chair in the living room where she had been listening all the time. "The children know there ain't no such thing as ghosts haunting you. I don't know why you insist on rehashing those old tales."

But Lena and the boys always pleaded with Grandmama to tell them more. Grandmama didn't even deign to throw Nellie a triumphant glance. She prided herself on being the bigger person in most situations. Lena had heard her tell an old friend that very thing one day as they sat on the side screened porch while her mother was in the kitchen cooking dinner. "You know, living here in this house that isn't really mine, and especially with Nellie who has always been spoiled rotten just because she's so pretty, I've had to be the bigger person in so many instances and just overlook a lot of things that a small petty person might have taken offense at."

The old friend had just reached over and patted Grandmama's hand, resting on the arm of one of the big wicker chairs, as though somebody had died.

The urn on the dining-room mantel was full of coarse gray material, like the vermiculite Nellie added to her potting soil. Lena knew what it looked like because the boys had told her so. They had taken the jar down once when no one else was home and looked inside. When they tried to make her look, too, she refused and ran away to hide behind the sofa on the porch until her mama came home. She had no idea what she would see down that jar. But she had an inkling that it would be something like looking at the picture of her dead baby aunt that had hung over her grandmother's bed. She had no intention of going looking for trouble.

In the center of the dining-room mantelpiece, between Granddaddy's ashes and Grandmama's china, was a posed portrait of Grandmama's family: Grandmama, Granddaddy, and her daddy and Aunt Sister as children. The photograph was nearly identical to the one of Lena's family on the mantelpiece in the living room: Nellie seated on the left, Jonah on the right, Raymond next to his mother, Edward next to his father, and Lena at age nine months in the middle sitting on what looked like a fern stand.

Everyone in Lena's black-and-white photograph wore a tight smile except Lena, who had only stopped screaming when the photographer's bulb flashed. The tears still glistened in her eyes in the photograph and her lips formed a surprised little "O" like a fish's mouth.

Despite her early encounter with her father's dead sister's picture, Lena loved photographs. She could sit and stare at the ones of her family for hours. Her father, picking up on any interest his children showed in a subject, had bought her a square, lime-green Brownie camera and film and demanded that the family assemble and stand still whenever she wanted to shoot their picture.

There was something right and prodigious about the family eating their big meals in the room that had become a mausoleum for a dead patriarch. It seemed to show the family's knack for making things important and inconsequential at the same time. Food, after all, was just sustenance, but it was also something glorious and rapturous for the family.

Lena heard her mother once mutter over a stack of fresh bloody beets, "You would think Jonah grew up in a house where there was never enough to eat instead of one that had Miss Lizzie's kitchen in it."

At the beginning of each meal Jonah looked around the table into each person's face, then said in a serious deep voice, "Let's say the blessing, please." His intonation quieted any chatter and everyone, including Grandmama who wasn't a Catholic but a Baptist even though she didn't attend any regular church service, made the sign of the cross and said to themselves, "In the name of the Father and of the Son and of the Holy Ghost, Amen." Then they all said aloud together, "Bless us, O Lord, and these thy gifts which we are about to receive from thy bounty, through Christ our Lord. Amen."

"Amen, Brother Ben, caught the rooster and killed the hen." That was Jonah, too. He said that nearly every day but especially when there was company. Then he would look around the table and everyone would smile or chuckle appreciatively as his grin seemed to bounce off the windowpanes behind Raymond's and Edward's chairs. And the sounds of the meal—cutlery against china, spoons stirring sugar into glasses of iced tea, heavy serving bowls being lifted and replaced on a fresh white linen tablecloth, requests to "pass the bread, please"—would take over for a while.

On some days Jonah would slap his hands and rub them together in delicious anticipation. "Good bread, good meat. Good God, let's eat," he'd say. And the meal would begin on that note.

On days when Jonah was in a bad mood—Nellie called it "having the devil in him," which always made Lena shudder when she heard it—there would be no joking after the grace was said. On those days the food would taste as delicious as always, but the atmosphere around the big oval table would feel as though they were eating in a prison. No amount of jocularity and teasing among the children or sweet talk or buttering-up of Jonah could lift the heavy pall that he laid over the table.

But some things never changed. After the soft clatter of dishes began, Jonah would address his mother, his wife, or one of his children, "And what did you do today?" It was a command not only to reply but to enlighten, engage, hold forth on the type of day that had passed since the last meal the family shared.

Lena always thought the question deserved some answer better than, "We saw a train on the way to school and it got to the crossing before we did and we had to wait all morning for it to pass. We were late. You got to write us a note for tomorrow."

But Jonah never wasted his time on writing notes to nuns. Nellie did that. He was more interested in the train.

"How many cars?" he'd ask as he leaned over on one arm of his chair—his was the only chair around the table that had arms—his graceful, neatly manicured hands poised in the air along with his question.

"Fifty-seven—and a caboose," Raymond would answer, proud that he had had the foresight to count.

"Fifty-seven? Um . . . must have been one of the Seaboard's if it was that long," Jonah would figure seriously.

This kind of talk satisfied her father. If none of the children had seen a train, or if Grandmama hadn't discovered an old pattern for a dress come back into style, then they would all discuss how much was paid for the corn or pole beans and whether the price was higher than the one last year, or if it was better the week before when the beans came from the farmer's curbside market rather than the new Colonial grocery store. Or Jonah would tell of the two men down at The Place who got into a fight over someone calling someone's woman ugly—even though Jonah said he had to tell the truth, the woman was ugly as sin and in his estimation wasn't worth fighting over under any circumstances: "Big old fat woman, you know her, Nellie, she's a big 'un"—and how he was going to have to replace the plate-glass window that one man had thrown the other through.

It was all part of what Jonah called learning to make conversation. "Hell," Jonah had said many times, snorting derisively, "knowing how to make conversation at the dinner table is one of the most important things you'll ever learn to do. Hell, you can sit over there with your mouth poked out if you want to, but I'll never sit at the table with somebody who sits there like they ain't got sense enough to make simple conversation, the least you can do is sit there and *look* pleasant. God knows, nobody wants to sit down to a meal of fine food and have to look across their plate at somebody with a unpleasant expression on their face."

Whenever Jonah lectured about conversation, Lena secretly thought that he was making a reference to Edward's stuttering. At one time all the adults thought they had a cure for it. Their father thought reading aloud would help improve Edward's speech. His mother thought extracurricular activities like the Boy Scouts would relax the boy enough that he would forget his nervousness and not stutter.

His grandmother kept her feelings to herself, but she too had had a theory. One evening, as the three children sat under the bright light in the sewing room and their mother listened to them read from their history books and readers, their grandmother crept into the room quietly with her right hand behind her back and sat down on the bed.

She motioned Lena over to the bed to sit by her. When the child sat down, her grandmother slipped her hidden hand between the two of them. Lena felt something cold and greasy on her thigh, but when she tried to look down to investigate, her grandmother said, "Sit still, Lena, and let Edward read."

Edward always read last because if he didn't, the other two children would become so impatient with his stuttering over words before their turns that they would start telling him to "come on and say it," and get their brother even more flustered. Even little Lena, who had started reading before she was four, could read as fast as Edward, who was five years older than she. He was just beginning to read from his large history book when their grandmother had come into the room.

" 'The government of the United States is di-di-di . . .' " Edward began, but he didn't get any further than that because when he began to stutter on "divided" his grandmother raised her hand from the bed and hit him square in the mouth with a fat greasy piece of raw meat with stiff black hairs sticking out all over it.

Everyone in the room except Grandmama screamed. She just stood back looking satisfied as the room dissolved into pandemonium. Raymond covered his head with his history book and ran into a corner yelling, "Good God from Gulfport!" like one of the winos down at The Place their daddy owned.

Nellie dropped the hand sewing she was working on and rushed over to Edward, who was spitting and sputtering and wiping his mouth over and over with the back of his hand. Lena, who had jumped up on the bed feet-first when her grandmama hauled off and hit Edward in the mouth, watched enthralled as her brother's face went through four or five different expressions—surprise, disbelief, fear, embarrassment, anger—after the blow landed on his lips.

"Miss Lizzie, have you completely lost your mind?" her

mother asked in a low voice as she wiped her son's lips with the first piece of material that she could lay her hands on, a piece of pink voile. "Hitting this child in the mouth with—what is that, anyway?"

"It's a cow's tongue, is what it is," her grandmother replied self-righteously. "And it's the only sure cure for stuttering. While ya'll around here with your fancy solutions to the boy's problem, his grandmama had to take matters into her own hands."

"Does that really work, Grandmama?" Raymond wanted to know as he emerged cautiously from the corner he had run into when the cow's tongue began to fly.

"Of course it does. If you hit the person right in the middle of a stutter, I know it works, seen it work lots of times."

"Ain't that right, Son?" Grandmama asked Edward, who still stood there like he didn't know what hit him, wiping his mouth and looking confused.

"Now, didn't that cure you, Edward?" she repeated.

All of them in the room held their breaths waiting to see the effects of the miraculous cure.

Edward spoke.

"Wh-wh-wh-what you do th-tha-that for, Grandmama?"

Lena could almost feel the disappointment in the small sewing room settle on all their shoulders.

Since then everyone had tried to accept Edward's stuttering and practice patience, especially Grandmama.

But while they were eating, there was so much else going on that Edward's stuttering was no distraction. At their table there were as many rules and regulations involved as there seemed to be in any liturgical service. Don't talk with your mouth full. Wait until the other person stops talking before speaking. Leave your napkin in your lap. Don't wave your knife around like that. Slow down, nobody's gonna take it away from you. Mabel, Mabel, big and able, keep your elbows off the table. Who's that humming? No singing at the table. These incantations were offered up with the meal like sacrifices.

Jonah hated paper napkins, said they were of no use. If anyone gave him one in a restaurant or at dinner in a friend's home, he'd make such a mess of it—shredding it, pretending it stuck to his fingers, asking for two or three more because one wasn't sufficient—that sometimes Nellie would reach into her purse, silently hand him one of her pretty lace-trimmed handkerchiefs, and pray he would just shut up.

At home the meal was over when everyone was finished, meaning when Jonah was finished. He'd take his linen napkin and wipe his mouth heartily, drop it by the side of his plate, and say sincerely, "Enjoyed my dinner," or "Enjoyed my breakfast." Nellie and Grandmama would say in unison, "Glad you did."

Then it was each child's turn to express appreciation for the meal. "Dinner was real good." "I enjoyed that." "Good candy yams, Mama." The enjoyment was genuine, the appreciation sincere. It was like the priest at Mass saying, *"Dominus vobiscum"* and the congregation responding *"Et cum spiritu tuo."*

The ritual didn't get stale from day to day any more than the liturgy did from Sunday to Sunday. It got richer.

Lena would sit at the table as she did in church, waiting to see if the patterns would be different one day, if the response would vary, if the communicants would hold back the response just for the devilment of it.

After the meal the ritual continued in the kitchen when Nellie told the three children it was time to let Grandmama come sit down and for them to clean up. Once, Nellie checked and found the boys rolling around on the floor fighting over the dishrag while Lena, standing on a kitchen chair, merrily washed dishes, still laden with food from dinner, in a sink overflowing with billowing white Ivory Liquid suds and lukewarm water.

Nellie's anger began at the white swinging door leading from the breakfast room and built as her gaze slowly swept the kitchen: turnip-green grease caking the edges of the plates and the big pot, overhung by a sickening overlapping of odors: meat juices and lemon rinds and squash and onion casserole, together with the buttermilk and eggs from the cornbread—all having had an extra hour to sit around in the heat of the kitchen and grow.

For the twelve years that Nellie and Jonah had been married, Jonah's mother had lived with them, forming an unofficial triumvirate to rule the household. In that time Nellie had picked up two skills from the older woman. One was cooking; the other was cursing. But unlike her mother-in-law, who Lena thought cursed in a straightforward average way, Nellie cursed in what Lena saw as curlicues and arabesques.

Lena's regal mother could and often did let loose with a curse that made the hair on her children's arms stand on end. "You children would make the Good Lord curse," she would scream at them. But Lena could never imagine the Lord saying, "You make my very asshole quiver," the way her mama did when they all got on her nerves badly, which was fairly often.

As soon as the children saw her in the kitchen doorway, reeling a bit with the effect of the scene, her eyes nearly closed, one hand gripping the heating pipe running from the cold furnace in the basement, they knew they were in for it.

When she recovered herself and opened her eyes fully, her anger rose another step and she segued from the swooning stage to the cussing stage without stopping.

"You little wild useless younguns!" she had screamed from the doorway, getting angrier and angrier as her gaze swept from the dried mashed potatoes, still in a pot sitting inside a frying pan of water simmering on a low burner on the stove, to the boys fighting on the unswept floor amid thin orange onion skins and sugar spilled from the large tin canister on the counter. Then she took a step toward the boys, arms outstretched to grasp them, and her foot cracked a pile of sugar scattered on the floor.

The sound sent quick shivers through her whole body. Right there her anger took a giant step up the staircase of rage.

"Get up off that damn floor! Get up off that floor this instant, you two little fanatical fools. Get up and sweep up this sugar. I can't stand to walk on sugar. You all know that! Dammit, look at this kitchen. I'd rather be in west hell with my back broke than have to depend on you all to do anything right. Can't ya'll do *shit?* Well, you gon' do it tonight, you can bet your little asses on that, if you have to stay up all night. Look at this floor, that stove, this table, that sink."

Then, on cue, Lena the baby, soaking wet all down the front of the plaid jumper that barely covered her fat little behind, standing with soapsuds in her hair, on her cheeks, soapsuds up to her armpits—little Lena sneezed. "Achoo!"

The sound, a tiny egg cracking in a raging storm, sent their mother even higher in her rage.

"Listen to that child, just listen to her! If you ain't got enough goddamn sense to do the job right—and God help your little ignorant asses in this world if you can't wash a damn dish right when you got hot running water at the sink—then you could at least keep your sister from wetting herself all up and making a mess at the sink. Lord have mercy! One of ya'll run get the mop. Cut off that water."

The water flowing from the faucet had filled the sink and was cascading over the sink's edge to the floor.

The boys, each eager for the honor of running to the back porch and retrieving the mop from its place high on a wall, and perhaps working his way back into his mother's good graces, rushed across the tile floor and made for the back door. When they both arrived there at the same time, they started up another fight on the spot, scuffling and struggling in the narrow doorway like two cheap comics, neither moving on to the task assigned to them.

Their mother made another dash for the sink to cut off the water and crunched more sugar underfoot.

"Damn, damn, damn!" she shouted as she pirouetted on the slippery granules.

Then she remembered the boys and turned to find them fighting in the doorway, and it seemed to be the worst situation she had ever seen.

"Jesus, keep me near the cross," she'd moan and shake her head slowly as if she were about to burst into tears. Her knees bent as she almost broke down to the floor, her pretty face contorted into a mesh of rage and misery.

"Lena ain't nothing but a baby. But she's got more sense than you two damn boys put together. How you both let her stand at that sink getting soaking wet . . . Come on, baby, we'll go change your dress. It's almost time for bed anyway. And child, don't you open your mouth to me tonight about going to bed. You'd think I was sentencing you to a slow death!"

Lena knew her sneeze was a tolling of the death knell. She had tried to stifle it, but it had burst out of her face with a force she couldn't control, drawing unwanted attention her way. At the mention of bedtime, her eyes began to fill with tears that threatened to brim over and flow down her face like the soapy dishwater had just overflowed the sink.

"Little witch, I'll whip your ass till it ropes like okra if you give me trouble tonight," her mother said, her sweetness souring on her stomach at the sight of the child's tears. "I want you to get upstairs, undressed and ready for your bath, before I come back up these steps. I mean what I say."

Then, turning to the boys fighting over the mop, she sincerely promised a slow death for both of them when their father came out of the bathroom if they didn't straighten up and fly right. It was all she needed to say to get them moving.

On some evenings in seasons other than winter, if Jonah didn't make the family take too long eating, or if the pandemonium in the kitchen clean-up didn't destroy the mood of the evening, they all congregated afterward on the side screened porch facing west. Full and content, they'd watch the sun set behind the tall pines and Mrs. Willback's garden. Then Jonah would retrieve his pistol from the top of the bookshelves and prepare to return to The Place for the night.

He would stretch and sigh and say, "Lawdy, Miss Clawdy," as if he dreaded a night of hard labor ahead of him, but Lena always suspected he enjoyed spending his evenings at The Place. Lena knew she always enjoyed the time she spent there after school and on Saturdays.

ELEVEN

❧ ❧

SATURDAY

Every Saturday morning the boys sat quietly on the edge of Edward's lower bunk bed trying to appear to listen attentively to what Nellie was saying to them about how much money to spend and how not to eat those hot dogs and ice-cream sandwiches that tore up their stomachs, and what time to come home. They both knew that if either of them showed the slightest sign of letting his attention wander during her instructions, she was as likely as not to cancel their Saturday ritual of going downtown to the Burghart Theatre for the entire morning and afternoon.

Their mother was still angry from three years before, when Raymond and Edward had gone to the theater as usual but, instead of coming home in the early afternoon as they were supposed to, had stayed and stayed there, way past dark. The car hadn't started, and Lena wasn't yet old enough to put the magic on it. Nellie didn't want to call down to The Place to tell Jonah to walk down Broadway and get the boys out of the movie house, because she feared he might kill them in his rage. And calling a cab would have been just as bad, because Jonah wandered in and out of the cab company any time of the day to talk with Joe Blount, the owner. She could just hear Joe Blount saying when

Jonah walked in, "Nellie called a cab Saturday night. . . ." So she had to walk all the way up Pleasant Hill in the dark and catch the bus and come all the way downtown to drag them home on public transportation.

When she got to the theater, it took nearly fifteen minutes to convince the ticket-taker that she was not trying to sneak in without paying just to see three cowboy movies, two cartoons, and a short. Jonah strolled through the red-leather double doors any time he wanted to, and the woman at the theater door wanted to make sure Nellie didn't think that courtesy extended to her. When Nellie got into the darkened theater she found the boys in the front row, just feet from the screen.

"If you don't get your little butts out of here, you better," she hissed at them.

They had had the nerve to *"sh-sh-sh!"* her. And Edward had asked her to wait one minute until they saw "this one part one-one-one-one more time."

She had a hissy fit right there in the front row of the Burghart Theatre, screaming and cussing and nearly crying with rage. She screamed so violently as she lunged across the knees of a row of little boys ducking their heads and craning their necks around her to see if Hopalong Cassidy was going to lose his hat in the final fistfight that even the projectionist woke from his half doze and peered out his tiny square window to make sure he had not missed something in this movie he must have seen already twenty-five times.

"I don't remember no cussing in this picture," the projectionist said to himself as he rubbed his eyes, scratched himself, and surveyed the screen.

He was just about to stop the projector and brace himself for the barrage of hoots and whistles and foot stomps and yells of "Hey, mister, Hey, mister, what's the matter with you up there?" when he spied the silhouette of a woman against the screen, waving her arms and brandishing her fist at somebody in the front row.

"Shoot," the man said to himself, "it ain't my department. Let the manager handle the fights."

Then he settled back on his tall barstool and dropped his chin back to his chest for a quick nap before he had to change the reel for the next feature.

Raymond and Edward's friends never let them live it down. They'd ask each Saturday as they all stood in line at the ticket booth, "Come by yourself today?" Edward or Raymond or both of them would have to light into the questioner for coming so close to asking, "Did you bring your ma?"

Sometimes Lena went with the boys to the Burghart just to get on their nerves, because she knew they hated for her to tag along unless it was a scary movie they could frighten her with later or a movie like *Carmen Jones* or *Manhattan Madness* with an all-black cast that nobody was going to miss. But usually she preferred to hang around at The Place on Saturdays instead. Especially if Nellie was working there.

Lena loved to watch her mother at work at The Place, selling half pints on the liquor store side, filling frosty glass mugs on the beer parlor side, writing cream-colored checks for the liquor salesmen from the big blue ledger, and tearing the checks off precisely at their perforated edges. It was like watching an entirely different person from the one who had given Lena life and went around the house with a whine or a roar in her voice all the time.

"Mama sure is good at being the boss," she told her father one evening after dinner as she climbed up into his lap, wrinkling the open newspaper he held in his hands. He sometimes sat and read the paper for an hour or so after dinner before returning to The Place.

Jonah furrowed his brow and tilted his head to the side as he looked at his baby daughter.

"What do you mean, baby?" he asked Lena as he folded the newspaper and dropped it on the floor next to the lamp beside his chair.

She shifted her weight and tried to find a more comfortable spot in her father's lap.

"I mean like when she's at The Place. She'll be doing all kinds of things at once, cashing checks, making sure Dear One doesn't sneak off without paying, telling Gloria and 'em what to cook, making Big Bill leave if he too drunk. That's being the boss, isn't it?" Lena asked. "That's what I see you doing when you're there. Except Mama don't play no skin on the counter like you do with Mr. Tyler."

Jonah laughed a rich deep chuckle that he reserved for his daughter's prattle. "She don't play no cards, huh?"

"No, but that's the only thing she don't do like you. So that makes her a good boss, huh?"

"Well," Jonah said slowly, considering the idea of his wife as boss for the first time in his life, "I guess Nellie does do a good job of helping out at The Place."

Lena laughed right out loud, spraying her father's face with spit. "Daddy, Mama shore do more than helping out at The Place. Helping out is what I do when I go outside and shake the tablecloth for Raymond and Edward when we all have to do the dishes. Mama do more than that."

"Well, of course she does," her father answered. "She does lots more than that, but it's all helping me out with my business."

"But that just don't sound right, Daddy—'helping out.' Lots of times when you stay out late, she gets up early in the morning and goes and open up The Place so you can sleep late. And the salesmen always say they glad Mama's there because she always know just how much beer and drinks you need and how much it gonna cost. And people call her Miss Nellie. Lay-Down and Yakkity-Yak even call her Boss Lady. And if Gloria or Estelle don't show up, she fries the fish and makes sandwiches."

"And you think that's more than just helping out, huh?" her father asked.

Lena shrugged her narrow shoulders. "Seem that way to me."

Jonah just grunted and looked off over Lena's head into the

growing darkness outside the big picture window over the sofa. When her father remained still and quiet for so long, Lena grew bored and slid down his leg and went off to see what everybody was doing in the kitchen. And when Lena returned to the living room nearly a half hour later to join the boys looking at "Father Knows Best," Jonah was still sitting in his chair staring into space, thinking about his wife as boss of his business.

Lena loved just about everything about the liquor store and juke joint downtown around the corner from the main business district. She even liked the smell of stale beer and cigarette smoke that engulfed her when her mother unlocked and swung open the double glass doors to the beer parlor side at eight o'clock on some Saturday mornings. Lena would look up at her mother and wait for her to say, "Uh, Lord, that stuffy old stank smell makes me sick to my stomach," as she always did. Then Nellie would turn all the way around to face the nearly deserted street and take a few quick gulps of fresh air before turning again and plunging into The Place and her duties there.

Not Lena. Without waiting for her mother, she would stick her head inside The Place, take a deep breath of the still musty air, and dash inside to plug in the lighted displays hanging on the walls. The square Miller High Life sign edged in golden neon; the black-and-white Black Label sign that seemed lit from within; the red-and-white "Coke Refreshes" sign; the sign shaped like a big can of Bluebird grapefruit juice: They all sputtered once or twice before flickering on. And although all of the signs, enticing customers to buy wine or snuff or cigarettes, lit and unlit, were coated with layers of grease and dust, they gave The Place the festive air of a carnival. That's what the smell reminded her of—a good time.

By midmorning on a Saturday, it was more crowded in The Place than anyone could imagine a jukejoint in a small town like Mulberry could be. But folks from surrounding towns and burgs even smaller than Mulberry who came into town to shop, pay bills, and window-shop would also stop by The Place to take a little drink and occasionally even a dance while they sent their children and sometimes their wives to the theater or the peanut shop for a while.

When Jonah had moved into the corner location, he had divided The Place into two rooms. The grill and beer parlor side was located in the L-shaped portion. And the small square liquor store fit into the L's missing corner. The whiskey store, which could be seen from the grill side through a panel of colored windows, was crowded with hanging promotional displays that nearly eclipsed the shelves of gin, bourbon, scotch, vodka, and blends.

On busy Saturdays—and there were no other kinds—there would be thirty or forty people sitting at the counters on the side and back of the cafe, eating or drinking. There would be another ten or twelve folks standing around the walls and jukebox. A few couples would be on the tiny dance floor, and the six small square tables would be crowded with as many people as could find chairs to sit down. And noisy. The noise in The Place on a Saturday was nearly as thick as the cigarette and grease smoke and the odor of beer, wine, and whiskey, drunk, digested, and belched back into the heavy juke-joint air.

Besides the music from the jukebox that patrons never let rest, there was the heady hum of conversation that always made Lena think of a swarm of giant bees that had attacked her and the boys in the plum groves behind Mrs. Willback's house. At regular intervals the hum would suddenly grow into a loud exchange of words that would sometimes end in a burst of laughter or more, even harsher words. If the words were angry enough they would turn into sudden slaps or flying fists. The news—"Fight, fight"—would travel along the bar as though it were a telegraph wire to the front and back doors and out to the street. Folks inside trying to get out would almost have to fight those standing at the doors trying to see in.

Then, like a summer rain shower, it would be over, dwindling like mist into idle threats or broken up by Jonah or one of "the boys" with a long stick from under the bar. And like a quick rainfall it would leave The Place cleaned and refreshed. Then the steady hum of music and voices would settle back over the room.

There was hardly anywhere on earth that Lena enjoyed more than The Place. She prayed that her father was serious when he got mad at the boys and swore he planned to overlook them and will The Place to her to run when he died. It made her heart race to think that she might one day be in charge of The Place. She wouldn't change the name or anything that she could think of. It would still be the Bluebird Liquor Store and Beer Parlor and Grill. And everybody would still refer to it as The Place.

She would always wear high-heeled mules and good-looking dresses like her mother did and not worry one bit about the smell of cigarette smoke and grease from the grill that got into her wool and cotton and linen fibers. She'd keep the same arrangement with Mr. Greeby down the street, who seemed to do all their dry cleaning for nothing. She didn't know what the agreement was, but she knew her father's penchant for deals and she knew she could never improve on any deal Jonah had made. He seemed to make deals all over town. He thrived on them. If he could get a product for less, whether or not he needed it, he was happy. He'd buy syrupy mandarin oranges by the gallon, knowing no one in the house ate them, just because he'd gotten a good price.

And The Place seemed to love Lena as much as she loved it. Women and a couple of men dressed like women, who sometimes smelled like they had doused themselves with ten or twelve tiny bottles of Hoyt's Cologne to hoodoo some man without washing under their arms and between their legs first, would sometimes sweep into The Place, scoop Lena up in their arms, and go sailing down Broadway with her as if she were some prized booty from a battle.

"Don't worry, Miss Nellie," they would yell over their shoulders. "I just want Emily Lewis at the candy store who think she got such pretty children to see what a truly pretty smart child look like."

Nellie rarely objected to the short trips these women took

Lena on up and down the street. After working more than ten years off and on at Jonah's place of business on the corner of Broadway and Cherry, she knew most of the people there as well as she knew her own personal friends. Jonah's business associates and poker and drinking buddies stopped by The Place all day, sticking their heads in the door to inquire, "Where is *he?*" as if "he" were some potentate whose whereabouts should always be known. But Nellie's friends never came by, even when they were downtown shopping. They never stopped in for a cold beer or a cold soda.

In fact Nellie probably knew the women at The Place better than she knew some of her friends. She knew which ones to trust and which ones not to trust. If some woman known for being dangerously unstable, like Cliona from Yamacraw, grabbed Lena and headed out the door, Nellie would just say to one of her "boys" standing close by, "Short Arm, go get my child." And Short Arm or one of them wearing a big white apron would hurry off importantly and bring Lena right back.

"Let me through, let me through," Short Arm would shout as he pushed through the crowd that always gathered on the corner outside on Saturdays, swatting folks left and right with his stump of an arm. If anyone even tried to speak to him, the short stubby man would puff up with importance and tell them, "Man, leave me 'lone, I ain't got no time to be messing around wif you. I don't play wid children. I'm on a errand for Miss Nellie. Got to get her child back from that fool-ass woman."

Short Arm would catch up with the escapee from Yamacraw with Lena riding fearlessly on her hip, snatch the child away with his good arm, and plunge back into the crowd with Cliona shouting after him, "You ignorant no-arm motherfucker, who you think you is? . . ."

"Big-mouth crazy-assed woman," he'd mutter as he stormed the crowds. "You okay, Lena? She ain't hurt you, did she?"

"Aww, Short Arm, Cliona from Yamacraw okay. She don't mean no harm," Lena would assure him.

"Yeah, most Negroes don't mean no harm to let them tell it.

But you got to stay away from folks like that. She crazy, baby. You got to stay away from crazy folks in this life. Heck I'm 'bout crazy, myself."

"Then what I'm doing with you, Short Arm?"

Short Arm just laughed. "Lena, baby, you a mess." Then he'd hurry to deliver Lena safely back to the counter in the liquor store and return to his job of stacking drink crates or putting cans of beer into the coolers.

On top of that, Nellie knew that Jonah instilled enough of a healthy fear in everybody who came to The Place that no one would be fool enough to let any harm come to Lena while in his or her care.

"All right, heifer, you let anything happen to my baby girl, you know I'll have to kill you," Jonah would warn the women if he walked past the peanut shop or the dry cleaners and saw Lena sitting atop the counter munching nuts or playing with an adding machine. The women would titter coquettishly at her father. But soon they would pick Lena up and take her back to The Place.

Actually there was little chance of anything happening to Lena, whether Jonah threatened them or not. Everyone on Broadway—whores, winos, boosters, family men, gamblers, flunkies, women with their maid's uniforms in big brown paper bags, roustabouts, store and theater owners, hard-working women from the box factory who were sometimes too tired at the end of the day to hold their heads up and drink their quarts of beer—all treated Lena like a precious commodity.

They all were tickled by the way Lena walked up and down Broadway looking just like Jonah spit her out.

"I bet I know who your daddy is," folks would yell at Lena from barbershop doorways and candy-store windows. She seemed to be the only regular of the strip under the age of ten, other than the children running in and out of the Burghart Theatre.

From the time Nellie had first brought her into The Place wrapped up in her yellow knitted blanket and propped her up on the counter of the liquor store in an empty Old Forester bourbon box, Lena had been treated like a princess by the denizens of the downtown strip. And she accommodated them by seeming to be what they thought she was—special—and by growing used to their wine- and whiskey-soaked breaths the same way she gradually grew accustomed to the taste of olives.

It wasn't hard to do. Besides, the folks at The Place were easy to like; they were interesting people. Everyone there seemed to have a story, and no matter how quiet they were around other people, they were eager to tell Lena their tales.

Out of the clear blue, for instance, Peanut—a shriveled little kernel of a man barely five feet tall with arms and thighs the size of a child's and a little bitty nut-shaped head—would walk into The Place, pull one of Lena's braids, and sit down at the end of the grill counter near her. Then he'd buy a pack of Wrigley's Doublemint gum, take out one stick for himself, and give the rest to her, even though everyone knew Lena could have anything she wanted that was for sale behind the counter. Peanut and Lena would sit there and chew their gum in silence for a while. Then he'd reach into the pockets of his tiny pants and pull out a quarter and hand it to her.

"Here, Lena, go play me some tunes on the jukebox," he'd say.

Lena would hop down from her stool, run toward the purple, red, and blue lights of the jukebox, and punch the greasy red-and-yellow buttons of *J30, A15,* and *P22* without even thinking. She knew just about everybody's favorite records on the nickelodeon because each tune seemed to have some special meaning for at least one customer at The Place. And each patron played that song over and over until the vending-machine man came, updated the records, and—usually over protest—took it off the machine.

Even Lena's mama had a favorite record. Weeks before Christmas the jukebox man would come in The Place smiling. "Well, Mrs. Mac, it's that time of year again," he'd say. And her mama would smile and nod her head as she continued to count out a customer's change.

In a few minutes all chatter and noise on the grill side of The Place would cease as the first words of Nellie's song came up on the jukebox.

"Bells will be ringing *(boomp-boomp, boomp-boomp)*, the glad, glad news *(boomp-boomp, boomp-boomp)*. Oh, what a Christmas *(boomp-boomp, boomp-boomp)* to have the blues *(boomp-boomp, boomp-boomp)*. My baby's gone *(boomp-boomp, boomp-boomp)*, I have no friends *(boomp-boomp, boomp-boomp)* to wish me greetings once again."

Charles Brown's smooth worn-out voice carried all over The Place and even out into the street, because the jukebox man would have turned the volume up loud to make sure Nellie could hear it over on the liquor store side. Then just about everyone in the joint would join in on the chorus, "Please, come home for Christmas, please, come home for Christmas, if not for Christmas, by New Year's night."

Nellie would slide aside the window that separated the grill from the liquor store and yell over the music, "Would you Negroes *please* be quiet so I can hear my damn song!"

Everybody in the joint understood that request. From the way patrons acted, Lena knew that in The Place, when your record, the one that came closest to saying what you felt, came on the jukebox, it was customary for you to stop in your tracks, bow your head, close your eyes, raise your right hand in the air above your head, stomp your foot, and command the entire place, "Be quiet, will you. That's my *song*. Lord, Lord, Lord."

Usually it was a slow tune that people claimed as theirs, like "A Change Is Gonna Come" or something by Sam Cooke or The Platters that had some special significance for the regulars of The Place. But there were those who consistently went for the upbeat tunes, like Jimmy Reed's "You Got Me Running" or Hank Ballard and the Midnighters' "Work With Me Annie," in which case they would close their eyes but wouldn't bow their heads and, instead of raising their hands over their heads, would just bend their elbows and pop their fingers to the beat of the song while rhythmically dipping their heads from side to side.

At that time Lena knew Peanut's favorite songs were all sung by Brook Benton. Funny as it seemed to everybody, Peanut pictured himself a lover and patterned himself on the smooth mellow Benton. Once, Lena had heard two women sitting at the counter say as Peanut walked by and brushed his hand across one's big ass, "Aw, don't pay it no mind. That ain't nobody but Peanut." Then they burst out laughing. "Girl, don't give me no little piece a' man," the dark little woman named Willie Bea said as she wiggled her sad narrow hips on the plastic bar stool. "Little as I is it's like rubbing a bunch of sticks together. Might start a fire." Then both women had laughed again.

When Lena came back from playing Peanut's songs on the jukebox, she took her seat on the stool and watched Peanut close his eyes and sing along with Brook, "Moonlight in Vermont." He even sounded a little like the romantic singer.

"You know, Lena, I used to have a pretty fair voice when I was a young man," he said as Brook's voice trailed off to music. "Sang with a little old band around here. Coulda made something of it, too. Ask your daddy. The girls used to be crazy 'bout me, used to just almost pass out when I really got to going, for real. But then I caught the TB and had to go away to the TB home. Folks never did forgive me for that. I got better, but I went away to nothing and so did my voice. Never did regain either one of them—my weight or my voice."

By then *A15* had come up on the machine's turntable, and Peanut lost himself in Brook's mellifluous tones again. Lena just sat there and chewed her gum and tried to picture Peanut in a pretty blue silk suit with his hair brushed back severely and waved with grease and covered by a stocking cap, his frame fleshed out to a healthy huskiness.

Peanut wasn't the only one. Even Stank, who worked in the fish house and walked Broadway with fish guts and blood smeared down the front of his apron and had a contingent of cats following him like he was their mother with her tits full, once told Lena about the time his brother fell into the Ocawatchee River while they were fishing on its banks. He jumped in, even though he couldn't swim a lick, and saved the boy's life.

"Yessiree, I was a hero for a day then. My mama made me a cake and the preacher made me stand up in church. Never did learn how to swim though. I always been scared of the water."

Transvestites sitting at the bar with scented powder lightly dusting their pockmarked faces taught her things about men and women long before she knew what to do with the newfound knowledge.

"Lena, baby, I've fattened my last frog for the snake," Seymour, who sometimes called himself Yvette, said bravely one day as he sat dejected and alone over a tall can of Miller High Life while his latest boyfriend was grinding shamelessly on the small dance floor with a skinny woman wearing a shiny wig. "I don't mind being the wax. I don't mind being the wick. But I be damned if I'm gonna be the flame."

All Lena could think of were the short votive candles that burned all the time in blood-red and sea-blue holders in the front of Blessed Martin de Porres Church and of the metal tray with the burned matches and quarters scattered in it. I didn't even know Seymour was Catholic, she thought.

Lena didn't always make friends easily with children her own age, but the folks at The Place were all eager to count her as a friend. Most she had known all her life. Many she had seen drunk and sober, high and low, broke and flush. Their habits were as familiar to her as her family's. And she vowed to herself if she ever got to run The Place, she would keep it open on Christmas, Thanksgiving, and New Year's just for them, no matter what the law said.

TWELVE

☙   ❧

HAIR

The summer vacation that took Lena and her brothers Raymond and Edward, her parents, her Aunt Sister, Uncle Jack, cousins James Junior and Jackie from South Carolina, and the family friends from Atlanta, the Stevenses, across the state to the Georgia coast the year she was seven could have been called *Colored Folks Going to the Beach,* like a painting. That's what her grandmother called it: *Colored Folks Going to the Beach.* She said it all month long as her family undertook the massive preparations for the two-week vacation. And she always sucked her false teeth in disgust when she said it.

"Colored folks going to the beach, *pshhht."*

She said it when Lena's mother came into the house carrying big thin brown paper bags filled with new shorts sets for herself, terry-cloth playsuits for Lena, swimsuits for the both of them, swimming trunks for Lena's father and brothers, and new white cotton undershirts and drawers and brightly colored towels for everybody. Her grandmother just watched the boys and Lena tear into the sacks of beachwear while they were still in Nellie's arms and muttered, "Colored folks buying beach towels." Then she sucked her teeth.

When her mother rounded up everyone in the house the

Monday before they left, to go downtown to Dannenberg's department store to purchase sandals—Red Goose for the children—her grandmother went along for the ride but refused to accompany the family into the shoe department. Instead she wandered through the sewing and notions section picking up spools of thread and cards of bias tape and putting them back while the others tried on white leather sandals and light brown ones with wide straps and chunky brass buckles. Every once in a while the old lady muttered to herself, "Colored folks buying beach shoes. They'll ruin those children's feet. Nellie ought to know better, ought to know those children's feet are still growing. They need support, not some little flimsy strap."

When the saleswoman in notions approached her grandmother suspiciously, Lena saw the old lady give her such an evil look that the pale white woman with the beginnings of a humped back actually edged her way back to her station at the big brown cash register without turning around to watch her step.

Most everyone in the house knew enough not to mention the trip directly to their grandmama. But Lena thought she was special, so later that week she ran to her grandmother in the sewing room to proudly display her new pair of red-and-white rubber flip-flops purchased expressly for the trip. The old woman was too outraged to speak right away. She just reached down and grabbed the rubber thongs off Lena's feet, flipping the child on her butt on one of her rag rugs, and flounced out of the room in search of someone who had "a little damn bit of sense" with whom to commiserate.

She found Imogene at her usual station above the ironing board in the kitchen and conferred on her the honor of a little damn bit of sense.

"Will you look at this little piece of shit Nellie bought to put on her child's feet, her baby daughter's feet! Now, is that crazy? *Psshht,* colored folks going to the beach."

Imogene, not wanting to jeopardize her job that only entailed some light cleaning, which she hated, and some heavy ironing, which she loved, just frowned without saying a word, spit snuff juice into the Maxwell House coffee can resting on the window-sill, and went back to ironing one of the boys' plaid cotton short-sleeved shirts and moving her feet to Ray Charles singing "Baby, What I Say" on the tiny transistor radio that hung around her neck on a string. That infuriated Lena's grandmother even further, so she flounced out of the kitchen too and, on the way back to the sewing room, threw the flimsy shoes as hard as she could under the long picnic table in the breakfast room.

Later Lena didn't dare ask her grandmother what she had done with the shoes, so she had to search the house for an entire day before she found them wedged between the deep freezer and the breakfast-room table.

Her grandmother had no intention of being part of *Colored Folks Going to the Beach.* That spring, when she had heard her son and daughter-in-law discussing the idea of the trip, she let them know right away not to count on her going along.

"No, thank you very much," she told them very politely, "but I'll just stay here and have a vacation from foolishness."

Lena couldn't for the life of her understand why her grandmother would not want to go on vacation to the beach in the first place, and why she was so vehement in her conviction that no other black folks had any business there either.

"Grandmama acts like she takes it personally that we're going to the beach," Lena told her mother, whom she found at the big white metal kitchen table shucking long ears of sweet white Silver Queen corn. Her father could never get enough sweet fried corn in the summer when it was plentiful, cooked just the way Nellie did it: First, holding the corn upright on the pointed end, she went over the outside of each shucked ear with a very sharp butcher knife, barely shearing off the very tips of each kernel. Each of the firm pieces of corn fell into the bottom of the big black iron skillet with a little *plink.* Then she went back over each ear with the flat side of the knife, scraping the cobs dry of all their milky juices.

"This is the only way to fix fried corn," her mother told her as she spit a long strand of silk from her mouth over her shoulder.

HAIR

The smooth reddish-brown skin on her face, chest, and bare arms would be dotted with spatters of corn juice. It seemed to Lena that her mother was polka-dotted with bits of corn milk all summer long.

"Now, you watch how I do this," her mother said as she added a handful of flour to the corn, washed the remaining flour off her hand into the mixture with about a cup of water, stirred the whole thing around in the big black skillet with her fingers, and put it over a low flame on the stove. "Heaven help you, you may get a man who loves fried corn the way your daddy does."

Finally she poured some hot fatback bacon grease into the corn, where it sizzled, and covered it with a big lid.

"I'm watching," Lena said as she sat with her chin on the table watching a fat green worm inch across the surface. But she persisted, "Mama, why is Grandmama so mad about us going to the beach?"

"What makes you think she's mad?" her mother asked innocently.

"I don't *think,* I know she is. She even tried to throw my new flip-flops away when I told her they were for the beach," Lena replied.

"Well, Lena, your grandmama's old, well older than the rest of us. Don't say I said she was old. And sometimes older people have different ideas about things than we do."

"Why?" Lena wanted to know as she made drawings in the layer of flour dusting the table.

"All kinds of reasons. Mostly because they grew up in a time different from ours. When your grandmama was little there were all kinds of things she wasn't allowed to do that you can do, like go into the stores downtown or to the county fair in the fall. Colored folks still can't do a lot of things, but you can do more than she ever thought about."

"What's that got to do with a vacation?" Lena wanted to know. "Seems like that would make you want it more."

"When your grandmama was coming up, and even when I was, the beach was one place that was just for white folks, not for colored unless you were taking care of somebody's white baby. It just wasn't for colored folks."

"Why?"

"Oh, you know how when white folks have something good, they make like it's no good for black people. Shit, you even hear colored people doing the same thing when somebody says, Let's go to the beach. 'I'm black enough,' they say, or, 'Colored folks and water don't mix.'

"When you been kept from something so long, sometimes you don't know how to act when you get to it."

"Oh," Lena said slowly as she trailed her finger through the flour.

"Do you understand, baby?" Lena's mother asked as she wiped up the child's picture from the table's surface with a damp dish towel.

"I think so," Lena answered and walked out of the kitchen to go sit with her grandmother in the sewing room. She loved her grandmama and didn't want her to think that she was being disloyal by going to the beach. But she had no intention of missing out on this opportunity. This trip was the first time in her life Lena would ever experience real freedom around water.

It wasn't fear of drowning that made her mother scream like a banshee every time Lena went near a body of water that was not in a bathtub or sink. It was fear of the child getting her hair wet, nappy, and tangled.

All Lena's life her long thick wiry hair had ruled her. It shaped what she was allowed to do, where she could go, how comfortable she was with her surroundings, what she did, how free she felt.

One of her earliest memories was of her mother combing her hair as gently as she could imagine anyone possibly doing it, cooing soothing words in her ear to distract her from the pain of the tugging and pulling it entailed. Until she was four years old, her mother sometimes combed her hair while she slept. She would go to bed, her long brick-colored hair freshly washed with coconut-oil shampoo and standing all over her head, and wake up with it smoothed and molded into four neat symmetrical plaits. Her mother told her it was magic that caused the transformation. All Lena knew was the "magic" gave her terrible dreams in which strange creatures chased her and cut off her head and swung it around in circles by her hair as they danced and shouted.

Ever since her birth, when she had come into the world with a head full of tight bright curls, soft and thick like the wool on a baby lamb, her hair had been a major topic of discussion, in her family and out.

"When I looked at you laying in my arms the first time, I knew all this damn hair on your head would be the death of me," her mother fussed and fumed as she sat on the edge of her bed and tried to pull the big black comb through Lena's shoulder-length nappy red hair.

"Owww!" was Lena's reply as she sat on the floor of her mother's bedroom, her little shoulders clamped between her mother's skinny knees.

"I'm sorry, baby, I'm doing my best not to hurt you. But you know how your hair is."

"It's not my fault it's long and nappy like it is," Lena said with her bottom lip trembling.

"Of course not. I just wish it didn't hurt you so much to get it combed."

"Me, too. *Oowwwwww!*"

"Sorry," her mother said automatically and kept on combing, bearing down on the job to hurry and finish. For as long as Lena could remember, and even before that, as she saw from her early pictures, she had had her hair combed in one of two ways. Either it was parted straight down the middle then divided again across the crown of her head into four equal parts which her mother braided into four plaits—this was her everyday hairdo. Or, on Sundays and other special occasions, the hair from the two top braids was combed together in one big pretty barrette and braided to fall down the side of her right cheek. The other two plaits were left to hang down her back.

"Whew, long-assed nappy red hair just like mine used to be before it all broke off when I started having you children," her mother kept muttering. "I feel like getting a pair of scissors sometimes and cutting it all off."

"Yeah, Mama, do that. Cut it off like Raymond and Edward's, real short."

"You mean to tell me you want me to cut off all your pretty long hair?"

"Yeah, real short too. Give me a skinny ball like the boys. Then I won't even have to see a comb. I can have me a little brush like them and wear a stocking cap to bed. Cut it off, Mama."

"Aw, but then you won't look like my little girl, you'll look like an old boy," her mama said, wrinkling her pretty nose at the last two words, then laughing at the thought of her baby without all her long rusty-colored hair.

Her grandmama, who could hardly stand to be in the same room when Lena was being put through the torture of getting her hair combed, was once walking by on the way down the hall to her own room and caught a snatch of this conversation. She came barreling into the room.

"Nellie, don't tell me you are actually considering cutting off that child's hair. I never heard anything so ridiculous in all my life. Cutting off that baby's pretty hair," her grandmother huffed.

Her mother resented the intrusion.

"Well, Miss Lizzie, my daughter and I were just having a private conversation of what if. But you're a fine one to talk, you who never lifted a comb to try to rake through all this hair."

"Now, Nellie, you know good and damn well I'd do anything I could for that child—she's my heart. But I can't stand to see her hurt and crying the way she gets when you try to comb her hair."

"Oh, that's right, make me the mean one, the one the child hates for hurting her and trying to make her look nice and neat," her mother said, her voice rising and cracking as she worked herself into a tizzy over something that had been decided years before.

Lena's mother swore that she hadn't had the luxury of expressing her true nature ever since she had had the responsibility of children—that she was sensitive, high-strung, and prone to be excitable, and had been ever since she had been a girl herself.

"Well, if you would just warm the child's hair out a little with a hot comb, it would be a lot easier to handle," Lena's grandmother would counter. She had no other retort and was on the defensive. Even before the suggestion was out of the old woman's mouth, she knew what Nellie would say.

"Warm it out? *Warm it out?*" her mother answered incredulously. "Shit, Miss Lizzie, you know as well as I do that the reason I don't straighten this child's hair—and God knows she could use it—is because of your son and his ideas."

"You goddamn right, you won't straighten that baby's hair because of me," Lena's father yelled from down the hall on his perch in the bathroom. No one knew he was even in the house. He liked to slip in and out unnoticed. Nellie said it was to hear what was said about him.

"Any fool knows you'd stunt the girl's growth of hair if you apply heat to it too early. Any fool knows that," he said. Her father was sure about everything he said, Lena had noticed.

"Yeah, any fool," her mother repeated.

"What's that, Nellie?" her father asked as he cracked the bathroom door another eye's width and threw his adventure book on the linoleum floor.

"I just said 'uh-huh,'" her mother replied with sour meekness.

"When the girl gets to be nine or ten, that'll be plenty of time to be straightening her hair," Jonah said, ending the conversation with a slam of the bathroom door.

Lena's grandmother felt somehow vindicated, and she strutted out of the room and down the hall saying, "Hell, cut off that child's hair—see what'll happen."

Shit, I'd cut it off myself if I didn't think they'd all kill me, Lena thought as she squirmed between her mother's legs while the woman tightened her grip and went back to the unpleasant task.

Despite the pain it caused Lena and everyone who had to deal with it, everybody in her family seemed to think her hair should give her some pleasure. It didn't. It was a burden. Sometimes it was even an embarrassment. Strange women in the grocery store would stare at her and say to one another in amazement, "Look at the head of hair on that child. Make her look just like a grown woman."

Even her best friend in first grade, Gwen, the quiet chubby little girl who was smart like Lena, knew the burden that Lena's hair was for her.

"You better be careful not to run under Miss Pratt's sprinkler, Lena," Gwen would shout as they both ran down the sidewalk of Ward Street after school. "Unless you want a whipping when you get home for getting your hair wet."

During the first steamy fall and final hot spring days of the school year, Miss Pratt, who had a well and didn't use the city water, which she had to pay for, watered her vegetable garden and yard every afternoon at 3:00 sharp for a good two hours. So when the Georgia heat was most oppressive, the neighborhood children—private school and public—knew that if they could make it to the end of the school day, they could take a refreshing dash across Miss Pratt's pretty green lawn through the shower of icy-cold water. Everybody, that is, except Lena.

Lena never had known the wild abandon of running in the spray of a garden hose without hearing her mother or grandmother calling from the house or garden, "Lena, if you don't get your little butt out of that water, you better." Or, "Lena, you get that hair wet and you and me gonna have it out." Or, "Lena, you know good and damn well you cannot cavort out there like that and get your hair wet. I refuse to let you go out this house once more with yourself looking like some wild savage because you played in some damn sprinkler and got your hair all nappy and tangled and then wouldn't let nobody come near you with a comb. No, little miss. Get your ass out that water."

The women had said it so often to Lena that they no longer had to be around to deter her when she considered running through some water.

In the weeks before their trip to the beach, there was as much discussion about what to do with Lena's hair for two weeks in all that moist humid air near the ocean as there was about the actual travel plans.

"Well, I don't care what you say, we gonna have to take a straightening comb with us to warm out that child's hair from time to time. Or do you want her to look like some wild thing the whole time we're down there?" Nellie asked Jonah in all seriousness, as if it were a pressing matter like, How we gonna pay this house note this month?

"Don't waste my time talking 'bout things that are already settled. You know what I said," her father replied over his plate at the breakfast table, as his wife jumped up and down getting more hot grits, more butter, more ice for his orange juice from the ice bucket on the breakfront. "The child's hair don't need straightening yet."

"Well, I don't know how you expect me to keep it looking nice when that ocean water and air get into it. I tell you, it's gonna rise like yeast bread," her mother replied, her voice high, as though she were being persecuted.

The discussion went on and on, from the breakfast table to the dinner table, with Lena sitting there pretending they weren't talking about her, and Raymond and Edward making monkey-shines when their parents weren't looking, one of them pretending to be a crying Lena getting her hair combed and the other one pretending to be their exasperated mother combing her bales of hair.

The problem was solved serendipitously for Lena and her family when Gail Goode, a shoplifter and loose woman (Lena's family called such women Broadway Jessies, alluding to the street they walked) strutted into The Place a few days before their departure with her own daughter proudly in tow for Lena's mother to see.

Lena, downtown at work with her mother that day, was playing behind the counter of the liquor store, exploring the ever-changing trove of treasures kept on the shelves beneath the cash register—pocketknives, sunglasses, tissues, silver dollars, packs of Sen-Sen, cigarette lighters, torn dollar bills, rusty nails, rolls of pennies, and decks of cards—when she heard the bell on the door ring. She didn't bother to stand up and see who had entered, but she did see her mother, who was sitting near the end of the counter and running the store that day, nearly leap over the counter in her excitement.

"Who did that child's hair like that?" her mother wanted to know immediately.

"Well, good afternoon to you too, Miss Nellie. And how are you today?" Lena heard Gail Goode's slow liquid voice and knew who it belonged to because Gail Goode was the proud owner of one of the biggest asses on Broadway.

"Oh, hey, Gail," her mother greeted the woman perfunctorily. Then, "This your little girl? She shore is cute. Now tell me, who did her hair like that?"

"I did," Gail answered proudly.

All Lena's mother seemed interested in was the child's hairdo. Lena knew it would eventually have something to do with her, so she scrambled from the dirty floor and peeped over the counter.

The little girl standing next to the Broadway Jessie with the enormous behind was a bit smaller than Lena, but her shiny black hair was every bit as long and thick.

Whereas Lena had her hair braided into four thick plaits, this little girl must have had her hair combed into a hundred thin braids cascading down on her shoulders like Shirley Temple curls. Someone had taken the time—Lena imagined that it must have been days—to part off a small section of her hair and braid it, then another small section and braid it, then another and another and another, until the little girl's entire head of thick, strong-looking hair was herded into long, tight manageable plaits that fell from her scalp to the ends of her hair where they curled into wiry little spools.

From behind the counter Lena could tell that the little girl did not like being the center of so much attention. She skipped around and fidgeted behind her mama's big butt to get out of so many lines of vision. But Nellie was having none of that.

"Well, you cute little thing," Lena's mother crooned from her stool at the end of the counter by the plate-glass window. When she wanted to, Nellie could get almost anything she wanted by being sweet. "Come on over here and let me get a good look at you."

"Go on, Shirley Lee, let Miss Nellie see your hair."

The child burrowed her face deeper into the cheeks of her mother's ass and wrapped her arms around the woman's thighs in shyness.

"Go on, child," Gail said impatiently. "Don't be acting like a fool when people talk to you."

The child saw she had no choice and peeped around her mother's hips, her head full of thin heavy braids swinging around her ears. Then she moved out to where Lena got her first good look at her and walked slowly over to Nellie with her chin tucked down to her chest and her eyes on the dusty cement floor.

The little girl had on a fancy pink polished cotton dress with a huge sash tied in back that was frilly enough for a party. On her feet she wore pink stretch socks trimmed with a narrow band of white lace and shiny black patent-leather baby dolls that were so free of scuffs that Lena knew they had to be new. And on the very top of her head someone had tied a wide pink satin bow on one of her braids.

Nellie lightly touched the girl's pink hair ribbon with the tips of her fingers and smiled. Lena saw her mother's eyes devour the little girl's hairstyle as if she were memorizing it.

"Well, I sure do like your hairdo, young lady," Nellie said to the child, who still hadn't looked up. "I have me a little girl just about your age, too. Come out here, Lena, and meet this pretty little girl."

Lena was going through a shy period herself, but after seeing how the other girl caught it for ducking her head behind her mama's big behind, she didn't dare pull the same stunt. So she stepped right out and leaned her back against the Schenley's gin sign pasted on the front of the counter.

"Say hello to the little girl," Nellie prompted.

"Hey," Lena said softly.

The other child looked up at Lena and smiled shyly, then dropped her chin back on her chest.

"Why don't you take Shirley Lee over to the other side and get you and her a nice cold drink," Nellie suggested.

Happy to escape the two women's scrutiny, Lena took the girl's hand and led her out the plate-glass door into the hot street, then back into the air-conditioned grill next door. The little girl hesitated a moment at the entrance when the blast of Bobby "Blue" Bland's rough blues from the jukebox hit her in the face, but Lena just tugged on her hand and pulled her into the sea of adults' legs that crowded the counter and dance floor. Lena knew The Place so well she could almost find the opening in the bar with her eyes closed. When she and Shirley Lee reached the entrance in the counter, they slipped under the lid and came out on the employees' side of the bar.

"Boo," said a voice right at their ears as they slipped behind the counter. Lena jumped higher than her little companion, but she just laughed at herself when she turned and caught a glimpse of hair the color of the inside of a baked sweet potato and the glint of gold. Gloria was sitting on the floor next to the grill with a stiff brush in her hand and a bucket between her propped-up legs.

"Well, look a' here, here's my girl. Miss Lena, I was wondering if you was ever gonna come over here and say hello. Or do you have you another friend now and don't have no time for Glo?"

Gloria was down on the floor, scrubbing around the bottom of the grill, which was caked with grease and dirt, because the health inspector was expected that week. But the waitress-barmaid-cook got around so much—in The Place and out—that Lena wouldn't have been surprised to find her anywhere. She was one of those women, Nellie had said, whose real age you couldn't tell but "considering how long she been out there, she don't look bad for whatever age she's going for."

Lena didn't know exactly where "out there" was, but she felt as if she knew just what her mother was saying. To Lena, Gloria almost always looked pretty good.

Gloria prided herself on working with what she had. Lena knew that because Gloria had told her so. "I may not have much left, baby, but I works with what I got."

Lena thought anyone with eyes could see that. When Jonah insisted that Gloria wear a clean white apron when she worked on the grill side at The Place, she wrapped the big stiff apron around her body to make a tight outfit like a sundress that showed off her shape. And sometimes in hot weather she didn't wear anything but a pair of panties underneath, Lena knew. Gloria had told her that too.

She had a gold tooth in the front of her mouth. And because she was always talking or laughing or popping a stick of gum, you could see the tooth flashing from all the way across the room, like a golden beacon.

And she nearly always had a black mole on her right cheek between her nose and her cherry-red lips. One day when she rushed into The Place without the birthmark on her face, Lena asked, "Gloria, where your mole?" And Gloria said, "Damn!" and ran over to the cheap mirror on the Kool green cigarette machine and hastily drew one in with the point of the red Maybelline eyebrow pencil she took from her big red purse.

Gloria seemed to enjoy talking with Lena as much as Lena enjoyed listening to her. Gloria was always anxious to talk about what she had done the night before, even though half the time Lena didn't understand Gloria's sly jokes at the expense of the string of losers and bums who slithered through her life.

"Lord, ham mercy, I'm getting too old for this here shit, excuse me, Lena baby, but I am," Gloria would avow as she hurried into The Place late and reached for two Stanback powders and an RC cola. She would put her quarter on the cash register and sigh. "Either I got to stop whoring around or stop working a steady job, one or the other. I tell you, I can't keep up both ends of this stick."

By then Lena knew what a whore was. She had insisted that someone tell her one Sunday morning as the family drove to Mass or she would ask Sister in class that next Monday morning. "I bet I miss half of what's said at home 'cause I don't know what it means," she said to the silent car.

Her father had kept the big green station wagon climbing up Forest Avenue at the same pace, but he looked over at his wife and said, "Tell Lena what the word means, Nellie." Lena excitedly jumped up on the back of the seat between her parents, wrinkling her pretty new navy-blue-and-white-dotted swiss dress with the big white sailor's color trimmed in red ricrac all down the front, to get in closer earshot.

"A whore," Nellie said evenly, "is a bad woman."

Lena waited for more.

Her mother didn't say another word.

Lena sucked her teeth in disgust like her grandmama did and fell back heavily on the rear seat between her two brothers.

"Is that all?" she asked in disappointment.

"That's bad enough," her mother said quietly.

When Gloria said she had to stop whoring around, Lena was quick to pick up on the word.

"Aww, Gloria," the girl said, "you ain't no whore."

Gloria looked at Lena in surprise. Then she reached in her purse and pulled out a dollar bill. "Here, Lena baby, go down to the peanut shop and buy us some candy."

Lena and Gloria were about to start one of their long conversations about life, but they were interrupted.

"I gotta go," Shirley Lee spoke for the first time, in a small nervous voice.

Lena and Gloria looked around in surprise. Lena was so engrossed in Gloria she had forgotten that she was still holding the little girl's hand. Shirley Lee was holding Lena's hand tighter and tighter, looking around The Place as if she were frightened by something.

"Let me get you girls a little treat," Gloria said and went over to the cooler for two orange drinks. After she handed each girl a bottle, she pulled two ten-cent bags of pork skins from the rack next to the Alka-Seltzer dispenser. With one hand she opened the cellophane bags, and with the other shook dollops of fiery orange hot sauce onto the rinds from a bottle on the counter.

By the time the girls had returned to the liquor store side of The Place with their snacks, negotiations must have been settled, because the next morning Gail Goode drove up to their house in her loud raggedy Chevrolet. She had come to comb Lena's hair into the same 'do that she had given her own daughter.

It hadn't taken days to do it as Lena had imagined, only the entire morning. The tugging and pulling that it entailed hurt Lena's tender scalp as much as ever, but when Gail Goode was finished, Lena couldn't have been happier with the results. She stood on a chair in front of the small mirror in the downstairs hall, the same mirror where she stood and lip-synched songs from long-playing albums by Dinah Washington and Billie Holiday and Dakota Staton, and looked at herself until her mother made her come to dinner.

She danced around all that evening and the next day slinging her tiny braids around her head. Sometimes she whipped them around so sharply that the ends stung her face where they landed. Her brothers swore they were sick of her and couldn't wait until she slung her hair around one time too many and her head went flying off into a corner.

Even her grandmother told her that if she didn't stop swinging her headful of braids around her ears like that she was going to get a headache for seven years like you got when you threw your hair outdoors and the birds used it for their nests. But she smiled when she said it because she thought Lena looked cute as a button with her braids. The old lady tried to count them, but when she got up to two hundred, Lena wouldn't sit still any longer and Grandmama lost count.

Lena didn't care what anyone said or thought. She was so pleased with her new hairdo that when she awoke the following morning and felt all the braids on her cheeks, she giggled. She felt she looked like a whole new exotic person.

When she overheard her mother tell her father, "And the best part is, no matter how wet she gets her hair, we won't even have to comb it again till we get back from vacation and she'll still look nice," Lena knew this new hairstyle was the best thing that had ever happened to her.

Maybe I *am* really lucky, like everyone says, 'cause I was born with a veil over my face, she thought. And my luck just took a while to start.

That very afternoon she put her new hairdo to the supreme test. While everyone else was off in different parts of the house preparing for the trip or ignoring it, she went into the kitchen pantry and closed the door. She stripped off her playsuit and panties and stepped into the striped tank-style swimsuit and white flip-flops her mother had just bought for her. Then she slipped out of the pantry, through the kitchen door, and down the back steps, peeping around corners and looking over her shoulder all the way to the water spigot under the back steps to make sure she wasn't seen.

She went straight for the water spigot and turned it on full force. Not giving herself time to lose her nerve, Lena ran full steam into the spinning jet spray of the lawn sprinkler.

The cold water hit her right in the chest and sent a shiver through her system. She screamed in shock and delight. As she turned and came back, the sprinkler spun around to hit her from behind, and she screamed again. When the stream of water came around a third time, it hit her on her butt and legs. Now she was completely wet from shoulders to feet, and she just laughed.

The fourth time, she ran into the spray head-on, and she yelped again when the water hit her in the right ear and soaked her face and hair. There was no turning back now, so she decided to enjoy this new experience.

She danced in the water's spray each time it came around, holding her hands out to make it cascade over her head. She pretended that the white stone birdbath in the middle of the yard was her partner and she danced around it, giggling at the sound of the drops of water hitting the surface of the water in the bowl. Usually when she danced, everyone laughed at her lack of coordination. But dancing in the water made Lena feel like a ballerina. The two redbirds—a bright crimson male and his mottled brown mate—that came each evening and bathed in the spray of the sprinkler appeared at the edge of the birdbath from the pine trees above and jumped around the rim of the bowl as if they were joining Lena in her dance.

She didn't notice she had an audience until she heard her mother's voice.

"Lena, you must be mad!" Nellie screamed from the porch where she stood with her grandmother and brothers beside her. "Get out of that water, get out of that water this instant!"

Lena had one wild idea of playing on as if she hadn't heard or seen her mother, but thought better of it when she remembered how angry her mother got when one of the boys ran from her while she was trying to whip him. She scampered out of the sprinkler's spray and up on the porch dripping wet. Before her mother could get her hands on her, however, Lena began explaining.

"But, Mama, you said it yourself, I heard you say it to Daddy, you said, 'Lena can get her hair as wet as she wants and we won't even have to comb it.' You said it, I heard you. You said it."

Her mother stopped in midgrasp, her hands about to encircle Lena's skinny arm. Nellie turned to Grandmama with her eyebrows raised slightly, and the older woman laughed and shrugged her shoulders.

Lena's eyes danced from her mother's face to her grandmother's face in expectation.

By the time Nellie said, "Go on, girl, enjoy yourself," the boys had peeled down to their undershorts and beat Lena back to the sprinkler, where they ran and played all afternoon until their fingertips and toes were wrinkled.

THIRTEEN

❦ ❦

BEACH

Three days later they packed the big green station wagon and headed for the beach.

Car trips were something at which Lena's family excelled. They had it down to a routine. Her daddy drove. Her mama sat in the front passenger seat. Each boy took a back window—Edward behind his father, Raymond behind his mother. Lena scrambled all over the car, usually starting out sitting in the middle of the backseat, then moving to stand in her spot on the hump in the middle of the floorboard, then climbing over to the middle of the front seat, then sidling over to sit between her mother's legs, then maybe moving back to the rear seat to fight with one of the boys for a view from his window. If there was nothing packed in the rear of the station wagon, she would sometimes climb back there, usually at the insistence of one of her brothers, to look out the wide back window and make faces and take off her shoes and wave her feet at the people in the car behind them. When her grandmother was along, the older woman sat between the boys in the back and didn't seem to mind Lena's wandering all over her.

The family took a car ride every Sunday after they all attended

10:00 A.M. Mass. Sometimes they just rode around town, where her father would stop from time to time at some run-down-looking house on a dirt street or back alley. He would get out of the car and go in to chat amiably or to demand matter-of-factly his "goddamn money." From the sound of her father's voice, Lena imagined this money that her father wanted from the people living at his Sunday stops as somehow different from ordinary money.

For one thing it was *his money*. He put the emphasis on that. So Lena suspected that the money—the dollar bills, fives, tens, and twenties—may have looked like ordinary money, but it was special, separate from the money he spent on the family food and utilities and clothes. Maybe it was money he won in poker and skin games. Perhaps it was money that came directly from the cash register downtown in The Place. Lena had thought for some time that there was something special about the money in the cash registers in the liquor store and in the grill side of The Place. Many times she had seen her mother stealthily slip a couple of twenties from the cash drawer into her pocket or purse while she was working behind the counter.

It had to be special money. That's how her daddy treated it. "Man, don't play with me about my goddamn money," he would yell as he walked out of one of the ramshackle houses, stopping to speak in a friendly manner to the older people sitting in swaybacked chairs on the porch. Then he would get in the car with his family and drive off to the next house, where he would want his goddamn money from some other person. Her mother would sit there in her Sunday finery, her slender hand on her throat, and smile out the car window with a look on her face that said, "My children in this car and I don't even know this man."

Other Sundays her father would head out of town to the countryside surrounding Mulberry to drive the back roads, smell the fresh air, and comment on the small patches of vegetable gardens country folks were growing in their yards.

"Look at those collard greens over there," he would say,

making all of them in the car direct their attention toward the garden with the huge shiny leaves of collards growing in neat bunches. "Now, those are some beautiful greens. Put down those comic books and papers back there," he would tell his children in the backseat. "Look out the window and enjoy the scenery."

Although the boys and Lena didn't dare say anything in protest, they would close the books and Sunday paper grudgingly. Then they would start taking out their anger on each other by pushing and shoving and pinching for more room or a better seat or view, or more air. They were miserable in the backseat watching the same scenery they had seen all their short lives, Sunday after Sunday, and they had to let somebody know it.

This trip to the beach was different. It was to be the longest trip the family had ever undertaken. Lena's father calculated it would take them all about eight hours, with rest, comfort, and lunch stops. He had calculated just about everything they were likely to encounter between their house and the Georgia shore. He didn't tell anybody, but he had even allowed time for them to get lost because he was to be at the head of the caravan leading three cars and ten people across the state. And he almost always got lost at least once during every road trip he took. He couldn't explain it or understand it really, but there was just something about a road map that seemed to dare him to strike out in his own direction regardless of what the lines and signs told him to do. In private Lena's mother said it was just so he could get mad when things didn't go according to his schedule. But Lena had noticed that it was her mother who always got anxious and angry when they got lost. Her father seemed to enjoy it, taking it as an opportunity to explore an area that they wouldn't have normally seen.

"Well, what do you know? I never knew that there was this little lake back here off this road," he'd say, sounding sincerely intrigued.

Her father had already told them that there would be no

reading during this trip. They could do that as soon as they got back home from vacation and started school. He wanted them to pay particular attention during the next two weeks to the things around them.

"As soon as we get out of this county," he told them over his shoulder as they pulled away from the house, their grandmother still waving to them from the steps of the side porch, "you'll start noticing how things are gonna change. The land, the way things look, the way they smell. Just watch."

Lena and the boys, wide-eyed with excitement over the trip and with no comic books to read, had to admit that he was right. Out the windows of the station wagon, they watched the familiar red Georgia clay of their own region gradually change to the rich black loam farther south and then to the light friable sandy soil of the coast.

The peach trees they were so used to seeing by the sides of the roads on their Sunday drives gave way to the broad pecan trees of south Georgia. After a hundred miles or so, the tall pines they knew so well seemed to grow shorter, into the knobby loblolly pines of the coastal region. Then, to their amazement, the trees seemed to take on an even stranger form.

The majestic oak trees they were familiar with began spreading their limbs and growing curly appendages like an old man's beard, which their father told them was Spanish moss. Then the sandy ground began sprouting palm trees, like those they had seen in pictures of desert islands.

The caravan of cars—first their big green station wagon, then Lena's aunt and uncle's black Ford sedan, and finally the Stevenses' brand-new 1956 red Cadillac—arrived at their small motel across the road from the beach long after dark because they had made so many stops across the state to eat and pee and stretch and rest. Lena could smell the sharp salty scent that her father told her was the smell of the marshes and the ocean, and she could hear the waves crashing against the shore, but it was too dark to see anything. And her mother insisted that the children get right into bed after a bath in putrid water that smelled like rotten eggs so they would be rested and ready to start their vacation early the next morning.

The motel they stayed in was owned by a short fat black man with a square fleshy face, who said his people came from Savannah. He had the unsettling habit of slapping his palm to his forehead, then slowly pulling his hand over his face and down the curve of his throat before he spoke. He wrapped up this ritual by thumping the middle of his chest with his fist once where his hand's journey ended. After seeing him do this the first night when he showed each family to its flat concrete block bungalow, Lena avoided him as much as possible. She lived in fear of watching the man pull his features into his hand like a cartoon character—maybe Popeye—and seeing them snap back like rubber into the shape of another face altogether.

The sulphur of the bathwater made them all smell like old-time beachcombers before they even saw the ocean. And that night Lena dreamed of the beach—or at least what she imagined it to look like from pictures she had seen.

The next morning Lena's father was the first to rise, getting the rest of them out of bed by singing loud choruses of "Shake, Rattle, and Roll."

"Get out of that bed, wash your face and hands. Get into that kitchen, rattle them pots and pans," he sang in his smooth tenor voice. "Shake, rattle, and roll."

He had them all laughing and dancing in the tiny kitchen of the small motel suite as grits bubbled in the pot and bacon fried in the skillet. Then they all dressed in their swimsuits and covers and headed across the street for the beach.

It was like going on a treasure hunt.

They started out walking in a group, but by the time they reached the wind-blown rickety fence along the well-worn path into the dunes, they were walking single-file. They all stopped every few steps to admire something completely new to their inland eyes: the wild white fiddle-leaf morning glories that crawled on dark green vines all over the dunes, the tiny sand crabs that ran from their approaching feet, the big holes in the sand that the men, sissy-like and skittish, swore were made by some kind of beach snakes. Raymond and Edward ran over to the biggest hole they could find in the sand, expecting to find a huge snake sticking its head out. Disappointed to discover no signs of life around the hole, Edward started to stick his hand down the wide opening. Four or five adults yelled at the same time. "Boy, don't you stick your hand down there! You may draw back a nub!" his father cautioned harshly.

Even for those in the group who had been to the beach before, this trip seemed like a whole new excursion into an unknown territory, an exotic exploration by pretty brown-skinned creatures perfectly at home under the burning midmorning sun.

Lena loved everything about the beach: the way the gulls and pelicans squawked and swooped above her, the way the air cooled the closer she got to the water, the salt she tasted on her lips when she licked them, the way the sea oats swayed gently in the ocean breeze, the tiny sanderlings scurrying away from the surf trying not to get their feet wet. She felt that she somehow belonged there at the shore, even though it was her first time even seeing the ocean.

She followed her first impulse when her group topped the final tertiary dunes and caught their first sight of the greenish-brown waters of the Atlantic. She threw down her bundles, kicked off her rubber thongs, and ran into the water, her many braids flying behind her like a bridal train. An incoming wave met her head-on and kissed her right in her face. She giggled like a flirtatious teenager and shook her head so her wet braids swung around her like a dog flinging water off its body.

She felt a little guilty when she remembered her grandmama back in hot dusty Mulberry. But after a few minutes of playing in the water and feeling the hot morning sun on her back, she ran up to her mother, her aunt, and Mrs. Stevens where they sat, all dressed in strapless skirted swimsuits, under two big red-and-white beach umbrellas her father had saved from a liquor promotion the summer before. There she wiped the salty water from her eyes and soon forgot everyone but the few black people in her group, who had the beach to themselves.

By midday everyone was spent from the sun, the playing, the sea air, and the big picnic lunch of fried chicken, potato salad, deviled eggs, ham and pimento cheese sandwiches, and lemon Coke that the women had found time to prepare during the morning. There were times when Lena hated the idea of having to grow into an adult woman on whose shoulders so much work seemed to fall. But like everyone else she sat down on the spread and ate until her face was greasy.

After lunch, while the women and men half-dozed under the big beach umbrellas, the children played on the sandy beach, careful not to go into the water without an adult or until an hour after they had eaten.

It was in this half-dazed state that Lena wandered away from her brothers and cousins, who were playing near the surf, kicking up sand and salt water in each other's faces in their exuberance. Her brothers had already forgotten the instructions given to them just that morning.

"Now, boys," their mother had said, trying to sound serious and stern as she beat eggs in a bowl for breakfast, "we want you to enjoy yourselves during this trip, but we also want you to take on some responsibility."

Lena, standing in the doorway of the small kitchenette, saw both sets of her brothers' shoulders sag at the news.

"Now, when we're out on the beach, no matter what other adult is there, we want you two to keep an eye on Lena. We don't expect you to kill your own damn fool selves in that water trying to save her or anything if she wanders in too deep, just make sure she doesn't get that far.

"Lena is just a little thing and doesn't understand like you two boys the respect you have to have for the water. Now, like I said, we want you to have a good time down here, too, but don't forget it's just like at home. Keep an eye out for Lena. She's our baby."

Lena found it easy to understand sometimes why the boys said they hated her. She hated it herself: always being considered a burden no matter how good she tried to be.

But when the idea hit her, she still wandered down the beach by herself without a thought to how the boys would have to pay for her absence when her mother discovered it.

FOURTEEN

❧   ❧

RACHEL

It was low tide. Lena didn't know it was called that, but she knew the ocean was different because she could now see the big brown pelicans congregate out on a long narrow sandbar that was not even visible a few hours before. Every now and then another three or four would glide by her, flying just inches above the waves, and swoop down on the island, insisting every time that their brothers and sisters find room for them to land. To Lena the birds looked ancient, like something from another time, before creatures like her mama and daddy and brothers walked the beaches.

As she strolled down the beach, she stopped for a while to watch a school of mullet leap and splash not three feet from where she stood at the water's edge. Lena could see the dragon-flies and sand flies and gnats hovering above the water's smooth still surface. Each time a big fat mullet, going after an insect, jumped out of the muddy water, the sun turned it silver-colored as it fell back in on its side, and Lena let out a little cry of appreciation.

When the fish moved on to another feeding spot, the girl looked down at her feet sunk nearly ankle-deep in the muddy sand of the ocean floor and saw the darting figures of minnows swimming fearlessly over her toes and behind her heels. She tried to keep her feet as still as possible because the smallest wiggling of her toes would produce clouds of mud in the water and disturb the tiny fish. To Lena there seemed to be hundreds of them, but then she saw that their shadows on the ocean floor near the water's edge doubled their numbers.

The child really enjoyed the feeling of communion with other creatures that the small fish playing around her ankles gave her. Bugs and small crawly things didn't bother her. The only thing that crawled on the ground she was truly afraid of was the black crusty roll-up bugs that her brothers delighted in throwing in her hair and dropping down the back of her blouse.

If Raymond and Edward were here, she thought as she watched the tiny fish play with her toes, they would feel called upon to go whooping and running through the water trying to catch the poor little things. Boys! Then she sucked her teeth in disgust the way her grandmother did and walked on.

The fine white sand, sparkling with glints of light like the glitter her mother sprinkled over her hair and on the costumes for her dance teacher's annual recitals, was hot between her bare brown toes. She wandered in and out of the surf to cool them off from time to time. To someone watching her from a spot in the dunes farther inland, Lena would have appeared to be wandering idly down the beach with no particular destination in mind, but the appearance would have been misleading.

Lena was looking for a particular place just a little farther down the beach, where the big rocks that lined part of the coast formed a low overhang facing the ocean. At that spot, she was sure, there was a curve in the beach that created a protected little cove where she could sit on the dry pure sand and feel the ocean breeze blow over her face and chest. She had dreamed about that very spot the night before as she slept with the smell of the sea in her throat.

When she saw the spot, she wasn't a bit surprised that it looked exactly like she had dreamed it would, with a big tree stump bleached white wedged among the rocks. In her seven years she had occasionally dreamed about places and things and events before they came to pass.

But she was a bit startled to find a barefoot black woman dressed in a long filmy maroon dress sitting on the huge stump of driftwood with her knees pulled up to her chin and her arms wrapped tightly around her bent legs.

The woman's hair, coming loose from short nappy braids, was wild and free in the wind. A heavy dark gray scarf of some rough cotton material, caught on one of the tree's short broken branches, blew just as wildly in the breeze beside her.

The woman was staring out at the water. She acted as though she didn't see Lena, but something inside the child told her she had. Lena continued walking toward the woman, although her best instincts told her to run back in the direction she had come. Her heart began to beat rapidly.

The strange figure continued to look out to sea as Lena walked toward her spot on the beach.

There was something familiar about the way the woman sat there. She looked as if she belonged there, but she also looked unaffected by her surroundings. The July sun, blazing like a hot tin plate in the sky, hadn't even raised a sweat on the woman's face and throat, which looked like they were made of old brown leather. But Lena could feel the rays burning her own scalp in the tiny parts between her braids.

Lena stopped and just stood there for a moment, digging her toes into the sand a few yards from the woman. The woman's washed-out-looking eyes swept away from some point far out to sea and moved around to Lena.

"Hey, Lena," the woman in the long thin maroon dress said in an easy, natural way. "My name is Rachel. I been waiting for you."

"Waiting for me?" Lena asked, her voice cracking with fear before she even felt it. "How you even know who I am? I don't know you."

"Oh, I knows all kinds of t'ings," the woman said. "Why don't you come over chere and set down by me?"

Lena was about to answer, "Do I have to?" when the woman said, "Or do you want me to come visit you in your bed tonight?"

The image of the woman coming to haunt her in the middle of the night instead of there on the sunny beach made Lena walk up to the apparition and sit down beside her immediately.

They sat there in silence for a long while, looking out at the baby waves gently lapping the sandy shore as the ocean breeze, soft as her grandmother's kiss, blew around them and lightly lifted Rachel's thin skirts around her knees. Hundreds of dragonflies zipped and darted through the air, going after the large mosquitoes, with the squawking gulls right on their tails looking for lunch. All the animal activity filled the air with humming, buzzing, and flapping.

The woman appeared calm and untroubled. Lena felt just the opposite. Now that she was sitting up close to the woman, the vise that had gripped her chest on first seeing her had tightened even more. The tightness made it hard for her to breathe and made the thumping of her heart against her rib cage seem more pronounced. Lena thought everybody on the beach would be able to hear her heart beat.

But when she looked up and down the beach, she realized for the first time that she had walked so far that her family and friends were no longer even in sight. And she began to panic.

"What's wrong wif you, gull? What you scared of?" Rachel sounded a bit annoyed.

"Lady, I'm scared of you."

"Shoot," the woman snorted and pulled the child closer to her on the tree. Rachel smelled like something out of the ocean: salty and wet all the way through, and her skin was scratchy with grains of sand. Lena now sat with her head full of the long reddish braids tucked under the woman's smelly armpit.

"You ain't got no cause to be scared of me. A child like you. You gonna see a heap more like me before you dead, too."

Lena shuddered at the thought and the feel of Rachel's clammy skin and clothes pressed next to her face, arm, and thigh.

"Feel good here on this log, don't it?" Rachel said as she slipped her arm from around Lena's shoulders and leaned her head back to catch the breeze on her throat. "Me and the peoples 'round here used to call the wind Tony. We used to sing, 'Blow, Tony, blow.' "

Lena just nodded dumbly. Her heart was still thumping like the machines at the paper plant, and when she tried to swallow, no spit came up in her mouth.

"When I was 'live, I used to love to come sit on this chere very spot. But I wasn't here much, much as I loved it, 'cause when I was 'live I was a slave."

"A slave?" Lena wanted to know.

"Yeah," Rachel answered.

"A slave? A slave like I read about in school?"

"A little thing like you can read?" Rachel asked with wonder in her voice. "How old you is, Lena?"

"Seven," Lena said.

"Seven. Hummmpph, I always wanted to read."

She just sat there a moment looking at the child, who sat next to her scratching mosquito bites on her thigh and staring back at her with big eyes. Then the woman seemed to remember what she was talking about and continued speaking.

"Years and years ago we peoples, black peoples, was all slaves up along in through this chere area. All up in through Georgia and down on through Alabama and 'ssippi and on up the coast, too.

"I warn't born here. I was born on a place up 'round Macon, where I was a slave, too, but they sold me off down chere when I was just 'bout a growed 'oman. I don't know why, just one day they just sold me, put me on a wagon with some pigs and goats and rode me off to this chere place . . . still to be a slave but a slave 'way from my ma and my pa and everybody I know."

"A slave?" Lena repeated in wonderment.

"The big house and barns and outbuildings and our cabins where us slaves stayed was set way back there," Rachel explained as she pointed inland past the sand dunes and sea grass that rose, then dipped out of sight. "The white man that say he owned us owned a whole lot of land and he grew rice 'long the river up the coast. You ever see fields where they grows rice, Lena?"

"No," Lena answered. She didn't know how to address the woman. Do you call a ghost ma'am? she wondered.

"Well, let me tells you, you don't never want to see it either. I didn't know not'ing 'bout no rice till I was brought down chere, but I had to learn mighty quick.

"Warn't no field really where they grew it, just a big old marsh where the river flooded every tide. It would be full of big old cypress trees with stumps that went way down in the mud and those palms with the sharp leaves that look like swords and all kind of t'ings growing in it. And the man which work us would say, 'Ya'll niggers go out there and clear that field today.' Us womens would have to tie up our skirt tails and go out there with the mens and work in that swampy water up to our knees. Water full of water moc'sin snakes and snapping turtles and 'gators.

"And the sun be beating down on you and ain't even no shade for what seem like a mile. And if they is, you better not get caucht standing under it. And the mosquitoes and flies and gnats, they be eating you up.

"And, Lena, every day be like that. If you ain't clearing a field, you planting or you weeding or you cutting and hauling. Every day."

"Every day? Even Sundays?" Lena wanted to know.

"Every day and some nights too, when the moon was big and bright. Going out in that marsh at night used to scare me to death. Sometimes there wouldn't even be no moon, and they send us out there to work with somebody holding a flambeau.

"But onst in a while, I take a chance and I slip off and come down chere to set. All I wanted to do was go by myself, set with my feets in this sand and let those cool, cool, moist breezes brush all over my tired body. I wanted the wind to blow right through me.

"I warn't trying to run away. Not then. Down chere I didn't even know which a-way to run. All I wanted was a little time down by the water. No working and sweating and hauling and caring for folks that warn't my own.

"This land right chere looked like the onliest place I was ever gonna know, the onliest home I was ever gonna have. I knew I had another home 'way, 'way 'cross the waters, but I ain't never been there or set foot on that soil. This all I know and I wanted it for my own. I wanted to feel and taste and hear this place that was all I knew.

"But the white folks say I warn't nothing but a slave. The missus she say, 'How dare you think you can just go to the ocean when you feels like it?' Just like that, she say it, 'How dare you? The onliest reason for you to go to the shore is to bring me a cool breeze back. Can you do that? Can you?' I'd say no, I can't do that. Then she say, 'Then what use is you going there wasting time?' "

Rachel stopped speaking and seemed to catch her breath. Lena remembered to breathe for the first time since the ghost started talking, it seemed, and Rachel continued.

"They beat me the first time they caught me chere. Beat me bad too. But I still come back. I had to breathe this air. I had to let it play with my skin. Shoo things out my body."

"You were a little girl to get a whipping?" Lena asked.

"No, I was a growed 'oman like I is now."

"And they still whipped you like you wasn't but a child?"

"They whipped me like I wasn't nothing. That what it mean to be a slave—you ain't nothing."

"What you mean, you ain't nothing?" Lena really wanted to know. She couldn't comprehend what Rachel was trying to tell her.

Rachel just looked at her. "Lots of people loves you, don't they, Lena?" she asked after a little while. "Don't they?"

Lena thought a second or two, then nodded her head.

"I'm glad. I'm glad you loved. Most times I don't think I was loved. Mebbe I was. My ma and pa loved me, I knows that, but they couldn't save me none. Sitting down chere at the ocean made me feel loved a little.

"There was something about the ocean that just kept drawing me chere, just tolling me to chere. It asked me questions that tore my heart. Questions I couldn't answer, but I couldn't stay 'way from chere neither."

"Late last night, up in our room at the motel with the windows open, I heard the ocean talking, too," Lena offered.

"Then you know what I mean. What it say to you?" Rachel wanted to know.

Lena turned shy and just shrugged her shoulders.

"Well, I tells you what it say to me. It tell me all the t'ings that coulda been, that could be.

"It sung songs to me of what I coulda been if I warn't no slave. What my mama coulda been. My mama before they sold me away from 'nem, she could sew anyt'ing with a needle and tread, anyt'ing. But she warn't no sewer, she was a slave.

"And my pa, he war a blacksmith. Best one in that whole county. That *whole* county. But him, he was a slave, too. And what about me? Maybe I wanted to make clothes for people, or stories, or pick a tune on the box for them to dance to or marry to or cry to. A slave can't do that. Not for real." Rachel fell silent again and let the sound of the seagulls and dragonflies fill the space her voice had left.

"It was bad?" Lena asked, but didn't really want to know. She had already heard more than she ever wanted to hear in her life.

"Little girl, you don't know how bad it was. Look at your legs, how smooth and clear they is. Look at mines, my whole body, so covered with scabs and scars and whelps. It was bad.

"And I ain't just talking 'bout the beatings I got, not that the beatings wasn't a big part of it. The beatings was bad, they make you strip down mother-naked. They didn't care none 'bout everybody seeing you without no clothes. Then they tell you to hug that tree or lay 'cross that log or stick your head in that fence, then they try to wear out that leather on your back, your neck, your behind, your head—anywhere. I seen folks—womens, mens—beat till the blood run down round they feets and stand in puddles in they brogan shoes. And seeing other folks beat was just 'bout as bad as it being you. I think the white folks know that, how bad it was seeing somebody else beat.

"Where I was born, up 'round Macon, they beat you through your clothes where the marks and blood don't show, but down here where I was they strip you mother-naked like you ain't got no decents, then they whips you.

"The white man that say he own us say, 'I don't care 'bout the marks, I take the loss.' That's what he say, 'I take the loss.' Like he know somet'ing 'bout loss. No, I was born to be something else than a slave."

"Then why were you a slave?" Lena asked.

"Didn't have no choice, child, what you think? But to be a slave on the ocean, I could not bear it."

A sleek white sea tern sharply traced in black flew directly over their heads, casting a brief shadow over Lena's face and leaving Rachel's untouched.

"See that bird, that beautiful, beautiful flying creature? When I lived they flew over me too, while I was working in the fields and late in the evening when I trudged back to my cabin to fall out dead tired on my t'in pallet stuffed with the Spanish moss that hang from the trees 'round here.

"Seeing them birds flying used to break my heart. I used to hear stories 'bout how our peoples used to be able to fly at one time. When I was your age, I used to try, try so hard I'd break out in a sweat just wishing, but I never could, never could fly."

Lena dropped her eyes to the sand and felt suddenly ashamed of the question in her mind.

"Course I wanted someone to love me," Rachel answered her silent question. "Course I needed a strong shoulder to hold on to; course I wanted to cry, and did lots of times. But it didn't do no good. T'ings was still the same when I woke up before first light each morning."

Sadness was overtaking Lena's feeling of fear. She wanted to tell Rachel, "I'm just a little girl. I don't want to hear all this. I don't want to know all this. Please, don't tell me any more." But Rachel just looked at the child's big brown eyes welling up with tears and slipped inside her head and thoughts again.

"Child," she said softly. "Do you know how long I been waiting for somebody like you to come along so I can tell them all of this, so I can share some of this? You t'ink I'm not gonna tell you now I got you here on my beach?"

Then Rachel threw her head back and began to shake all over, her short nappy braids quivering with her. She opened her mouth wide, wider than Lena thought anyone was capable of doing. Her lips stretched back farther and farther, exposing more and more of her brown-and-pink gums. Then she started moaning and howling like something from the grave, long and low like a werewolf out of a scary movie. Lena started to cover her eyes with her hands and bring her knees up to her ears, the way she always did during the scary part of movies when she sat in the balcony of the Burghart Theatre with her brothers, but she couldn't move her hands to her face. She couldn't move at all.

At last Rachel settled down and sat quietly on the log, rocking from side to side.

"But I didn't feel so bad when I took a chance and come down here to set awhile," Rachel finally said.

"Did they beat you some more when they caught you down here again?" Lena couldn't understand why she asked these questions. She didn't really want to know the answers. They seemed to pour out of her mouth without her permission.

"No, little girl, they didn't beat me. When I warn't where they thought I oughta be, they sent a boy to come look for me. His name was Johnny. He was a nice boy. He had a club foot and fetched things and did errands and such around the place. He was just slow and the white folks holler at him for it, but he couldn't no more help it than the man in the moon.

"Johnny come and he beg me to come back. He found me sittin' on this chere tree stump that had been hit by lightning and then had fell in on the beach.

"I was just setting here watching it get dark. Johnny was real scared for me. All us black folks, we all lived in fear. Always afraid, scared of the beatings or of getting sold away or of something. He come running up, calling my name, 'Rachel, Rachel.' I heard him long 'fore I saw him.

"When he caught sight of me setting on this tree stump he stopped dead still up on the cliff back there. Then he come running down the path to the beach down here where I was setting.

" 'What you hollering my name for, Johnny?' I asked him.

"He say, 'Rachel, Rachel, they send me for you. They say you better get your black ass back to the cabins fast as you can run. Rachel, you got to do it. They come here, they kill you.'

" 'They already done that, Johnny,' I said then.

"The boy was looking back over his shoulder like something fixin' to jump out the bushes and grab him, then turning back, straining to see me in the growing darkness.

"I told him, 'You go on back, Johnny. Tell 'em you can't find me. I'm staying right chere on this log.'

"The boy stood there dancing from his good foot to his bad foot for a while, then run off in the direction of the big house.

"When I heard the hosses' hooves, it was pure-T dark. And the tide that was dead still when Johnny come looking for me was turned around and coming in fast. Just like it is now," Rachel said as she pointed to the water's edge creeping back toward them.

Lena looked out at the ocean a ways off from their feet in the sand. The surf was being whipped up by the wind. The churning of the ocean had made foam like dingy soapsuds that blew onto the beach and skittered across the sand around the legs of the tiny sanderlings and larger seagulls standing with their beaks to the wind.

The girl was surprised to see how quickly the water's edge had inched back toward them. The sandbar full of pelicans had disappeared under the waves, and the sun was no longer directly overhead. She knew it must be getting late in the afternoon. Her own braids blew in the wind like Rachel's hair and she longed to get away from that fishy odor that rose from the apparition's clothes and being, but she still couldn't move from her spot on the log.

She tried to creep her foot along the white sand a bit at the bottom of the crab-eaten log, but when it wouldn't obey her command and move, she didn't dare try to get up and walk away. She wasn't even sure that she really wanted to leave Rachel crying and moaning on the beach, until the woman said she could go.

Does the tide come in that fast when she's not here? Lena wondered to herself.

"I'm always here," the woman answered and lifted her chin in the air. "This is where I wanted to be, this is where I *choose* to be, and this is where I is.

"Like I was saying, this is where I was setting when them two white mens—the man which owned the place where I was a slave to and the man which worked for him—come riding up on their big snorting hosses. In the dark they sound to me like they was come riding from hell.

"I could feel those hosses' hoofbeats hitting the earth and echoing through my chest, but I warn't scared. Not a bit that time, 'cause I knew I warn't gonna go nowhere. They reined in them hosses and come to a stop right up there above us," Rachel continued, jerking her head over her shoulder in the direction of the overhang behind them.

" 'Rachel!' one of 'em screamed down at me. I was surprised they could see me in the dark. They most likely couldn't. They must a' just knowed I was down here.

" 'Rachel, you black bitch, who the hell you think you is, making us come out here in the dark to look for your black ass? Get on back to the house, you gon' regret the day you ever saw this here water.'

"But I didn't say a word. The tide was coming in fast, I could feel it around my feets already. And I knew that the path leading up to the overhang where they stood was under water itself by then. I just sat there listening to the ocean, to what she had to say to me 'bout what coulda been.

"I reached up and pulled this chere scarf off my head. Wropped one end of it 'round my right arm here at the wrist, then wropped the other end onto this branch of the log. Had this here long apron. I ripped it off from 'round my waist and tied my other arm best I could to the other side of this log.

"By then the water was almost up to my waist, and it felt good and cool on my body.

" 'We oughta just leave your black ass down there,' one of the mens said.

"I didn't say nothing. I just smiled. It happened real quick, faster than I thought it would. The tide rose so fast I hardly had time to t'ink of my ma and pa back at the place up 'round Macon, then I thought 'bout this here man name Daniel and how his eyes look when they drove me away from up there. He looked so sad that I was going away.

"And the last thing I remember as I heard them two mens trying to ride down that watery path and cursing when they find out they can't get down there to me is I hope don't nobody's eyes never look that sad for me again. 'Cause I was glad to be going. I was going to the ocean and couldn't nobody ever stop me from going there again.

"I been chere ever since, but you the onliest one I ever talked to. You special, Lena."

Rachel settled back on the log so solidly and contentedly that Lena thought the ghost might just disappear into the wood. The child sat as still she had before. When a big stinging deer fly landed on her left arm and began biting her, she swatted it with the palm of her right hand. The swift movement of her own hand surprised her. She could move once again. Get up and walk away, she told herself, since Rachel was back to looking out to sea as she had been when Lena first saw her. But now it was Lena who held herself there. She knew in her heart there was something she still had to share with Rachel, just as the woman had shared her story with her.

"Grandmama say colored folks don't belong on the beach." Lena's voice was barely a whisper.

Rachel turned her whole body around so she was facing Lena. Then she reached out with her damp leathery hands and grabbed the child's shoulders firmly and dipped her face down until it was level with Lena's. She spoke right into the girl's mouth.

"Don't you believe that," she said very slowly. "Don't you believe that, Lena. Black folk belong here. You belong here. Don't believe black folks don't belong on the beach. Don't never believe black folks don't belong nowhere. Don't be afraid, Lena. Claim what is yours. I died to be here on this beach, Lena. Don't never forget that. You belong anywhere on this earth you want to."

The smell of the ocean—salty, fishy, alive, green—was so strong on Rachel's breath blowing into Lena's face that it made the girl a little dizzy. And the woman was holding the child's shoulders so tightly in her hands that it was beginning to hurt.

"Lena!" her brother Raymond's harsh voice broke through the sea air.

"Girl, where you been?"

Lena jumped up from the log, breaking Rachel's grip on her. She was in a state of confusion. For a while she had forgotten that her brothers even existed. Seeing them running up the beach toward her and Rachel's protected cove seemed to make stars spin before her eyes, as if two worlds had collided before her.

"Lena, wh-wh-what you doing up h-here all by yourself?" Edward demanded angrily as he reached her first and grabbed her skinny bare arm so hard it made her wince. But Lena could see the relief in his eyes.

"Good God, Lena, what made you go off by yourself like that?" Raymond asked. He was as mad as Edward.

Lena didn't know what to say. She saw the boys looking right at her where she stood next to the log, but they didn't say a word about Rachel.

Just to make sure, Lena turned around and looked at the woman in the thin maroon dress. She was still there and had gone back to staring out to sea.

"Lena, pay attention." Raymond grabbed her hand and pulled

her sharply toward him. "Do you know you almost got us killed? What you wander off for by yourself like that? Mama an' 'em still 'sleep, so they don't know you gone."

"Yeah, if th-th-they did, they'd b-b-be makin' two little wo-wo-wooden overcoats for us right now. Daddy woulda sk-skinned us alive."

"Yeah. You're more damn trouble than you'll ever be worth," Raymond agreed as he took her other arm and pulled her away from the log back down the beach in the direction of the motel. "Come on, let's get back. And quick too."

Coming behind them, Edward gave Lena a push and muttered, "You old pop-eyed fool."

Lena couldn't take any more. Seeing Rachel, hearing the ghost's story, knowing she was the only one who saw her and that she better not tell anyone or she would get sick, then having Raymond and Edward shoving and pinching her like she was nothing. It was all too much.

She pulled away from her brothers' grasp and flung herself down on the hot beach sobbing, the ends of her hundreds of plaits falling into the sand.

The sight stopped Raymond and Edward in their tracks. They had never seen anything like it, had never heard their baby sister cry like that before: deep heart-rending sobs that shook her whole body. They were immediately repentant.

Dropping to the sand beside her, they sat her up and tried brushing the sand off her face and arms and swimsuit.

"Shhhh, don't cry, Lena, we sorry. Come on, stop crying, we sorry we yelled at you," Raymond said in gentle tones.

"Yeah," Edward added, as contrite as his brother, "we were just scared you had gone off and got in the water and drowned. You know you ain't got no business going off by yourself on this beach."

"Yes, I do. Yes, I do, I belong on this beach. We all do. We do, too, belong down here," Lena kept repeating to her puzzled brothers.

"Lena, you know you don't have any business going off being

by yourself, especially down here where you don't know anybody," Raymond tried to reason with her.

"Yes, I do, yes, I do," Lena kept saying. "I belong down here
on this beach. This ocean is just as much mine as anybody's. It's
yours too, Raymond. We colored folks, we belong on the
beach."

"Girl, what you talking about?" Raymond demanded.

"I do, too, belong down here. I belong on this beach, Raymond, I belong anywhere on this earth I want to be," she insisted.

The boys exchanged glances and decided not to press their
baby sister about what she meant. They knew she was as likely
as not to say something that would confuse and scare them. And
they had had enough of a scare for one day when they realized
she was missing.

"Okay, okay, y-y-you right, Lena, w-we do belong here. I
know w-wh-what you mean. Now, stop crying."

Lena was calming down some now. She was trying to stop her
sobs. But they kept escaping from her chest in little hiccuping
sounds that shook her whole body. And her face, especially her
nose and ears and eyes, was red and strained. The boys knew that
their mother would be able to tell right away that Lena had been
crying.

"Come on," Raymond suggested. "Let's get in the water and
cool off."

The sudsy waves rolling into the shore with the tide were like
a refreshing cool drink against their bodies. But Lena couldn't
help shuddering a bit at the feel of the salty water on her skin.
It made her think of Rachel, whom she could still see sitting up
on the beach on her bleached-out tree stump. And when an
especially big wave came in while Lena wasn't looking, covering
her head and face, going up her nose, and putting a salty taste
in her throat, she had to fight a panicky feeling that she knew
must have been like the one Rachel felt when the tide came in
and she was tied underwater to that tree.

When she emerged from the wave, spitting and sputtering,

her heart racing, her eyes stinging, she heard the boys laughing at her histrionics. She was about to get angry with them because they obviously didn't understand the importance of what she had just experienced. She was going to tell them that they were stupid and unfeeling and didn't care about anything but not getting a whipping. Then she looked up at Rachel and saw a smile on the woman's leathery face. She was laughing, too, just like the boys. Throwing her head back, showing her throat and teeth. She was laughing at Lena flopping around in the water's edge like a clown doll trying to find her footing in the shifting sands under her feet, snot hanging from her nose, hundreds of plaits heavy with ocean water trailing down around her ears.

It was the first time Lena had seen a smile on the visage of the ghost, and it raised so many emotions in the girl that she didn't know whether to laugh herself or cry. Instead she threw her head back into the next oncoming wave with her braids dangling behind her and flopped her entire body spread-eagle like a puppet into the surf. She knew it must have looked funny.

The ocean rushing into her ears filled her head with salty water, grains of sand, and what Lena knew had to be the sound of Rachel's laughter.

As soon as the boys saw Lena laughing again, they were so relieved that they did everything they could think of to please her and make up for their nastiness toward her. Edward found a long narrow silver-and-black feather floating on the water, which he shook nearly dry and gave to the girl to stick among her many braids made thick and bouncy by the moist salt air and seawater.

They found two seashells almost exactly the same, with swirls of blue and yellow in their whorls, and promised to show her how to make them into earrings for her pierced ears when they got home.

At the water's edge they acted like clowns, too, standing on their hands with just their feet sticking out of the water, to make Lena laugh as they walked back down the beach toward the contented black people just stirring from their afternoon naps.

Nellie nudged her sister-in-law and Mrs. Stevens, lying on either side of her on big yellow beach towels. "Look how happy the children look," she said as they watched the boys swinging Lena between them, walking down the beach toward the women. "I know I don't give them enough credit sometimes. But those boys do look out for their baby sister."

Lena enjoyed the rest of her vacation at the shore, going down to the clean sandy beach every chance she got, her skin turning as rich and brown as a berry from hours in the sun, her braids becoming woolly and fat from the water and bright red from the sun. She had become what the motel owner called a real beach bum, a native of the coast. But there was one thing she couldn't bring herself to do. She couldn't eat the big blue crabs that her father bought from the black fishermen on a rickety nearby dock and the women steamed up in huge black pots with hot peppers and salt until the creatures were orangy red.

Their smell reminded Lena too much of Rachel, whom she never saw again on the beach.

Driving back to Mulberry didn't take nearly as long as driving to the coast had. They didn't get lost once, and they made fewer stops than before. At one little store in the middle of nowhere, the caravan pulled over. The men went into the woods to pee, and the women and children went into the store to buy cold drinks.

"That child look just like a little pickaninny," the fat smiling white woman behind the counter said, pointing to Lena.

"Well, bitch, she ain't no damn pickaninny," her mother replied, looking dead into the woman's faded flat eyes and not dropping a stitch. The woman was dumbfounded. She couldn't seem to find her voice as Lena's mother laid down the correct change on the counter for the cold drinks and the deposit on the bottles that Lena and the boys had picked out of the ice-filled cooler, grabbed Lena's hand, and strutted out the door.

Her mother got back in the car and never said a word about the exchange, but as soon as they got home, Nellie and Grandmama sat up most of the night loosening all the braids from Lena's head and twisting the thick waved hair into four balls.

The next morning, her mother got in the big green station wagon and drove Lena the short distance up the street to Delores' Beauty Parlour.

FIFTEEN

❧ • ❧

MAMIE

The early Georgia morning was already hazy hot when Lena's mother sent her up the street to the neighborhood beauty shop. The shop was located on a dusty red clay street in a buttercup-yellow wooden shed-like structure behind the home of the proprietress. The sign out front near the dirt driveway portrayed a woman, vaguely black, with a waved hairdo. Actually it was a drawing of a white woman with a paint-darkened face. Beneath the picture it said, *DELORES BEAUTY PARLOUR.*

The route Lena took from her house to Delores's was a familiar one. She had been going that way for two years. The street climbed for seven blocks past homes and gardens and stores until it reached the peak of Pleasant Hill, where the area's city bus service began.

Lena made the short walk up the street to the shop last as long as possible. She paused at the dusty window of Mr. Gibson's tiny grocery store and counted the four loaves of Colonial bread— there were never more than half a dozen—along the counter. If she had walked in and asked to buy a loaf, the owner, a tall man with stooped shoulders, would have muttered to himself, "Lord, people just coming in buying *all* my bread."

Although Lena looked forward to having clean straightened hair, she did not relish Delores's casual style of cosmetology. The previous spring the beautician had burned a spot on the left side of Lena's face when the greasy handle of the hot curling iron had slipped from Delores's hand and, in falling, grazed the child's cheek. Lena had sat up front in church that Easter with her head bent down, embarrassed by the scar. She tipped her straw hat forward and hoped to keep her burn a secret.

Her grandmother had walked up the street, a damp dish towel still tucked in her belt, to curse Delores out for her carelessness. And her father had personally thrown Delores's skinny boyfriend out of The Place because of his old lady's mistake. But that fury had faded with time as the small scar on the girl's face had vanished with the help of cocoa butter. And besides, Lena's hair was more than anyone in her family could, or wanted to, handle. Each time her mother tried to wash, comb out, and straighten the girl's long wild hair at the kitchen stove, the attempt had ended in misery. The older Lena got, the thicker and more tangled her hair became. And her mother, who was no expert with a straightening comb, burned her scalp and the top of her ears often.

The whole thing weighed too heavily on the household. For days after the simple hairdressing, Lena's cries seemed to ring through the house. The ghostly cries seemed to give more validity to Grandmama's belief that because Lena was born with a veil over her face she was indeed touched by the supernatural.

Instead of sitting on a chair in front of the kitchen's gas stove to get her hair fixed, Lena was back at Delores's, where, her mother was convinced, a trained cosmetologist could handle her hair a bit less painfully.

As the girl reached the shop, a few feet away from the open screened door, she began to smell the fruit-scented hair preparations that had become the trademark and community-wide joke of Delores Beauty Parlour. Months before, some sweet-talking salesman had come by the shop offering Delores an unbeatable deal on what he called "a famous formula 'specially made for the colored hair." Besides adding luster and aiding in the growth of hair, this lean, smooth young man had told Delores as he slowly reached across her enormous breasts to pick up a bottle, all the products had a "light, fruity scent."

Delores, long known around town for her weakness for skinny men, bought six cases each of the fuchsia-colored shampoo, pressing oil, and conditioning cream from the drummer who then disappeared into another sales territory, where his long brown frame played havoc with some other lady's good sense.

The coconut-pineapple odor of the hot pink hair products overwhelmed even the smell of burning hair that was nearly palpable in a shop where hair was straightened with the twin force of heat and metal. Despite the customers' complaints that the sticky-sweet, heavy smell of the hair preparations made them sick to their stomachs, especially when combined with the heat of the hot comb and curlers, Delores continued to use the stuff, determined to prove that she had not been hoodwinked by the skinny young man in the shiny blue suit who talked with a golden toothpick dangling from his mouth.

Old men, walking in twos down to the corner store for tobacco, would pass the beauty shop driveway, stop, sniff the air a few times, look at each other out of the sides of their eyes, shake their gray heads, and break into streams of laughter as they walked on.

As Lena opened the screen door to the shop, the door screeched an announcement of her arrival to the four women there. They turned in unison to scrutinize the newcomer and cut their conversation off abruptly when they saw the skinny-legged little girl standing in the doorway.

Although the women in the shop had stopped their talk as soon as they saw Lena at the door, they hadn't done it early enough. From outside the shop, Lena had heard the friendly rough talk that she had come to associate with the shop and the sweet smell of hair products.

"Did you get to go to that big gospel caravan at the auditorium in Macon last Sunday?"

"Go to it? Girl, I will have you know I were even invited

backstage. I know the lead singer in The Three Luminaries. Rev. Roland introduced all us at a revival last year."

"Lord, girl, the lead singer? You know the lead singer? The one with all that curly hair and that big bass voice way down in that big ol' chest of his? I wonder if he got any hair on that chest. Uh, uh, uh?"

"I don't know. Ask Delores, she the one who know the man."

"That is right, Delores. You say you know the man."

"Now, just 'cause I know him don't mean I know all 'bout up under his clothes. Lord ham mercy. He sing gospel music, **for** God's sake."

Although she wasn't supposed to hear it, the talk was as familiar to Lena as the red lipstick-stained cigarette butts floating on the last bit of Coca-Cola and spit in the bottom of bottles left sitting around the shop. As familiar as the little electric radio on a high shelf always tuned to gospel music interspersed with commercials for Nehi Orange drink and hair pommade jingles— "I'm glad I found that Long-Aid in the pretty pink jar." As familiar as the small copies of *Jet* magazine and larger copies of *Sepia* lying around on upended milk and cola crates for the customers' enjoyment and enlightenment.

"Will you look at the fingernails on this man here!"

"Miz Wilson, don't you know that's the first thing I saw when I picked up that new issue of *Jet* this morning."

"Disgraceful."

"They almost needed another page to show all of 'em."

"Disgraceful, just disgraceful. For a man to let his nails grow over like that."

"What man? What's disgraceful?"

" 'New Jersey Man Claws Way Into Guinness Book of Records. Postal Worker Charles E. Byington Grows 5-Foot Nails. "I can still stamp a letter postage due," says father of 3.' "

"Oh, that makes me sick to my stomach."

"He wouldn't have no three children with me till he cut them nails."

"Can you imagine what his feets must look like?"

Lena smiled shyly as she climbed the two wooden steps to the shop, entered, and let the dusty screen door close behind her. Three of the women there she recognized as Delores, the shop's fleshy owner, and two regular customers. One of them, a school-teacher wearing a red-and-white polka-dot dress, sat waiting her turn in one of the four chairs, with a white hand towel wrapped around her head. Delores was straightening the other customer's short salt-and-pepper hair with a smoking hot comb; but as she paused to look at Lena, the beautician let the hot comb hang loosely from her hand, the habit that had caused Lena's burn the previous spring. Lena winced and looked away to the back of the shop.

"Good morning. Mama says for me to get a shampoo, dandruff treatment, press and plaits, no curls," Lena recited her instructions as usual. But this time she did it with less thought than usual. Her full attention was riveted to the fourth woman there, who stood at the back near the shop's only window, deliberately drying fruity-scented combs and brushes and smiling as she listened to the schoolteacher's talk.

Lena guessed that the fourth woman was a new girl working for Delores. As long as the child had been coming to the shop, there had been a rapid procession of young women at Delores Beauty Parlour. Helpers, Delores called them sometimes. But usually the beautician just referred to each of them as "my new girl," even though they ranged in age from their late teens to their late twenties.

They appeared and vanished with regularity, usually coming from tiny Georgia towns like Quitman and Barnesville, willing and anxious to learn a trade under Delores's guidance. She taught them very little past wash and press, however, keeping the secrets of curling and croquignole, a specialty of hers, to herself. Disgruntled, they all eventually left after only a few weeks, to be replaced by other girls as excited and eager to please and learn as their predecessors had been.

This new young woman leaning on the back windowsill

looked up at Lena briefly then returned to her conversation with the towel-wrapped schoolteacher.

Lena was awestruck.

She had seen pictures of Lena Horne and Dorothy Dandridge in copies of *Ebony* at home and in movies at the Burghart Theatre, and she thought the women in her family were just as lovely. But this was as close she had ever come to such a clearly beautiful woman outside that sphere. It immediately made perfect sense to Lena that someone who looked like the new girl should be in the beauty business.

I want to be made to look just like that, Lena thought as she hung back near the door of the shop.

The new "new girl" looked to be about twenty years old, no longer a teenager but barely so. She was tall and sturdy-looking, not heavy but robust. She appeared able to take care of herself. There were lifted buckets and raised axes in her body frame, not artificial pink roses encased in glass. She was what Lena had heard other women derisively call "big-boned." But this woman wore her size proudly like a suit of armor. In fact this new young helper looked to Lena like a warrior, with her broad hands and strong-looking arms and legs.

The pair of black patent-leather Mary Janes she wore on her big wide feet just made her appear overgrown. She was too stately to look ridiculous. She made the slightest movement—like the shifting of the weight of her hips on the windowsill—with the grace of a falling feather.

When Lena learned later that the young woman was from a point on the Georgia coast between Savannah and a town too small to have a name Lena recognized—making it smaller than her own little town—she was not a bit surprised. The woman had the same raw country air of health that her cousins from Wrightsville gave off. Lena could almost smell it. The new girl was nearly bursting with good health. The orange smock she wore over a green blouse and black cotton skirt pulled tight across her shoulders, her body teasing the seams with its heartiness.

Lena felt she could stand there staring at the new girl's strong solid body all day, but it wasn't only the woman's sturdy body that left Lena spellbound. It was her face. Round, full, and oily, beautiful past the point of reality, the new girl's face looked out of place in the small dusty shop. But then Lena could not imagine a place of suitable matching beauty existing anywhere in the world.

The woman had deep deep, dark skin that gleamed with the patina of natural oils. Her skin was taut, glowing, and flawless, stretched over a face that was rounded at the cheeks and chin to the point of healthiness but just shy of chubbiness.

Her black hair, as shiny as her skin, was straightened hard and pulled back into a short ponytail held by a red rubber band. The hairdo left her head free of unnecessary extras, unencumbered. Lena tried to imagine that countenance with any of the big pearlized and glassy earrings her mother kept in a golden leather box on her dresser. But it was a wasted exercise. The pretties paled next to this face.

Her eyebrows, thick and unruly, made dark unexpected statements across her face. Her short curly eyelashes gave her face a slightly surprised expression. And her eyes, with flecks of gold sparkling in them, were alive with something that Lena did not immediately recognize but knew that she admired.

Looking at the woman's face was like looking at the beautifully elegant dark wood piano that her grandmother kept in the music room but allowed no one to touch since Jonah had decided one day to stop playing. When the young woman spoke, Lena half-expected to hear the tinkling of piano keys. But what she heard from the back of the shop was enough to make her start: the sounds of a lowland geechee. Here and there the woman with the gleaming face pronounced a word so strangely to Lena's ear that the girl giggled at the plain foreignness of the sound. The lilting voice put Lena in the mind of something—maybe a movie she had seen, but she couldn't remember which one.

Pointing to a customer's purse on the floor, the new girl admonished her to "Watch your sat-*chel.*" And in talking about a pot of collards one of the customers had cooked the night before, she said, "I like all vege*tables,*" as if the word were pronounced like "kitchen table."

Lena understood most of what the women said, but coming as the words did from this woman's rich, beautiful mouth, Lena could not be sure if they were ordinary words or strange exotic ones.

"Lena, this here are Mamie," Delores said as the woman with the glorious face rose from her perch on the windowsill, walked up to the little girl, and stood directly in front of her with her arms crossed loosely under her full breasts. She was even taller than Lena had first thought. Lena only came up to the woman's rib cage. Delores continued, "She are going to be doing your hairs from now on. Looks like I have got myself so many new heads to do that I are surely going to need some help."

Lena had noticed that Delores routinely forgot each "new girl" and talked about the latest arrival as if she were the first and original "new girl."

Delores, a pretty woman who weighed over two hundred pounds and moved as if she were always wearing an easy-to-wrinkle taffeta dress, talked "proper," stretching grammar and pronunciation all out of shape with her airs. Lena's father called Delores's manner of speaking "talking full of 'ers' and 'bers,' like folks from the North." Lena knew little about the North. But from what she could tell from folks' stories, she imagined it a veritable Tower of Babel with everyone trying to talk "proper" all at once. Atlanta was the farthest north of her middle Georgia town she had ever been, and there, she had noticed, people spoke with a few "ers" and "bers" of their own.

As Delores continued to chatter, Lena saw that her own right hand was halfway up to the new girl's face before she even realized that she had reached out to touch the woman's full shiny cheek with the backs of her little girl's fingers. She stopped her hand in midair, clenched it into a fist, and, hunching her shoulders, quickly brought it back down to her side without a word.

At age nine Lena felt too old for this spontaneous touching, but it came as naturally to her as a baby reaching for a gold locket. From the comments her mother and grandmother made around the house, she knew she would be leaving little-girl status soon, and only because she was the baby of the family had she been allowed to prolong the stage as long as she had. At her house *"Awww,* she just a baby" had recently been giving way to "You know you too big a girl to be doing that."

But Mamie had already seen her abbreviated gesture and gave her a little conspiratorial grin. Without speaking, the full-faced apprentice beautician put her large hands on Lena's shoulders, turned her around, and guided her to the back of the shop and the lone steel sink with a black rubber neck rest attached to its lip. A red vinyl chair with metal armrests was placed in front of the sink with its back up against the rubber neck rest. Mamie sat the girl in the chair, shook out an orange plastic drape cloth, wrapped it around Lena's thin shoulders to cover her red plaid shorts set, and secured it at the back of the girl's neck with a tuck. Lena felt she was in the hands of an expert, not a large country girl at her first paying job.

Mamie was to do Lena's hair at that basin that Saturday and every third Saturday until the girl was twelve. In all that time, Lena never missed an appointment. Even with bad weather, summer vacations, visits of relatives from up north, rehearsals for school pageants, and illnesses in the family, she could think of nothing more important than seeing Mamie.

Before Mamie had come to Delores Beauty Parlour, Lena had always kept her eyes closed tightly during her entire shampoo for fear of the sting of fruit-scented suds. Now, with Mamie's face shining down on her, Lena could not force herself to lower her eyelids and shut herself off from the only opportunity she might have to stare directly into her hairdresser's beautiful face.

From time to time during the shampoo and rinse, Mamie would smile down at Lena, and the little girl would be struck anew by the wide-open radiance, the pure, clean beauty of that face, untouched by any flaw. It was a face that beckoned response. Lena just had to smile back at her.

At the sink in the back of the tiny shop, it seemed hotter, if possible, than in the front, where the metal combs and curlers lay burning all day over the open rings of gas fire. Few breezes stirred through the open front door or the back window. As Mamie stretched across Lena to reach some shampoo on the shelf above the sink, the cotton material of her smock would strain at the seams and soak up perspiration on her shoulders and under her arms. At those times the young woman smelled to Lena like the dirt outside her home when a sudden rainstorm hit the dust and the aroma of earth rose up all over the neighborhood. As quietly as possible, Lena would inhale deeply.

In the tiny shop's year-round heat, Mamie would work up more suds in Lena's hair. Heavier and thicker when wet, it pulled Lena's head back into the sink, exposing her throat to the shop. Mamie didn't handle her hair delicately, the way her mother did. She maneuvered it like a woman washing a big bath towel by hand. As she scrubbed, pearls of sweat formed on the brow and upper lip of the young beautician's face. Like liquid jewels, the perspiration formed and rolled off Mamie's face unattended as she continued to work up more fruity suds. On Mamie's skin, greasy smooth and taut, the sweat looked like the beads of water that Lena had seen her grandmother accidentally spill once, only once, onto her prized upright piano from a vase of flowers.

Sometimes Lena tried to catch a drop of perspiration as it rolled down Mamie's cheek and fell off the soft curve of her rounded jawbone. If she could catch one droplet, the girl was certain it would roll around in her palm like a drop of mercury from a broken thermometer. But since Lena never wanted to be obvious about what she was attempting, she never succeeded—not in more than three years of Saturdays—in capturing that one drop.

What she did capture from Mamie, however, was far more precious for Lena than an imagined jewel. With only a few sentences, Mamie gave Lena the gift of curiosity. She let drop the germ in Lena that grew to the desire, the yearning, the obsession to know and understand her world.

"It's never been book sense I was after, no," Mamie would say to Lena as she straightened the very edges of the girl's thick sandy-colored hair without so much as warming the skin around her face and ears. "What's been important to me is the whys of things. And that you can't be learning through no books. No, indeed not. That's the kind of knowledge has to be learned through people, through finding out things about them. All kinds of people, all kinds of things. Things they don't even know they know.

"You know how you find out things? You just keepa asking and asking and digging and searching. When you find out things about folks, you find out things 'bout life, you find out things 'bout yourself. And the puzzle is always just sitting there just waiting for somebody to come along and figure it."

"People always telling me stuff," Lena offered shyly.

"Well, course they do," Mamie had responded with a smile. "People just naturally love to tell things to a curious little something like you."

But this explanation of Mamie's came much later, after Mamie had discovered that Lena got the thin wide scar on her left calf by backing into the grill of the upstairs bathroom heater while she was drying off; that she was seven when she was vaccinated against polio; that her fingernails were unusually small compared to her hands; that she and her friend Gwen had once stolen two candy bars; and that her grandmother played the numbers with Delores, the neighborhood numbers lady.

When Lena would slip into the shampoo chair on her Saturday mornings, and like two old women on a porch, she and Mamie would slip comfortably into whatever space the end of the girl's last appointment had led them two weeks earlier. And though most days Mamie joined in the hubbub of business and socializing that was a black beauty shop during Lena's visits, the two talked mainly with each other. Delores and her other customers rarely interrupted them, hardly noticing their talk, so naturally did they communicate.

As Mamie began Lena's shampoo that first Saturday, another

of Delores's customers entered the shop, and the dusty screen door screeched again.

"Uh, I wonder why that creaking door bother me so?" Mamie asked aloud as she soaked Lena's hair with a jet of steaming hot water.

"Me, too," Lena said softly, hesitantly.

"Me, too, what, child?" Mamie asked like an old woman, her voice curious, not unfriendly, as she continued to work the pink shampoo into Lena's hair.

Lena froze. Fool! she thought. She had no sooner imagined her worst fear than it had happened: she had said something stupid to this woman whom she had only to remain with and gaze upon. Sometimes it seemed even her thoughts haunted her. Clamping her lips shut tight, and keeping them that way, she hoped she would be forgiven.

As soon as Mamie had spoken her question, she had felt the skin of the child's scalp tense under the pads of her soapy fingers. She leaned forward and looked directly into the girl's upside-down face for a moment, then she stood up and continued talking as if Lena were a longtime, trusted friend who had instinctively said the appropriate thing.

"Well, you know, that noisy door just makes my neck hairs just stand on end," Mamie explained. "Makes me scared. Other people, they always say that that noise sets they teeth on edge, but me, no. It's my neck hairs, and you know why? The noise remind me of the time I was little and these little kittens—to be sure, I didn't know they was kittens at the time—was outside my window all night just a-screeching and a-yelling and crying for they mama who wasn't there.

"I was up laying 'wake all night, too, too scared to look outside and make sure it wasn't some dead thing from the grave making them howling noises, and too 'shamed to wake anybody else up in the house to go look for me. Whew, always make my neck hairs all prickly, that noise." She shook her broad shoulders with a fastidious little shudder.

Lena had little time to consider the strangeness of this

beautiful-faced grown woman she did not know talking so freely with her. If Delores had not just introduced her, the girl might have suspected Mamie of being a ghost. As Mamie effortlessly washed, combed, and dried Lena's hair, causing her no pain, she was off on another subject, easing in a question here and there. Lena's throat was sometimes too dry for her to reply, but no matter. Mamie was in control.

Mamie made Lena think about herself, her family, her school-mates, her looks, and her dislikes, the things that made her sad, angry, joyful, tearful, confused. Mamie showed her how to delve into all these things with a question and come up to the surface with answers that somehow soothed and excited her at the same time.

There was only one topic that Lena was truly afraid to put under the microscope of her questions. But one Saturday, after she was sure she saw the visage of a young child float through her bedroom the night before, she screwed up her courage and brought her fears to Mamie.

"Mamie," she asked while the woman rinsed the fruity-smell-ing suds from her hair, "do you believe in ghosts?"

"You mean hants and spirits and such, child?"

"Uh-huh," Lena said, already sorry that she had brought it up.

"Well, course I do," Mamie said with a smile.

Lena felt a relief so strong that she feared she might burst into tears. She had been so afraid that Mamie would laugh in her face, call her silly, a little girl afraid of ghosts. She should have known better. She should have known Mamie.

But even after she asked Mamie the question, she could not bring herself to say what she really wanted to say. "Mamie," she wanted to say. "I see ghosts." She had never told anyone, and she felt she never would. Besides the sickness that started to envelop her whenever she began to tell someone of her ghostly visitations, Lena knew the way most people reacted to such talk—even her own family, who claimed to know her better than anybody else in the world. They talked of her being born with a veil over her face and of seeing ghosts over her shoulder and of putting the magic on things, but they did not really believe in half the stuff they talked about.

After some weeks it was settled between Lena and Mamie. Each appointment became a couple of hours of instruction in "questions." It always began with a question.

"Lena, child, how many children in your family?" Mamie asked one Saturday morning.

"Just me and my two brothers, Raymond and Edward," Lena replied, pleased that the questions had begun for another Saturday.

"No other ones?"

"No, Mamie."

"Umm, a little family?"

"Little? It's not so little, Mamie. There's me and Edward and Raymond and Mama and Daddy and my grandmama. She lives with us. Then there's other folks."

"Other folks?" Mamie sounded interested, but her tone was still as casual as before and she continued with Lena's shampoo.

"Yeah, like Dear One and Yakkity-Yak an' 'em. The ones from The Place. They don't live with us either. They just there all the time, in and out."

"What's The Place?

"It's the whiskey store and grill. The place Daddy own. Grandmama just turn up her nose when they come to the house to do some heavy work or bring a case of Coca-Colas from The Place. She says they're just old beer-heads and winos and drunks."

"Old winos?" Mamie had that same casual, interested tone in her voice.

"Oh, Grandmama doesn't mean anything by it. Besides, it's really not true. They're not all just old winos."

"How do you know?"

"I know."

"How?"

"I know because I know Frank Petersen's not an old wino. And I know I never seen him drunk. He just takes a drink."

"Frank Petersen?"

"Uh-huh. He's my friend."

"Oh." Mamie said, satisfied for the time being.

Lena, now as enamored of Mamie's entire being as she had at first been of her face, latched on to the instruction as a way of touching her, of getting close to the woman. The girl still remembered her first inclination to reach out and touch Mamie's shining face.

In the early weeks of their friendship Lena had let Mamie do most of the talking and querying, seldom contributing to the conversation. But as she grew comfortable with Mamie and her questions, she began taking part in their ritual, passing along tidbits of background about the customers at Delores's or repeating a stray old wives' tale just for the sake of tearing it apart to look for truth.

When she left the shop to reenter her own life, Lena took with her a piece of Mamie, the questioning part. Around her own house she gingerly began investigations about events, family, neighbors, situations that interested her.

At school she gently made incisions into the backgrounds of most of the nuns who taught at Blessed Martin de Porres and discovered facts about their heritages that might have embarrassed them if they had noticed her investigation. Her schoolmates would have gotten whippings if their parents knew the things Lena got them to tell her about their households.

Lena was surprised by the flood of satisfaction and accomplishment she felt on having uncovered some rag of information that had gone undetected before. From Mamie she had learned the private joy of discovering.

As far as Lena could see, only she had been privileged to share Mamie's wealth of questions and knowledge. She wanted to keep it that way. She hadn't even told her mama or grandmama what a special person Mamie was. Only her breathless wonder that she had Mamie all to herself kept Lena from standing up in the middle of the beauty shop and testifying like the women she and her brothers heard crying inside revival tents. "Yes, Lord, thank you, Jesus. You saw what your child cried for and you answered her prayer. Thank you, Lord Jesus."

Lena knew she was free to ask Mamie questions whenever she wished. Mamie had never backed away from any of her inquiries. This meant she could ask Mamie questions about herself, too. Mamie's "You'll never know, child, if you don't ask" was not a platitude for her; it was a motto, a banner. But the child never did ask for personal information, and Mamie never volunteered it.

Whenever Lena thought of the many details she didn't know about Mamie, it made her heart race the way it did when she saw ghosts. She didn't know Mamie's exact age or birth date. She didn't know who Mamie's people were, or if she had any family. She never saw the young woman in the store or at church or strolling down the street in the late evening. And the child never asked why. She preferred to keep Mamie a mystery.

Even when, three years after their first meeting, Lena showed up for her regular hair appointment and found Mamie, like the other "new girls" before her, vanished, gone from her wooden stool in the shop, the child did not ask Delores any direct questions about her disappearance or whereabouts. It was not that Lena did not ache to know, was not frantic to know where Mamie was. The girl, by then almost a teenager, just did not ask. It seemed to be somehow breaking their rules.

Instead Lena sat in the shampoo chair at the back of the tiny shop, turned to the new girl, a shabby and faded replacement for Mamie, and asked her, "Is it scary to come to a new town to live and work?"

The young woman just stared at her vacantly.

It took much longer to wash and straighten Lena's hair than it had in a long while. The new girl fumbled and tugged, putting some of the pain Lena had nearly forgotten back into her hair. When she finally finished and clumsily removed the drape cloth from around Lena's neck, Lena leapt from the chair and dashed out the door and back down the street.

She passed Geraldine Hardeman's grandmother's house without a sideways glance. And when she got to Sarah's old house she even forgot to feel lonely.

By the time she got home, it was two hours later than she usually returned. Her head throbbed from her new beautician's work. She hadn't eaten all day and her empty stomach growled and snarled. Mamie's disappearance had upset her and made her long for the familiar. When she entered the kitchen, she was relieved to find that, as far as she could see, nothing there had changed. Most importantly, Frank Petersen was still there washing dishes at the sink. And from the aroma of coffee in the air, Lena knew the man who was her best adult friend now that Mamie was gone had made a fresh pot for her.

SIXTEEN

❧ ❧

FRANK

"Will somebody get that stinking wino out of this house with that stinking Pall Mall. This ain't no damn juke joint, you know, this is a home." Grandmama was furious. She swore she smelled a whiff of smoke upstairs in her bedroom. "It was just a whimp, a mere whimp of that nasty cigarette smoke, but I smelled it all right." And she knew, just knew, that that "stinking wino" with his stinking cigarettes had been in her room, in her own personal room, and had been smoking in there and now she was sure that she'd never be able to get that odor out of her clothes and personal things.

"A person's bedroom is a private and sacred place, or at least it's supposed to be. Hell, it's the only little spot I have in this whole house that I can call my own and I be damned if I'm gonna let some nameless riffraff invade it."

Lena wanted to say, "He ain't nameless," but she had better sense than to say anything.

"And I bet he had that greasy hat of his laying on my bed, too. Any fool knows that's bad luck. No man will ever lay there now!"

Grandmama had already dragged Raymond from his bed,

half-asleep, insisting that he come into her room and smell it, too. When he couldn't smell anything, the old lady roughly ejected him and grabbed Edward coming out the bathroom and nearly threw him through her bedroom door to "hurry up and smell it before the damn smell goes away, for God's sake." But he couldn't smell anything either. "I swear I can't, Gr-gr-grand-mama," he said. He too was ejected.

Grandmama looked for a moment to Lena standing silently in the hall next to her own bedroom door for corroboration but dismissed the notion with a suck of her teeth. She realized that Lena would staunchly stand by Frank Petersen and deny any smell of smoke the same way the child would have denied it if someone asked if her grandmama played the illegal lottery called "the bug" with Delores the hairdresser.

"That's right," Grandmama huffed when she finally tracked Frank Petersen down as he sat on the back porch steps smoking a filterless Pall Mall. "That's where you better be if you must smoke. Dirty habit, none of my people ever did it. And a good thing, too. You better not come into my room again with even the odor of cigarette tobacco about your clothes."

Frank Petersen took a long drag on his cigarette—it was one of a mere three or four that he smoked the entire day while he worked at Lena's—and looked out into the woods on the other side of the stream. He wouldn't turn to look at the old woman or even to acknowledge with the tilt of his head that she was there at the top of the cement steps fussing down at the crown of his graying head. When she finally ran out of steam and couldn't think of anything else to berate the man about, she turned and headed back into the house muttering, "I don't know why I even bother."

Lena waited in her hiding place with her back pressed against the wall in the breakfast room awhile because she knew that Grandmama was known to double back on a target if a stray thought hit her as she wandered away and everyone was sure she was finished. Lena never wanted to get caught in the crossfire of her grandmother's rage. Even though Grandmama sometimes sounded like Lena's mother in her tirades, her fits of rage were different from Nellie's in intent. Nellie was mostly rant and rave. Grandmama was action.

When Lena was sure the coast was clear, she'd slip onto the back porch and quietly sit on a step below where Frank Petersen still sat smoking his bent cigarette.

"I'd die the death of a Chinaman before I'd ever go into that woman's room," he'd say calmly, then stub the cigarette out carefully on the cement step and throw it out into the yard with a flick of his slender fingers.

Lena had never heard Frank Petersen refer to Grandmama by name. She was always "that woman," "she," or "her." And Grandmama returned the favor by calling Frank only "that stinking wino," "he," and "him."

It had been a running battle between the two of them—Grandmama and Frank Petersen—ever since he first showed up at the screened porch door when Lena was eight.

The family had just sat down to dinner when there was a knock at the door.

"Now, who the hell is that?" Grandma asked and made as if to push her chair away from the table and stand up, even though she had no intention of actually rising. But Nellie reached over and laid a hand on the woman's wrist to stay her just the same. She looked over at Raymond with a raised eyebrow. But Edward was quicker. He jumped up and headed out of the dining room before Raymond had a chance to respond to his mother's signal.

"Whoever it is, tell 'em we're at the dinner table and can't be disturbed," Jonah said across the table to Edward's retreating back.

"Then you come right back. I don't care who it is," Nellie added. "We're waiting to start dinner."

Edward disappeared and returned right away. "It's a man," he said.

"Who is he?" Nellie asked.

Edward snapped his fingers and said, "Oh," then dashed back to the porch.

Grandmama just shook her head, looked at Nellie, and sighed, "Lord, Lord, Lord."

Edward appeared again. "He sa-sa-say his name is Frank Petersen, you sp-sp-sp-spell it with an *e-e-e-e-e-e.*"

"Did you tell him we were eating dinner?" Nellie asked.

Edward snapped his fingers again and ran off.

This time both Nellie and Grandmama rolled their eyes to heaven and let their heads fall back against the high backs of their dining-room chairs. Raymond stretched his long legs under the table and nudged Lena's foot. They both started laughing. Jonah, trying not to look exasperated, laid a hand on either side of his plate and examined his neatly trimmed nails.

"Well, what does he want?" Nellie asked when Edward returned, beginning to breathe hard.

"Say he got some Co-Colas from The Place. Wh-where you want 'em?"

"Jesus, keep me near the cross! Edward, don't you know where we keep the drinks?" Nellie said, her voice threatening to rise.

Jonah finally lost patience with the whole scene. "Edward, Son, tell him to stack those drinks on the back porch, show him where it is, and tell him to put 'em with the other drinks and put those empty bottles he finds on the porch underneath into the truck."

While Edward hurried off, Jonah explained, "That's Frank Petersen. You know him, Nellie, from down at The Place. You said you needed somebody 'round here to wash windows and take down those heavy curtains. He can help 'round the house too. He's about the most reliable of those Negroes who supposed to be working for me. He can be here whenever you need him."

By then Edward was back in his seat and the meal was about to begin. But when Jonah took one bite of his pole beans, he said,

"These beans cold." And Grandmama and Nellie jumped up in tandem and began snatching bowls of food off the table to take them back into the kitchen to reheat.

It seemed that Grandmama never forgave Frank Petersen for the cold beans that day.

When Lena wandered into the kitchen later that evening for some more banana pudding, she found a strange thin man standing at the sink washing dishes. Her heart started to thump a few beats faster, and she took a couple of steps backward before she remembered the man who had knocked on the door during dinner.

He was a dark slender man, almost tall, with a frame that looked supple and wiry even while he was standing still. As many times as Lena had been at The Place, she was sure that she had never seen him there. He had the kind of demeanor that she would surely have remembered. Back straight, shoulders relaxed but level, feet planted firmly a few inches apart on the linoleum floor, he made washing somebody else's dishes an action of dignity.

She stood next to the refrigerator for so long watching the back of the man's head that he felt her stare raise the hair on the back of his neck, and he turned at the waist, tilted his head—one ear over his shoulder—and said, "Good evening." Then, without waiting for a greeting from her, he turned back and continued washing dishes. Quietly Lena took a small bowl from the cabinet and a big serving spoon from the drawer next to the sink. Then she stood in the open door of the refrigerator and spooned her banana pudding into the small blue-and-white bowl in silence. When she turned around, the man was still at the sink with his back to her, but he had his right arm, soapy to the forearm where the long sleeve of his white shirt was rolled up, stretched out beside him, his slim elegant hand open, palm up.

Lena was used to picking up silent signals from all around her. She licked the big spoon clean of banana pudding and laid it in the man's outstretched hand. Still not bothering to look at her, he dropped the big spoon in the sink of soapy water and handed her a clean smaller coffee spoon from the drain for her banana pudding.

"Thank you," she said to the side of the man's face. Under a stubbly gray-and-black beard, his skin was the color of old snuff spit and double-etched with lines. In addition to the deep lines around his mouth, nose, and eyes, his entire face was entrenched with fine wrinkles crossing and crisscrossing each other like a dried river bed. Where his beard stubble stopped, right above his Adam's apple, the hairs grew thin and slightly curly.

"My name is Frank Petersen, you spell it with an *e,*" he said.

"Thank you, Frank Petersen," Lena said.

"You welcome," he replied to the heavy skillet he was washing, seeming to forget her right away.

She turned and walked as slowly as she could toward the breakfast-room door, hoping he would invite her back to sit at the kitchen table and keep him company the way her grandmother did. But by the time she reached the door, he hadn't said a word.

Minutes later, when she returned to bring her empty bowl back into the kitchen, he was gone.

Although Frank Petersen almost never spoke directly to Grandmama, he had a hundred responses to the complaints and accusations she lodged against him all day long. If he walked into the room she was in with a broom or mop in his hand, she would brush past him and say, "Get that thing out of my face. And don't be trying to brush up against me," even though Frank always made sure not to come anywhere near her.

After letting her pass, he'd say under his breath, "When nine catch ten, that's when I'll be trying to brush up against that woman."

Or if Grandmama found him standing at the sink washing dishes, she'd say to the room in general, "I think I'll go out and weed the garden till things clear out in here." Then she'd grab her big straw hat with the polka-dot streamer trailing down from it, which Nellie had bought and hung for her on a hook by the kitchen door, and she'd head outside.

Frank Petersen would wait until the old lady had descended the cement steps and was well out of earshot, then say, "You got diamonds in your back. You look better going than coming to me."

Each time Grandmama shot a comment in the man's direction, Lena pretended to pay no attention, continuing to do whatever she was doing, but actually she was always hoping to hear her favorite retort from Frank Petersen: "Excusez-moi." Except Frank would pronounce it, "Ex-cusez-*moi*" and roll his eyes in his head and wiggle his shoulders in an exaggerated Gallic shrug.

"That's the Frenchman's language, Lena-Wena," Frank had explained to Lena. "It means 'excuse me,' yet it means more than that. And then, not exactly that either because you can't say in our language what you can say in their talk. Talk means a lot more to a Frenchie.

"I learned that over there, too," Frank would say casually, seeming not to want to brag about his travels and experiences. But he talked quite a bit about France. "Now it may not be that way now. May be a different place nowadays." He told Lena that he had been there in World War II, "the big 'un," and had served proudly in the artillery unit of the 135th.

The two of them would sit on the back steps in the warm and the cool weather. While they both shucked corn or while he plucked plump squab clean of their gray feathers, Frank would weave long, detailed stories of his time in France. He told Lena of the red wine drunk in château cellars while the artillery boomed overhead; of green green countryside so lush you wanted to take a bite out of it; of fresh crusty French bread crisp and hot from the oven of some pretty mam'selle. The air in France, he said, smelled different from the air in Georgia. It was all different: the sky bluer, the fog softer, the trees greener. Frank made it sound wonderful.

But Lena found out years later, after he had died and left all his things to her, that he had never even been to France. It was only his dream to go there. In fact he had spent all of the war years in a dusty army town in Arkansas, peeling potatoes and washing mountains of dishes and glasses in a greasy spoon on the edge of camp, where feckless young men came to drink and pick up women and tell tales of France. The recruiting officer had laughed out loud at him when he showed up to enlist, already a man in his forties.

"We may be fighting a war, buddy, but we ain't that much in need. Next."

But, God, he had wanted to go to France. To join the army and train and go to another continent to fight and love and experience life there.

And whenever he told Grandmama "Ex-cusez-*moi,*" it took Lena and him right to the outskirts of Paris. Even after Nellie finally heard him say the phrase under his breath and laughed at his speaking French, he didn't let it weigh down his dreams. He just looked at her haughtily, raised one eyebrow, and said, "Well, ex-cusez-*moi.*"

"You sure are silly to be an old man," Nellie told him irritably. But she really didn't take Frank seriously.

"Heard you were down on Broadway the other night drinking that cheap peach wine and wanting to turn the place out when you got 'bout drunk," Nellie would say with a sly grin as Frank Petersen took a load of clothes downstairs to the machine in the basement.

He would just cut his eyes at her and dismiss the comment with a soft snort as he continued on down the basement steps. But later, if he heard her upstairs in the hall doing her exercises, her thighs slapping against the wood floors, he'd grab hold of a door or the banister and yell, "Hold on, Lena-Wena," and pretend the whole house was shaking.

Looking back from adulthood on those days when Frank Petersen came to their house nearly every day with his red-rimmed eyes and his stories of traveling the world and living by his wits, Lena sometimes thought she should have suspected that he had been mostly lying, embellishing his life for a gullible little girl. But then, just as quickly, she would remember the jaunty way he wore his battered hat; the time he sat down at their untuned piano while he was dusting it and played a snatch of a rousing ragtime before Grandmama flew into the room, a tiny outraged bird, to stop the desecration; the funny drawing he once made of her on the back of a brown paper bag, exaggerating her long face, big eyes, and pointed witch's chin. And she couldn't help but be swept up in his dream self all over again.

When Grandmama complained directly to Jonah about her dislike for Frank, her father always said the same thing. "For God's sake, Mama, the man shows up every day he's supposed to and does anything you ask him to. That's more than any of those half-wits and idiots do who work for me."

But as far as Grandmama was concerned, Frank Petersen had so many other drawbacks.

" 'Early in the morning in the middle a' the night, two dead boys rose to fight. Back to back they faced each other, pulled out their swords, and shot each other. Two deaf and dumb policemen heard the noise, came and killed the two dead boys. If you don't believe my story is true, ask the blind man, he saw it, too.'

"You believe that, Lena-Wena?" Frank asked Lena one day after reciting the bit of nonsense for the children's enjoyment.

"Some of it," she said sincerely, hoping he would ask her what part. But he didn't. He just chuckled at the thought of Grandmama being annoyed that he taught her and Raymond and Edward such things. The boys, who were teenagers when Frank first came to the house and usually didn't hang around the man as Lena did, loved the rhyme and knew the piece of silliness by heart. The first time Grandmama heard them recite it for their friends, she immediately recognized its source and sucked her teeth.

"Too damn bad you can't learn your schoolbooks as quick as you pick up that stupid-assed shit," she'd say fiercely.

And Grandmama had other complaints. The whole time Frank Petersen worked at the house, he refused to keep to a set schedule. Even though he came to work early in the morning and always stayed until late in the afternoon, it seemed he came and went when he felt like it.

If Grandmama decided she wanted something done and discovered he had already left for the day, she just *hmp*ed and latched on to his departure as another opportunity to berate the man.

"Gone already, huh? I'm not surprised," Grandmama would say as she leaned over her sewing machine to look out the window down the long dirt drive to see if she could still catch sight of him. Lena always thought she looked with longing after Frank. "Probably been sneaking a drink all day from the liquor caddy. Probably drunk as a skunk by now. Probably *had* to leave and get out of here while he could still walk upright."

Lena kept silent, but she knew that Frank Petersen hadn't been drunk. She knew what drunk looked like. And in three years she had never seen Frank Petersen there. Lena knew that he hadn't touched any of the bottles of liquor on the caddy in the dining room, either. He didn't need to. Frank carried his own bottle of Growers peach wine with him at all times. And whenever he felt like a drink, usually at the end of the day, but never in the mornings, he would reach into the folds of his pants for what he called "a taste or two." He drank right from the bottle wherever he happened to be when the need hit him and didn't seem to mind if Lena stood by and watched his Adam's apple dance up and down as he drank.

He took his drink, smacked his lips, and replaced the bottle in the pocket of his baggy pants. Then he went on with his work. Lena had watched him closely and he never seemed changed by the wine. After practically growing up at The Place, seeing folks getting drunk, saying, "Hey, baby, sugar, how you doing, baby, pretty li'l thang, you, how you doing today?" slurring their words as though they had pieces of Juicy Fruit in their mouths, Lena felt confident that she knew what a drunk person looked like.

Lena knew a wino when she saw one. They were men mostly,

with names like Yakkity-Yak, Sass Ass, and Slack, names they had picked up somewhere after tossing their real names aside as too much trouble to keep. They were nothing like Frank Petersen.

But one Saturday morning when she was twelve, soon after Mamie had disappeared from Delores Beauty Parlour, and Frank Petersen still had not shown up more than two hours after he usually arrived, Lena began to worry. And for some reason she couldn't get the thought of Growers peach wine out of her mind.

Most Saturdays, when Frank Petersen arrived, he would heat up a pot of coffee and sit down with Lena in front of the television set—she on the floor, he on the pink ottoman that matched Nellie's pink reading chair, with the steaming cup dangling between his knees—and watch a few minutes of "Mighty Mouse" or "Pixie and Dixie" or "Merry Melodies" before he got to work.

But it wasn't until midmorning, when Popeye was singing his final stanza of "I'm Popeye the Sailor Man," that Lena looked out the French doors in the living room and saw Frank Petersen coming slowly toward the house. She knew in a flash he was drunk, really drunk.

For one thing, he was walking like an old person, which, despite his graying hair and stories of the old days, she didn't think he was anywhere near being. Lena couldn't think of Frank in terms of age. He never complained that he was tired or his bones ached or his legs gave out on him, the way Grandmama or Mother Josepha at school did, and she knew both those women were old. The laws of time and nature just didn't apply to Frank Petersen as far as she was concerned.

Usually he walked briskly, with his body slightly aslant, his head and shoulders forging the way through the air for the rest of his body. When he was in a real hurry, he swung his arms sharply by his side with his hands clenched in loose fists. But this morning Frank Petersen was walking with his shoulders hunched over, legs stiff, arms hanging limply at his sides. He seemed afraid to step down hard on the ground for fear of jarring loose some old bone or muscle that would never have time to heal before he died.

He bypassed the screened porch, his usual entry, and headed around the side of the house on his way to the back porch, stepping on each faded pink flagstone that lined the walk to the back of the house as if it were a fragile lily pad afloat a deep pond. The way he walked made Lena think again of winos huddled down in doorways all night waiting for The Place to open and give them a dry, comfortable place to spend the day.

Watching him in the bright morning light was like watching a strange stage show through the living- and dining-room windows. She felt she knew the character but that he was different, maybe dressed in a bizarre new costume.

But that wasn't it exactly, either, because although he looked strange, Frank Petersen was wearing his usual getup, the same one he had been wearing three years before, when she first saw him: baggy dark brown trousers held up at his thin waist by a worn leather belt, a white long-sleeved cotton shirt bleached thin and brilliant in the morning sunlight, stiff black lace-up shoes, and the dusty brown felt hat so battered out of shape by wear and time that it no longer fit into a specific category. It could once have been a Stetson or it could have been a derby. But this morning, instead of wearing it at what he called a jaunty Parisian tilt, he wore it pulled down low on his brow, as a farmer would.

He also had on the pair of black frame sunglasses Lena had bought for him at Woolworth's downtown with her own allowance when he complained that the bright morning sunlight was beginning to give him headaches.

When the weather turned cold, he added to the outfit a thin brown suit jacket that didn't match the pants. Then, when he came into the house, he'd remove his hat and put one of the large white starched butcher's aprons he always left hanging on a nail on the kitchen porch right on over his clothes, coat and all. He'd put on the apron, cross the strings behind his back, and tie it closed in front with a bow.

Sometimes he even left his weary-looking hat on after tying on his apron and kept it on all day. So on some winter days he would stand at the kitchen sink doing dishes in his hat, coat, and apron. He would push his coat sleeves up to the elbows so he could plunge his slender leathery hands into the steaming dishwater, scalding the way he liked it.

Although Grandmama would suck her teeth at the strange picture he presented, everybody else in the house kept silent about it. Of all the women who had ever come to the house over the years to help Nellie and Grandmama with the cleaning, no one of them had ever been as reliable as Frank Petersen.

When Frank disappeared from Lena's view out the side of the dining-room window around the back of the house, she raced through the breakfast room and reached the kitchen door just in time to see him trying to make it to the top of the steps of the porch outside. When he got to the top step, he sighed heavily and leaned forward, bracing his hands on his thighs to get his breath back. Then Lena watched him wearily remove his hat and put on his big white apron. Something about the way he held his head made Lena know he couldn't stand any noise that morning, so she didn't say anything.

Silently she unhooked the latch on the inside screen door and pushed it open. Frank walked in in that same old-man way and brushed past her without saying a word, which was unusual for him. He didn't even bother to raise his head or throw her a glance as he shuffled across the black-and-white linoleum tile to the white metal table next to the sink and sat down heavily in a chair with his back safely to the sunlight streaming through the open window. Moving as if it might be his last effort, he put his elbows on the table's surface and rested his temples in the up-turned palms of his hands.

Lena, who felt as comfortable with Frank Petersen as she felt with anyone in the world, suddenly didn't know what to do in his presence. Maybe he needs a cup of coffee, she thought as she examined the top of the man's head still resting in his hands at the table. She went immediately over to the stove and turned on the gas under the blue tin pot of coffee left over from a fresh pot Frank had made at the end of the day before.

Frank Petersen still hadn't moved, and it was silent in the bright yellow kitchen. Lena stood at the stove and watched him for a while before deciding to start his day for him the way she knew he usually did. She walked over to the sink and began running hot water onto a big dollop of Ivory Liquid, then stood back and watched the sink fill up with clouds of suds. When the suds stood over the top of the sink's rim, she turned off the faucet and began putting dirty glasses into the water. Lena could see Frank Petersen flinch each time she clinked a fluted beer glass or tall tea glass with Coca-Cola gummy in its bottom against the sink, so she stopped that.

The kitchen was so quiet, she was almost afraid to move. It was so quiet that when the coffee boiled over on the stove, the sizzling sound startled her and Frank and she knocked a glass into the sink with a clatter. Frank shot her a murderous glance from between his fingers. And for the first time that morning, she looked right back into his face, because although she had heated the coffee up, she didn't feel responsible for the noise it made. And she was growing more and more uneasy about Frank showing up in such a strange condition. Angry, in fact.

Their eyes met only for a moment. Then Frank dropped his head back in his hands. When he made no move to get up, Lena rushed across the room to the stove and turned the gas flame off. Using a dish towel that was hanging on the refrigerator door, she moved the pot from the front to the back burner. Then she went to the cabinet for two coffee cups and placed one on the table directly in front of Frank Petersen and the other across the table from him.

Still in silence she went back to the refrigerator, opened the door, and reached inside for the red-and-white can of Carnation evaporated milk sitting on the top shelf amid jars and bottles and bowls of food. Each time she made a trip across the room she noticed that her lanky bare legs sliced through the shafts of orange morning light pouring into the room and stirred up thousands of dust motes in the air.

After taking the dishrag off the refrigerator door again, Lena stopped to take the hot coffee pot off the back of the stove and brought the coffee and the can of milk to the table.

There she stood completely still and silent at Frank Petersen's elbow with the pot of coffee in her hand like a highly trained waiter in a posh restaurant. When he finally slid his elbows off the table and slowly leaned back in the straight-back chair, she poured the steaming coffee, nearly as thick as syrup, into his cup and then filled her own.

When she returned and sat at her place, she tugged at the leg of her white shorts and tucked one leg under her thigh to keep her skin from sticking to the yellow vinyl seat.

"You gonna ever stop wearing them white shorts?" Frank Petersen spoke for the first time, not lifting his eyes from his cup of coffee.

"Not till they split," Lena said, looking up at him, glad he was talking. "I like 'em. Tight, just like they are."

The room fell back into silence.

When Frank Petersen didn't reach for the can of evaporated milk, Lena pushed it across the tabletop to him. But he still refused to pick it up. Instead he sat there taking great searing gulps of the hot coffee black, even though Lena knew he took his coffee the same way she did: with sugar and lots of cream.

Frank Petersen's eyes were so red and puffy, Lena didn't understand how he could see out of them when he raised them and looked directly at her. "Humph, you probably just wearing them shorts for those little boys from up the street who come flocking down here," he said.

Lena looked up at him in surprise because she could tell that he wasn't kidding her.

"Who you mean?" Lena asked. "Ronnie and Charles and them? You know they just come down here so they can play pool down in the basement."

"That's what you think?" Frank had an ugly sound to his voice that made Lena as uneasy as his swaying in his chair did.

"Shoot, that's what I know." Lena sucked her teeth in disgust. "Frank Petersen, you know good and well those boys are Edward's friends."

But he wasn't listening. "Yeah, keep messing around with those boys, you'll have a baby 'fore you twelve."

"I'm already almost thirteen," Lena snapped back at him, but she didn't feel as confident and sassy as she sounded. Frank Petersen's talk of boys and having babies was making her flustered. She had never really given much thought to the boys who pretended to come to the house to see Edward but spent most of the visit trying to flirt with her. They were closer to her age than to Edward's. But to Lena they weren't serious suitors, just fools she had known all her life who tried to impress her with fancy pool shots.

"You sure are mean today," Lena said finally.

Frank Petersen finished off his coffee while it was still steaming and pushed the drained cup an arm's length away from him on the table. Lena could tell he was no longer looking at her, but she couldn't pinpoint exactly where his red watery eyes were focused. A fine misting of sweat was beginning to cover his sagging face and he swayed a bit in his chair. Tired of fighting the battle to keep his head up, he let his chin fall to his chest.

Lena had to know. She remembered that Mamie once said, "Child, sometimes the easiest way into something is the straightest way. If you want to know something bad enough, then be a woman in your own shoes and just ask."

"Frank Petersen," she asked, "you drunk?"

"Humph." He laughed shortly to himself. "My name is Frank Petersen, you spell it with an *e*. I'm not drunk."

But when he laughed, he lurched forward in his chair and had to brace himself against the table's edge. Lena had been around The Place enough to know that a firm denial of inebriety was a sure sign of drunkenness.

"I've never seen you drunk before," she said, trying not too hard to hide her disappointment. "I didn't think you got drunk. I thought you just took a drink."

Frank thought for a while, then said, "Lena-Wena, you think too much of me."

And Lena didn't know what to say to that. So they sat silently again, eyeing each other across the white metal tabletop. The girl saw that Frank was looking at her the way he did when he was trying to decide whether to teach her something new or let her remain ignorant. He must have made up his mind because after a while he deliberately placed his hands flat on the table in front of him, palms down, and leaned forward toward Lena.

"Bessie Mountain came back to me last night," he said in a whisper.

Lena could barely hear him, so she leaned forward, too.

He repeated it. "Bessie Mountain came back to me last night."

Lena was about to say, "Who? Big ole fat Bessie Mountain?" because that was all she had ever heard anyone call the huge woman who had once been Frank Petersen's woman but had moved on years before to someone else. Everyone teased him about Bessie Mountain, even Nellie. But Lena caught herself in time and just nodded her head at Frank's revelation.

"She came up to my boardinghouse last night," he continued softly. "Walked right up the stairs and into my room like she belonged there. I looked up and she was standing in the door.

"Humph, she as big as ever. Nearly filled up the whole doorway. But she looked good to me." He closed his eyes and sort of chuckled at the memory of the fat woman in his room.

Lena was leaning closer and closer to him, trying to catch his every word as he continued to whisper in the quiet house.

"I said, 'Bessie, what you doing here?' She say, 'I come back to see you, sweet man.' And my heart just dance because that's what she used to call me, 'sweet man.'

"Then she came over to where I was sitting on the end of my bed and stood over me and rub my head right there," he said, pointing to his gray temples, "like she used to. And I laid my head against her big belly, like I used to."

Frank Petersen and Lena were leaning so close to each other now that she could smell the sweet fruity peach wine gone sour on his breath. She moved in even closer to the man when he began to speak again, still in a whisper.

"We stayed like that for a long time, her with her hand on my head, me with my head on her stomach. Mostly because I was scared to move. Lena, I coulda stayed like that forever. But I did move 'cause I knew it couldn't last. I pulled back my head and looked up at her. She had that 'I'm after something' look on her face. And she just laughed with her big mouth open and her teeth showing 'cause she knew I know that look."

He paused.

"You know what she came back to me for after all these years? You know what?" Frank Petersen demanded.

Lena finally found her voice. "No, Frank Petersen, what?" she asked.

"She came back to me for a piece of money, a piece of money, like I was John Dee Rockyfeller or somebody. I ain't gonna tell you what she wanted it for. I'm too 'shamed," Frank said, dropping his gaze briefly to the tabletop, then raising it again. "But I gave her what I had—just a few dollars and some coins and her old gold ring.

"She put her fingers, soft puffy fingers, on my head again, right here," he said, pointing again to his temples, "called me sweet man and left. I heard her flat feet going down the steps and down the hall and on out the house. I couldn't get the sound of those feet out my mind all night."

He paused, and Lena thought for a second that he was going to continue. But he was finished. And the girl and the man both slumped back in their chairs exhausted and sat looking past each other's head in silence.

When her father went out the front door and let the screen door slam behind him, Lena nearly knocked over her half-full cup of coffee at her elbow in her surprise. But Frank Petersen didn't even flinch. He sat like stone and didn't bother to reply when Lena asked if she could do anything for him.

As quietly as possible Lena rose and finished the few dishes in the sink and swept the kitchen floor, being sure not to sweep any trash and good luck out the door. By the time Grandmama and Nellie came down to fix a late breakfast, they hardly noticed how slow and silent Frank Petersen was and how busy Lena was.

SEVENTEEN

❧   ❧

SCHOOL

Lena began each school day by standing in line in front of the three-story red brick schoolhouse. All the girls, dressed in pleated navy-blue skirts and white blouses, stood in one straight line, and the boys, in neat blue trousers and short-sleeve white shirts, stood in another straight line beside them.

Lena had attended Miss Russell's small kindergarten in the front room of the teacher's house as her brothers had before her and her mother and father had before them. She began Blessed Martin de Porres in the first-floor room of Sister Ann's first grade. The next year, when she was seven, she moved up to the second floor of the three-story schoolhouse to Sister Mary Hespian's second-grade class with the same boys and girls who would be her classmates for the next eleven years. Second grade was the last time she would be in a room with only one grade until she was elevated to the third floor and high school.

Although the public-school children sometimes taunted Lena and her classmates, saying they went to a poor folks' school, the Catholic-school children were never daunted by the classroom setup. They knew their parents paid tuition of thirty dollars a month for their education.

"You aren't some of those *public-*school children," Mother Josepha would boom in her nasal, Northern accent. "You attend parochial school, *pri*vate school. And I expect you all to conduct yourselves as such." The nuns at Martin de Porres, Sisters of the Blessed Sacrament, dedicated to teaching American Indian and colored children, could say "public school" as if it were something nasty in their mouths. Besides Miss Russell, Lena had had no other teachers than nuns. They were all women from the North whose first assignment in the South seemed to be her school. They spoke lovingly of Boston baked beans and ate so Mrs. Claver said, strange flat patty squash and the roots of turnips but threw the greens away.

They were all white, something that the black students quickly forgot in the struggle just to survive twelve years at a Catholic school. Lena thought of their skin color as part of their uncomfortable-looking black-and-white habits.

But school wasn't hard for Lena. She loved learning, and because she was smart and her parents had money and contributed regularly and generously to the school and church, the nuns went easy on her. She relished going to her classroom, where so far everything had gone smoothly. She prayed daily that the ghosts that still haunted her would never invade her school.

Meanwhile the other girls in her class were beginning to get giggly and flirty with the same boys they had ignored the year before. But Lena found it hard to be truly swept up in passing love notes and writing boys' names on notebooks. And since her first dance she had been as wary of boys as she was of ghosts.

She hadn't really wanted to go to the harvest dance sponsored by the church's Catholic Youth Organization. Despite her ease with the patrons of The Place and her flirty nonchalance around the boys Edward brought home to run in the woods and play pool in the basement with, Lena was still shy in situations in which she wasn't absolutely sure of what was going to happen. And unlike her classmates, who seemed to glide effortlessly into the latest dance steps, Lena had the coordination of the white girls on "American Bandstand" and embarrassed herself and her partner each time she took to the floor. Her friends tried to be patient with her when they came to her house to practice the latest moves. But Lena spent most of the visit sitting on the attic steps watching her friends do the Stroll and Madison in front of her.

However, Gwen, who had already bought a new dress, was determined that they both go. It was the first dance that the nuns had allowed the eighth-graders to attend.

"We've all got to go. You know how vengeful nuns can be. If we don't take advantage of their great generosity, they'll get back at us. They won't let us come to a dance till we're eighteen," Gwen had warned.

And on the day of the dance Lena was caught up in the excitement of preparations along with everyone else. Her grandmama and Nellie had collaborated on her mint-green party dress, combining the high neckline of one pattern with the trendy bouffant *poi de soi* skirt of another. It was all sleek lines and fitted bodice.

In it she felt like women she had seen at The Place who burst into the joint shouting, "Uh-huh, watch out! I feel like I'm gonna take somebody's man tonight." And those brassy women, Lena had noted, usually ended up doing just that.

But much of Lena's brass was dulled when she discovered that the nuns had slipped in a group of students from the colored academy for the blind without telling any of the CYO members. They assigned each Blessed Martin de Porres student the responsibility of a blind boy or girl for the evening.

The blind student Lena got was a slim, solidly built boy named Henry with three pimples on the side of his nose. His hair was closely cropped and he wore a brown suit that was a bit too small and a white shirt.

Emboldened by how pretty she looked in her mint-green dress and low-heeled pumps, Lena took Henry's hand and led him across the dance floor to the refreshment table. She was stunned to discover that his hands were callused across the top of the palms. How could a blind boy play so vigorously that he got calluses on his hands? Lena had imagined that this shy gentle boy, like most blind people, sat around all day listening to sounds and staring into darkness. Henry's hands felt like those of a ditch digger.

She knew rough play on playground equipment could have left his hands that way. Lena's mother had forbidden her to play on the iron things and still checked her hands for calluses to make sure she wasn't swinging around a pole throwing her legs up in the air. Nellie had told her she was a young lady and shouldn't go around showing her panties to anyone who cared to stare.

That warning was as close as Nellie had come to discussing sex with her daughter, until the day she found the girl sitting astraddle the spool railing at the foot of her grandmama's four-poster bed and screamed, "Lena, get down off that thing. You hurt yourself down there in your matchbox, you never will have any children."

The injunction had left Lena a little confused until she and her girlfriends caught two teenagers under the bleachers at a public-school football game. "I bet she gets a baby," Lena's friend Marilyn predicted as the girls continued to peer through the cracks in the bleachers at the copulating pair. "You play with fire, you get burned. You play with pussy, you get fucked."

When a slow record began playing, Lena impulsively grabbed Henry's hand and led him out on the floor. Whatever activity Henry was used to, dancing was definitely not part of it. The two of them stumbled around, stepping on each other's feet, until the laughter of her friends drove them back to their chairs.

Responsibility for the blind boy had worn off sections of Lena's sparkling party veneer. She was ready to ditch him even before it occurred to her that Henry couldn't even see how pretty she looked in her green party dress.

When she looked into his eyes, Lena discovered thick-looking milky pupils unlike any she had ever seen before. And unless she spoke, the two of them sat there in silence. Once, when he tried to edge his strangely callused hands toward hers, Lena cleared her throat loudly and startled him motionless.

When the boy finally got up enough nerve to say, "You smell good, Lena, I bet you're pretty," Lena felt the germ of annoyance turn to terror. She snatched her hand away and hissed, "How do you know how I look?"

The boy was so flustered he couldn't answer. Lena jumped up and ran to the bathroom. Once it had occurred to her that the blind boy might not really be blind, and that he resembled the creatures that haunted her, everything else seemed unimportant. She spent the rest of the evening trying to avoid him, but the nuns chaperoning the dance kept bringing him to her whenever she tried to hide.

"Lena?" the boy said hesitantly, reaching out his callused hands each time he was led to her. The very sound of the boy's voice speaking her name made her shiver as if a cat had walked across her grave.

But Lena's clumsy dancing and wariness about boys didn't deter their interest in her. They knew her family made their living on things they considered dangerous—liquor, gambling, and loans. The allure of danger made the boys hot.

"Your daddy's not here with his pistol, is he?" one boy asked each time he showed up at Lena's house under the pretense of shooting a game of pool.

Gwen laughed at Lena's allure. "If the nuns knew how much boys came by your house, they'd call you an occasion of sin," she joked.

Lena and Gwen thought they knew all about nuns. But later that year, when the girls arrived at school and discovered the nuns racing up and down the wide staircases of the schoolhouse on the trail of a rumor, they began to question their own knowledge.

As the nuns ran about, their rusty black and sparkling white veils, starched to the consistency of cardboard, flew out behind them, coming perilously close to exposing their black, brown, red, and gray crewcuts to the ever-vigilant eyes of the students. The holy women had gotten wind of an accusation that some student's mother had inadvertently passed on to her child.

"Those nuns just hiding behind those veils," the mother was supposed to have said. The student had overheard the comment, picked it up, and brought it back to the crowded classroom.

The rumor, begun on the third floor of the school among the older children and overheard by a child on the second floor, quickly spread among the students on the lower floors. The phrase was repeated over and over, word for word as the mother had said it, because most of the little ones had no idea what it meant. Each child told it exactly as he or she had heard it to the next little pair of ears, and then they dissected it.

"Does it mean that they have horns that they are hiding behind those veils?" asked a little girl in second grade.

"Maybe it means they are really bank robbers and thieves running from the law," suggested a boy who was always being sent home for insisting on wearing his cap pistols and holster over his blue-and-white uniform.

"Could be they men behind them veils?" Marilyn, considered the most mannish of Lena's classmates, suggested slyly, pointing to her crotch.

In a frenzy of truth-hunting, the nuns rushed through the school and its grounds pouncing on students and bringing them to the principal's office on the third floor for questioning.

Meanwhile Lena and her friends—Brenda, Wanda, Dorothy, Lois, Carroll, Marilyn, Deborah, Caryl, and Gwen—stood in the schoolyard by the gray metal swing sets, hastily getting their stories together. "Now, when she asks you who said it first, just say you never even heard it before," Marilyn instructed the girls standing around the playground like a covey of jaybirds in their navy-blue pleated skirts and white cotton blouses. By the time a nun swooped down on them, they were all nodding their heads in agreement.

So when Sister Mary Augustine, looking like the visage of death with her long bony face and her deep-sunk gray eyes, appeared at the principal's door and beckoned Lena—next in the line of students winding all the way down the staircase—to come in and stand before Mother Josepha's gleaming dark wood desk, the girl marched in without a qualm. And when the hefty, red-faced nun behind the desk asked, "Who did you hear this from? Whose mother said this thing?" Lena threw her shoulders back, stuck out her chest, and opened her mouth to speak.

"I don't know what you're talking about, Mother, I never even heard anything," was what she intended to say, just as Marilyn had told them to. Instead a voice from deep inside her that she had never heard before boomed, "It was Cynthia's mother."

The voice was a man's or a grown woman's, husky and deep—it certainly wasn't Lena's voice. The words came out of her mouth in a rush of hot air. Lena covered her mouth with her hand, but it was too late. The words the voice had spoken were the truth.

The nun standing on guard with her back to the principal's closed office door seemed as startled by the voice as Lena herself had been. The thin blond hairs of her eyelashes fluttered over her pale eyeballs a few times and her nose began to twitch. The nun had taught Lena in sixth grade and knew just what her prize pupil's voice sounded like.

But the principal, thrilled at the ease with which her interrogation had elicited results, immediately jumped from her seat in the wooden swivel chair, shoved her colleague aside, and threw open the door. Reaching back to drag the tall, stunned Sister Mary Augustine with her, she flew out of the office past the line of Lena's friends awaiting their turns under the hot lights of interrogation.

Left in the office alone, Lena leaned against a cream-colored wall. The bones in her body turned to jelly; she slid down the wall and slumped onto the floor. The strange, unsummoned voice coming out of her mouth stunned and scared Lena worse than any ghost ever had.

She hadn't seen any ghosts or apparitions since she had suspected the blind boy at the dance was a spirit, and she was trying to forget she ever had. But that voice coming out of her mouth made her face it: no matter how many pretty dresses her mother and grandmother made for her, no matter how many good grades she made in school, no matter how high she scored on her reading tests, no matter how pretty her hair looked after she came from Delores Beauty Parlour, there was something wrong with her.

She was like a fancy birthday present all wrapped up in flowered gift paper and tied with a pretty bow. But for all the festive wrapping, there was no telling what was underneath. You couldn't take her out. She might say or do or see anything.

While Lena was immobile on the floor of the principal's office, other demons were afoot. "Lena told! Lena told!" The word spread through the school as rapidly as the original rumor had.

Her classmates were astonished at the news. "What kind of traitor is she?" Dorothy asked the other girls under her breath while Sister Louis Marie taught the eighth-graders on the other side of the room.

"She's not like us, that's why," hissed Wanda. "She never was and this proves it."

"Remember how she was always asking that stuff like, did I think tables and chairs talked when people were out of the room?" Deborah said. "And how bad she treated that poor blind boy at the dance that time. Running around the hall like she was crazy?"

The girls' outrage took on epic proportions as the day went on. When the principal rang the big cowbell dismissing classes for the day, Lena almost had to fight her way home.

Gwen was the only girl who would walk with her. When Lena tried to come up with some acceptable, natural explanation for why she told on Cynthia, Gwen just shrugged and said, "It's no big thing. Everybody's acting like you killed somebody."

Lena went to bed that night without eating dinner, even though her grandmother had prepared stew meat with potatoes, and turnip greens with their creamy roots left unmashed specifically for her.

"But, baby, it's your favorite," Grandmama pleaded, trying to entice her downstairs from her bedroom.

"Well, tell her to come down and sit at the table anyway," Jonah demanded when he walked in and saw the table set for only three. Now that Raymond was also away, at college in Tennessee, Jonah was almost beginning to regret his decision to send Edward to military school.

"I really don't think Lena feels well," Nellie said. "She's been quiet as the grave since she came home from school. She didn't even have anything to say to her buddy Frank Petersen today. You know she's a young lady now. She may just be having cramps."

"Hell, just 'cause you a young lady don't mean you can't sit up at a table and make conversation while everybody else eats," Jonah said. But after a while he put the paper down, went upstairs, and knocked on Lena's bedroom door.

"I come to visit the sick," Jonah joked as he stuck his head in the door.

"I'm not sick," Lena said from her spot on the bed with her schoolbooks around her. "I just don't want any dinner."

"Well, that sounds sick to me. You know your grandmama made stew meat just for you," Jonah said from the doorway. "If you don't want any dinner, you can at least come down and keep us company at the dinner table."

"I just don't feel like it, I just don't feel like sitting at the table and making conversation. Just this once, I don't feel like it." It wasn't that she wasn't hungry; she was. People in her family never seemed to lose their appetites, no matter what. But she had just had one of the worst days of her life. She did not feel that she could rally her strength to sit at the table and pretend that everything was okay while she ate the delicious meal.

Jonah tucked in his chin and looked at her as if she had spit on the floor. "Who the hell you think you talking to like that?" he wanted to know.

"I'm sorry," Lena said automatically.

"Well, you damn well better be and you also better learn to change your tone of voice. What's the matter with you tonight?

I think you better just stay your ass up here for the rest of the evening till you learn how to talk to people."

Jonah thought that his baby girl had such a strange haunted look on her face that even he couldn't bring himself to chastise her any further. He left the room and didn't even wait for her reply, "Yes, Daddy."

After Jonah closed the door and went back downstairs, Lena stopped looking vacantly at the books on her bed and returned to staring at the ceiling. She closed her eyes and concentrated, as Mamie had taught her to when she did her hair at Delores Beauty Parlour.

What was that voice like? What did it put me in the mind of? she asked herself, thinking that Mamie would be proud of her attempt at objectivity.

The voice wasn't exactly like the strange ghosts that had been appearing to her off and on for as long as she could remember. Those apparitions—an animal, a woman, or a floating creature with no head—all had some form, some shape that she could see. Even though the shapes they took invariably frightened her, at least they were things that were discernible.

This voice had no shape or form. It didn't come out of the night or first dark or the mirror or a picture. It came out of her. Was this thing now *in* her? Was it now a part of her, this thing she had feared the most?

It was as if some demon had taken possession of her body.

That thought struck her like a slap in the face. She sat up on her bed, still covered with the summery white eyelet spread and the ruffled valance around the edges dusting the floor, and stared off into a corner as she remembered something her teacher Sister Louis Marie had said a couple of weeks before.

From time to time the nuns at Martin de Porres, from the first grade on up, calmly terrorized their students by telling stories they represented as factual about their adventures in the western United States, where they had taught American Indian children.

"I saw things out West," said Sister Louis Marie, "that I never would have believed if I had not witnessed them with the two good eyes the Good Lord gave me and heard it with my own ears. I saw people, little innocent children, possessed by the devil, whose eyes blazed with the fires of hell and whose voices were no longer their own. Young women who spoke with the voices of men and men who sounded as if they were animals. Children who had clawed their bodies raw with their own fingernails.

"It was the devil in those poor people, the very devil that I saw with my own eyes. But the church in her infinite wisdom knows the power of Satan and has holy implements like holy water—demons cannot stand the touch of holy water; it burns the very skin of the possessed one—to drive the demons of hell out."

Now the nun's words churned red and ugly in Lena's mind, reminding her of faces she had seen in the night.

Jesus, keep me near the cross! Lena thought, using her mother's favorite phrase. Maybe that's it. Maybe I'm possessed, too.

EIGHTEEN

❧   ❧

MAGIC

The next morning Lena wanted
to skip breakfast and get to the church long before school was
to begin. But she knew that if she even looked as if she wanted
to miss two meals in a row, her mother would put her in the car
right then and take her to St. Luke's Hospital's basement for a
visit to Dr. Williams—even though Nellie was beginning to
dread visits to the doctor there. She did love to stop and look at
the luscious yellow, red, and white display of rosebushes climbing up the back of the hospital like the eighth wonder of the
world, but she said she got sick and tired of trying to dodge old
Nurse Bloom and her barrage of questions about Lena and all
that old-fashioned shit about veils and spirits and second sight.
"The last time I took Edward there, when he broke his arm, she
had the nerve to say she just knew in her bones I was going to
be coming there soon with an emergency. I started to say, 'Well,
I wish the hell you had called and told me what the emergency
was going to be. It would have saved poor Edward a lot of pain
and me a lot of trouble.' "

"Nellie," Grandmama had retorted sharply, "you so quick to
dismiss anything old folks say. Nurse Bloom may not be a bosom
buddy of mine, but I shore respect what she say."

Nellie had just sucked her teeth. And Grandmama hadn't spoken to her for the rest of the day.

So Lena rose earlier than usual, while the house still slept, and dressed hastily. Then she went downstairs by herself in the quiet house and began frying bacon in the big black spider and put the pot of water and salt on the gas fire for grits. When Grandmama and Nellie, awakened by the smell of breakfast, walked into the kitchen tying their robes around them, Lena wasn't a bit surprised.

Food got such a hold on this family, she thought.

"I see your stomach woke you up bright and early this morning," Grandmama said with a chuckle and a sly look at her daughter-in-law as she took the long fork from Lena's hand and turned the strips of bacon in the pan. "Look at her, Nellie, the girl got the white mouth. I may have to smear some of this bacon grease around your mouth before you pass out. That'll teach you to not join us for dinner."

"Taught us, too," Nellie said as she took the butter from the refrigerator door and bread from the box on top next to the cake box. "It was so lonesome at that table without you, baby. I don't know what we're gonna do when you go away to college."

"Well, that's a long way off," Grandmama said huffily, as if she were offended by even the idea of Lena leaving the house and the family for four years.

This morning, more than usual, Lena was grateful for the easy flow of conversation that seemed always to envelop her family. Now the talk made it easier for her to slip away. By the time she had wolfed down her breakfast, grabbed her books and blue cardigan, and headed up Pleasant Hill, it was only about a quarter after seven.

She hurried past Sarah's old house, cut through the dirt street where her friend Lois lived, and crossed the big street that led to the public elementary school, past the old library that was now a housing project.

The Blessed Martin de Porres school and churchyard were still empty when she walked slowly up the stone steps to the church with her schoolbooks clutched to her chest. Inside the church the air was damp and cool, heavy with the incense the altar boys burned when Father O'Donnell held the beautiful gold monstrance above his head during Benediction. On Sundays the scent made Lena sick to her stomach—empty since midnight so she could receive Holy Communion.

Someone else—probably the priest's housekeeper—had already been there. Lena saw flames on a couple of the small votive candles flickering in their blue and red holders at the side of the altar. Taking a deep breath, she reached her trembling right hand into the small font next to the church's door, dipped into the well of holy water, and made the sign of the cross with her eyes closed.

But the holy water did not sear and scorch her skin as Sister Louis Marie had said it would a person possessed by the devil. Lena stood a moment in the middle of the church and stared at her wet fingertips as tears welled up in her eyes. When she wiped the salty drops away from her lashes, the tears mixed with the holy water and still no steam rose from the mixture.

She didn't know whether to feel relief or disappointment. On the one hand it meant that she was not possessed, as she had thought the night before. On the other it meant she was right back where she had been when the voice had issued from her throat in the principal's office. She knew there was something different about her, but she didn't know what.

She headed slowly down the carpeted aisle toward the altar, genuflected, and slipped into the nearest pew, directly under the choir's loft, letting her body relax against the smooth oak seat. She had never been in the church all by herself before. It was peaceful just sitting there beneath the gaze of the Christ on the cross and the statues of Mary and Joseph and Martin de Porres and the beautifully simple Stations of the Cross carvings. It never crossed her mind that anything scary could happen there.

She couldn't remember ever sitting this far back in church. It seemed that she had always sat in front in the children's pews, with the nuns directly behind to thump a head or pull an ear of anyone who dared to talk or appear inattentive during Mass. Back where she sat now, in the adults' seats, she got a different perspective.

Compared to the simple tables in the Western mission churches the nuns described, the altar at Blessed Martin de Porres was grand, with gold candlesticks, lace-trimmed linens, and the heavy red leather-bound gilt-edged missal.

But for all its fancy trappings, the church wasn't the least bit intimidating to Lena. For a little while in fact, Lena considered staying there. Not just for the morning or for the school day, but for the rest of her life. She could live on the white wafers that stuck to the roof of her mouth during Communion, and the amber-colored wine that she knew was kept in the sacristy off the altar. She could wash in the baptismal font at the side of the altar near the candle tray, but there was only room for a whore's bath. She wasn't sure what she would do for a toilet. She guessed she could sneak downstairs to the bathroom in the church hall at night and not be seen. But she knew she couldn't hold her pee all day.

For a little while it was pleasant sitting in the cool church, weaving a fantasy of living there, imagining her pretty clothes hanging on a rack in the back where the ushers stood during Mass, her lotions and powder and deodorant sitting on the altar next to her comb and brush. But, she thought with a deep sigh, what was the use of weaving a stupid future for herself like that? She couldn't live in the church any more than she could go to the nuns for help. There was no running away from herself. I've come this far, she thought. I'm thirteen years old, I'm not a baby anymore. I can't run and hide, and I can't pretend everything is just fine. But, Lord, what am I gonna do?

The sound of the big cowbell calling the students to stand in line for the opening of school was her answer. Lena emerged from the church feeling older and more responsible than she had been half an hour before when she had entered the building.

But she wasn't prepared for what awaited her at school.

All the girls were standing as usual at the school gate. When she walked up to greet them, they all turned away in unison and, as if according to plan, hurried to stand in line.

Her tattling on Cynthia had ostracized her. Days after the incident Lena would turn in class to pass a silly note along to Wanda or Dorothy, and the girl would look straight ahead as if she didn't see or hear Lena. Or worse, Wanda or Dorothy would raise her hand and complain to Sister Louis Marie, "Sister, Lena's talking and disturbing my work."

No matter how hard she tried to fight back the tears and hold her chin up, she couldn't pull it off. Reprimanded by the teacher, she would sit in her seat with tears rolling down her cheeks, the titters of her friends dancing around her like demons.

Lena thought that after a few days, when the voice didn't manifest itself again, things would get better. The girls would tire of the silent treatment and break down and be her friends again. But she was wrong. As the fall days grew chillier and chillier and winter became a fact, the girls became frostier and meaner.

"Look at her over there with her funny-looking self," Deborah said during recess on the first day as she and her friends watched Lena come out of the school building, her brown paper lunch bag in her hand. "Think she cute just 'cause she think she got a shape. I wouldn't have no titties and big butt like that for nothing."

"Yeah," Brenda added, "and she ain't hardly got no legs."

It was a feeding frenzy: each girl took a trait of Lena's in her mouth like a thick piece of flesh and gnawed it to shreds with anger and envy.

They laughed over Lena's nervous habit of biting her nails. Then they decided to hate her long red hair when she wore it in a ponytail. They hated her hair more then than they had when she had just got it done at Delores Beauty Parlour and wore it loose and wild and hanging down.

She was the last to be picked for any ball teams or tag teams. When they clustered in the school yard in groups of three and four pretending to be The Supremes, or Martha and the Vandellas, they closed ranks against Lena and pretended there was no room for one more.

When they ran out of things to hate her for, they turned to Gwen, Lena's one remaining friend, called her fat and laughed at the gap between her two front teeth. That hurt Lena as much as the unkindnesses they hurled at her. But Gwen only shrugged and acted as if she couldn't care less. She had read somewhere that gapped teeth were a sign of passion and prided herself on her smile.

"Shoot, they weren't ever that nice to me anyway," Gwen tried to reassure her friend. "Don't let 'em see you cry."

It was some time before Lena's family noticed that she seemed unusually moody and lost. Then one day it struck her mother that none of Lena's friends other than Gwen ever came around to visit.

"Well, Nellie, our baby has never been one to have a whole lot of children running in and out the house," Grandmama reassured her daughter-in-law when Nellie brought up her concern one day in the kitchen.

"I know, Miss Lizzie, but do you think it's healthy for her to have just one friend at her age? Why, she's a teenager now. The only person she's ever on the phone to, it seems, is Gwen, and they've been friends since first grade."

"Well, if you ask me, old friends are the best kind to have. Those are the ones you need to keep," Grandmama said.

"I just don't know if it's a good idea for her to be up under grown folks so much," Nellie said. "If it's not us, it's Frank Petersen. And if she's not with him, it's the folks down at The Place. I just think she ought to be stretching her wings a little bit now that she's growing up and learning about all kinds of people."

Grandmama sucked her teeth. "You got to face it, Nellie. She's not like you when you were a girl—always having to rip and run the streets to this place and that, getting into this and that just to keep entertained."

Nellie bristled.

"She's a reader and a thinker," Grandmama said. "The last time I was at St. Luke's to have Dr. Williams listen to my heart—what for, I don't know, I'm strong as a Montana mule—I was talking to Nurse Bloom about Lena and how smart and bright she is. That old nurse said she wasn't a bit surprised. She was there at the birth and says she knows how special Lena is."

"Well, Miss Lizzie, I was there at the birth, too, you might remember. I don't know about all that veil-over-her-face shit, but I do agree with you that our Lena is special," said Nellie.

"Our baby ain't got to be a little hot-butt fast girl to satisfy *me,*" the older lady said.

Nellie slammed down the lid on a pot of field peas boiling on the stove. She knew her mother-in-law well enough to know what she was getting at. "Dammit, Miss Lizzie, how many times do I have to tell you that Raymond was a premature baby before you get it into your head? He came two months early. That's all. Hell, the boy is more than twenty years old now. What's over is over."

The rest of the afternoon was taken up with the two women arguing moral values, all concern about the recent change in Lena momentarily forgotten.

Coming in from school, Lena had heard some of the women's sharp talk. She decided to detour upstairs to her room instead of going through the kitchen as usual. As she pulled off her navy-blue skirt and looked for an old pair of jeans to put on, she thought about her family's attitude toward her, always telling her she was special.

She remembered with a smile how she used to "put the magic" on stuff when she was a little girl. How everybody in her family expected her to be able to rub her hands across the surface of anything that didn't work right so it would magically be fixed just by her touch. They didn't ask her to do that anymore. Now that she thought about it, she couldn't remember when they had stopped, just as she couldn't remember when they first started expecting her to do it.

Sometimes the things she remembered seeing and doing when

she was younger seemed like a dream to her now. Had she really seen the ghost of a slave named Rachel on the beach? Did the baby in the picture that was probably still leaning against the wall in the attic really try to pull her inside the frame?

It could get very confusing. Real people could become as unreal for her as the ghosts were. With a twinge of guilt she remembered the blind boy Henry, whom she had suspected of being a ghost. She sometimes even doubted whether she had really had a beautiful beautician who taught her how to ask questions.

Deep down she knew that the ghosts she saw were real. She could feel her heart beat harder just thinking about some of them. But somewhere along the line she had decided that the best way to deal with the ghosts and visions was to push them far back in her mind and pretend they were unreal. She imagined a whole pile of scaries somewhere in her soul, covered up with an old khaki canvas tarp like the one Frank Petersen threw over the cord of wood stacked up by the front door porch. Perhaps, she thought, that's where the voice came from, from that pile of memories and visions.

Putting the magic on stuff, she mused quietly. She was a little embarrassed by the childish idea, but she was alone and willing to give anything a try.

She sat up straight on her bed in her socks, white blouse, and panties, her head high on her long neck, her legs crossed like an Indian's, and tried to remember the kinds of things that used to go through her head when she had put the magic on stuff. But she couldn't remember a thing about what she had thought in those days when she got their big green woodie started or the television picture unscrambled, so she cleared her mind as best she could and began rubbing her right hand over the left side of her body.

She started at her bare brown shoulder and let her right hand follow the contours of her left arm, past her vaccination mark, past her slightly ashy elbow, over her forearm, her wrists, and her knuckles until she stopped at the fingertips of her left hand.

When she finished that, she did the same thing with her left hand over her right arm.

Then she returned to her broad shoulders and, with both hands, slowly rubbed the entire length of the front of her body, paying special attention to her breasts, where she felt her heart beating. Gently she brought her hands down over her smooth thighs, slender legs, and ankles—down to her narrow feet with the scar on the left instep where a frying pan full of hot lard had mysteriously fallen off the stove, and on to her slender toes.

She could only reach so far on her back, but she crossed her arms over her chest, stretched them as far as she could around, and ran her fingertips down the side of her spine. Then she ran her hands the rest of the way down the backs of her thighs and legs to her heels.

She thought she should pay extra attention to her head. She rubbed both hands over her forehead, across her temples, and around the crown of her head where her thick hair was pulled back into a ponytail, and she did it again before moving to her throat, from which the voice that tattled on Cynthia's mother had come.

"There!" she said aloud and continued sitting on the bed in silence waiting for something to show her that putting the magic on herself had worked. But it seemed too much like tempting fate, like asking something strange to walk into her room. Finally she jumped up and ran out to the telephone in the upstairs hall.

She was surprised that she could even remember her classmate Lois's phone number. It had been a long time since she had dialed it, but it came right to mind. "That's a good sign," she said aloud.

When Lois answered the telephone on the second ring, Lena thought, That's another good sign. She swallowed and spoke right up.

"Hello, Lois? This is Lena."

There was a pause. Then Lois said in her flattest voice, "Yeah, what *you* want?"

Lena's heart sank at the sound of her former friend's voice.

But Lois didn't give her a chance to come up with anything. "My mama want to use the phone," she said. "I got to go." Then she hung up.

Lena held the dead phone in her hand for a moment, still hearing the loud click of the broken connection. For the first time, she allowed herself to feel the anger at her ex-friends that had been simmering since the girls had stopped speaking to her. Who the hell does Lois think she is, hanging up in my face like that?

Instead of slamming the phone back on the receiver, she decided to dial another number.

"Hello?" Lena said timidly when the line was picked up.

"Hey, girl," Gwen said immediately. "Whatcha doing?"

Lena longed to say, "Gwen, I see ghosts and hear voices and all kinds of things." But she was afraid she'd lose Gwen, too.

Saying anything to her family was out of the question. Lena remembered the frightening convulsions she suffered when she had tried to tell when she was younger. She was sure that even Grandmama, who claimed to have a belief in all kinds of things, wouldn't be able to help her. Nobody could help her. What good would it do to tell them?

There didn't seem to be anything anyone could do. Whatever was inside her making her see and feel things no one else saw and felt was stronger than anything in her everyday world. Sure, her family would love her and pet her up after she went into convulsions. Dr. Williams would make a house call and take her temperature and give her a sedative. Her mother and grandmother would lay cold compresses on her head. But the ghosts would still come back whenever they felt like it.

NINETEEN

❧ ❧

SLEEPWALK

Three nights later Lena began walking in her sleep. The first time it happened, Sunday night, Nellie woke at about midnight to find Lena standing by her bed, her arms sticking out from her body at an angle, her hands clenched into fists, her gaze fixed straight ahead at some point over her mother's head, her mouth hanging open.

"What is it, baby?" Nellie asked groggily. "You can't sleep?"

"The wolf. It's attacking me," Lena said in a strange voice.

"Wolf? What wolf, sugar? What you talking about?" Nellie was trying hard to come awake and see what Lena wanted.

"The wolf tried to grab my throat and tear it out. It tried to kill me," Lena said. It didn't sound as if she were answering Nellie's question, but rather just talking to herself.

In the moonlight streaming into the room at the foot of the bed, Lena looked to Nellie like a phantom. Dressed in her favorite long white flannel gown, her hair pulled back into a ponytail and wrapped around one pink sponge curler, she hardly resembled the pretty teenager Nellie was used to seeing.

The sound of Lena's voice was like that of some girl her mother didn't know. It gave Nellie a chill all over. She reached over to her night table and clicked on the lamp for some light to reassure herself, to cut through the darkness.

Lena didn't even blink at the bright light in her face. She just stood there staring at her parents' headboard. Now that the light was on, Nellie could see the muscles in the side of her baby's face flexing and contorting.

"Jonah, Jonah," Nellie whispered to her husband, who was snoring soundly next to her. "Wake up, Jonah. Something's wrong."

When he didn't stir, Nellie shook his shoulder sharply and repeated, "Wake up, Jonah. Something's wrong with Lena."

Jonah shot awake, flailing his arms and snorting. "What's a matter with her?"

Nellie just put her finger to her lips and pointed to the girl standing still as a statue next to their bed. "I think she's still sleeping. Look at her."

Jonah sat up and leaned across Nellie to look at his daughter intently.

"Lena, baby," he said.

"Shhh. Don't startle her. Not while she's still sleep. If you wake her up while she's sleepwalking, they say she'll go crazy."

"Well, then, dammit, what we gonna do?" Jonah asked, exasperated.

"Let's see if we can get her back to her room," Nellie suggested.

They both led her into her room and tucked her stiff body back into bed as quietly as possible, trying not to awaken her.

Nellie and Jonah stood over their sleeping daughter for a while to make sure she was soundly asleep again before returning to their own bed. The air in their room was thick with thoughts they were reluctant to express. They were both frightened by the sleepwalking.

Nellie tried to act casual the next morning when Lena came downstairs hungry and ready for breakfast, unaware that she was a somnambulist.

"You sleep all right last night?" Nellie asked as she poured beaten eggs into the frying pan.

"Pretty good," Lena answered as she sipped her orange juice. "How about you?"

"Oh, just fine," her mother answered quickly.

Nellie had had every intention of telling Lena that she had sleepwalked into her parents' room the night before, but now that she was faced with the task, she felt unsure of herself. Somehow she suddenly felt that this was something she had to protect her daughter from. She remembered how, just three days before, Lena had almost burst into tears when Miss Lizzie had teased her about never dreaming of a winning number for her to play in the "bug."

We've told this child too much foolishness about herself as it is, her mother thought. She doesn't need to know that she's walking in her sleep now, too.

But as soon as Lena left the house for school and her grandmama went into the sewing room, Nellie got right on the phone to Dr. Williams's office.

"Oh, it's nothing to worry about, Mrs. Mac," Dr. Williams reassured her after hearing the story of Lena walking in her sleep. "Young folks do that sometimes. Puberty, adolescence—it can be a hard time for some children. And the sleepwalking, that could just be Lena's reaction to it. I'd be surprised if it ever happened again.

"Besides," the doctor added, chuckling, "you know the old folks say you don't have to worry about a child like Lena. You know she's one of my little lucky babies. The old folks say nothing bad's gonna happen to her."

Nellie hung up the phone relieved. Many of her friends over the years had deserted Dr. Williams for other physicians—"good Jewish doctors," they called them—and the integrated county hospital. But Nellie never even considered it. She still felt the same aura of care and healing at Saint Luke's that she had felt when her children were born there. She was one of Dr. Williams's fiercest supporters. Now, as relief flooded her head, washing away the sense of foreboding that had been there since the night before, she knew why.

Still, for months afterward, she and Jonah continued to keep an eye on Lena. Waking in the middle of the night, Nellie would slip into Lena's room on bare feet to make sure she had not wandered away in her sleep. When Jonah came home in the early-morning hours—from The Place or playing poker or screwing around—he would peep in before he lay down for the final time. But when they always found her safe in bed, eventually they relaxed their vigils and slept through the night.

As soon as they did, Lena began her night wanderings again.

In the darkness of early morning she would rise from her bed and head out her bedroom door. Never pausing to check her surroundings, she walked down the steps and out the front door of the house. An hour or so later she returned, climbed back into bed, and fell into a blessed dreamless sleep.

Her night wanderings went on for six months at two- or three-week intervals without anyone in the house becoming aware of them. Then Lena got suspicious.

"Lena-Wena, you're gonna have to start wearing shoes even when you're just walking around the house," Frank Petersen told her one day as he changed the linen on all the beds. "The bottoms of your sheets are just full of dirt."

She just turned up her nose at the suggestion. "I hate wearing shoes and socks," said Lena, who went around the house in her bare feet long after the weather had turned chilly.

"You know, your feet gonna be wide as bateaus if you don't start wearing shoes more regular," Grandmama said. But she dropped the subject when she realized that she was agreeing with Frank Petersen.

Lena ignored them both, but she began to notice that her feet did seem dirtier than usual some mornings when she took her bath. Then, a few months after Frank Petersen complained of her dirty feet, Lena awoke to find her feet and the end of her gown not only soiled but also soaking wet. And stuck between the toes on one foot were two or three shreds of slimy brown leaves.

Lena almost let out a scream. Where did the wet leaves come from? Had a night visitor left them there between her toes as a reminder of the visit? Had she dreamed so hard about wading through water that she actually became wet? As she sat on her rumpled bed, biting the cuticles around her thumbnail nervously, Lena was reminded of something she hadn't thought of in years. She couldn't put her finger on it, but it seemed so important it kept intruding on her fear and confusion.

Lena raced to the bathroom and, thankful that it was empty, frantically rinsed the material off her feet. As she watched the debris spin down the drain, Lena wished the terror that it raised in her could be as easily washed away. But she knew that nothing having to do with her was ever solved that easily.

For days after that she checked her feet first thing in the morning for signs of wet and leaves. Each time, her feet came up dry. But the question still nagged at her while she ate breakfast and tried to make small talk, while she sat in class and tried to concentrate on the Crusades, while she undressed again for bed: how could she get soaking wet without knowing how it happened? But before a week had passed, she discovered just how.

One night the pressure of her bladder tugged her awake. She slowly opened her eyes. But she didn't see the familiar surroundings of her room—the pink walls, the chest of drawers by the closet, the vanity table prettily trimmed in pink ruffles and covered with bottles of Shalimar and jars of Dippity Do and Noxema. Instead she found herself sitting in the middle of the woods behind her house, propped up against the rough bark of a big pine tree with the moonlight in her eyes. She knew she was deep in the woods: she couldn't see an electric light or the roof of a house nearby or hear the sound of a living thing around her.

For just a second, Lena thought she might still be dreaming, but she could feel the cold wet ground beneath her and the scratch of the tree's bark against her back. Her feet and gown hem were wet and sandy.

This time she didn't even try to hold it back. In the middle of the woods, deep in the night, Lena threw back her head and howled like some wild thing, like a wolf. She cried as she had not allowed herself to cry since she was seven years old. She screamed until her throat was raw, and she clutched at her long hair, pulling it out of the ponytail clip. Then she lay on the ground among the brown pine needles and slick leaves, shuddering and gasping to catch her breath, dry heaves wracking her body.

"Oh, God, help me, help me!" she prayed as she felt the cold seep into her bones from the damp earth. She closed her eyes and tried to remember some time when she felt safe and warm. But all she could recall were the apparitions and voices that still made her shiver.

Now I'm wandering around at night through the woods and doing God knows what all, and I can't even remember any of it, she thought as she sat on the damp ground, hugging herself against the cold and rocking back and forth, scraping her back on the tree. I can't keep on like this. I've got to get far away from here, I've got to get away from here, I've got to get away from here!

Lena sat rocking on the cold ground, not bothering to wipe the tears from her face.

But her immediate problem was finding her way back home and doing it before anyone discovered she was missing. If Mama and 'em find out I'm wandering around in my sleep, they'll never let me out of their sight again. But if I can't get away from here and all this crazy shit, I may as well be dead.

She got up, brushed herself off, and started walking, stepping in and out of beams of moonlight. At every step she just knew she was going to run into some frightful rotting creature, maybe the one that had lured or brought her into the woods in the first place. But she couldn't bear to stand still and wait for daylight.

She seemed to be walking in circles, getting nowhere. But after an hour or so she heard the sound of falling water and, following it, came to a small clearing in the woods where a stream flowed over a huge flat boulder and cascaded gracefully into a small dark pool five or six feet below.

Lena had found her brothers' secret swimming hole, the one she had yearned to see when she was a little girl forbidden to wander in the woods. She was so happy to find something she recognized, something she could connect with the world of reality, that she sat down on the banks of the pool and cried again.

It was no longer as dark as before. She jumped up and began running along the banks of the stream. If she stayed with the course of the water, she knew she would eventually come to the spot behind her house. By the time she got there, the sun was almost peeking through the pines behind.

"Don't let anybody be up early," she prayed as she carefully slipped past the kitchen door she must have left wide open and quietly ran up the steps to her bedroom.

She longed to go into the bathroom and wash off the dirt and debris that still clung to her feet, but she didn't dare make that much noise. So she just scraped her feet against the painted wicker wastepaper can in her room, changed from her wet nightgown into a clean one, and climbed wearily into bed. She was exhausted, but she didn't dare sleep. How would she ever sleep again?

When she shifted in bed under the sheets and the heavy quilt her grandmama had made especially for her, her gritty feet rubbed together like two pieces of sandpaper.

She was reminded of Rachel. The fine grains of sand on her damp feet, embedded in the creases weaving between her toes and under her pink toenails, put Lena in mind of the watery woman whose skin and clothes felt rough and scratchy when she rubbed against her.

Lena had long ago put down to fantasy the memory of sitting on the beach on a washed-up log next to the woman who said she was a ghost. In fact she had tried to put the memory of all the ghosts and specters that had wandered through her bedroom and her head all her life out of her mind. But now, with the feel of wet sand on her feet, the memory of the slave's ghost was so sharp, the woman seemed in the room with her.

What was it she told me? What was it I was never supposed

to forget? Suddenly it seemed important to remember everything about the experience on the Georgia coast that she had
spent years trying to forget.

She closed her eyes to recreate that day when she had wandered away from her family in search of the protected cove she
had dreamed about. When she felt herself slipping off to sleep,
she snatched herself alert and sat up with her back against the
headboard. Then she remembered.

Rachel said I belonged there on that beach. "You belong
here. You belong here." That's what she kept saying, Lena said
to herself. She said I belonged anywhere on earth that I chose
to be.

But even as Lena repeated Rachel's words to herself, she felt
they weren't intended for her. The last thing in the world she
wanted was to belong to the spot of earth she found herself on.
She didn't feel she belonged there in Mulberry, on Forest Avenue, in Pleasant Hill, at Blessed Martin de Porres School. Just
getting to be fifteen years old in that spot had been so taxing for
Lena that it seemed any minute she might crack down the middle
and fall apart. In fact she yearned to get as far away as she could
from the place she called home.

All her terrors, the sleepwalking, her childhood memories of
ghosts, her skewed premonitions, the hatred the girls at school
still harbored toward her, all the things that had frightened and
haunted her all her life were connected with the town of Mulberry and her close familiar home.

I can't trust anything, Lena thought.

TWENTY

❦   ❦

GRANDMAMA

"Grandma, am I still shaped-up like Mama's people?" Lena asked as she looked over her shoulder at her body, naked except for white bra and panties, in the full-length mirror in the sewing room.

" 'till the day you die, baby," Grandmama said, clenching a mouthful of straight pins between her teeth. It was sometimes dangerous to hug or kiss Grandmama while she was sewing. If the pins in her mouth didn't prick Lena, the needles stuck in the front of her dress did. Lena had learned long ago it was best to hug her grandmama from behind and only kiss the top of her head, where her hair was balding, when she came home from school and found the old lady sitting at her sewing machine.

Lena could tell by looking in the mirror that she had the same body and frame her mother had. She had the same big low butt, the same long waist where no belt felt comfortable unless it was nearly resting on her low narrow hip bones, the same slender legs and fragile-looking ankles. She also had her mother's beautiful breasts, not so big they weighed her down, but big enough that they played a perfect counterpoint in front to her big behind and made her resemble an S when viewed from the side.

This seemed to make the link she felt with her mother real and tangible. Something that she could look in the mirror and see. Something that all those people who thought Lena strange could look at and compare and say, "Yes, indeed, that's Nellie's child, all right." She might be crazy as hell, nervous and jumpy for no reason, but she was Nellie's child. Her body proved it.

It made her feel less like a changeling left for her family by mistake and more like the special baby girl they thought they'd gotten.

Ever since she awoke in the middle of the woods, Lena lived in fear that others, especially her family, would discover the secret of her visions and voices and be forced to take some action. Lena held on to anything that would make her feel more anchored to what she imagined other people's lives must be like. The problems she knew others faced—no job or money, an alcoholic relative, physical abuse, being evicted—never seemed so bad when she compared them with hers. Shit, at least they don't see things, she thought.

"We'll have this outfit finished, except for the handwork and hemming, before your mama gets home from The Place this evening," Grandmama said, holding up the straight white wool skirt she was making for Lena to wear to the school talent show. Lena put on a lightweight pink cotton duster and sat on the bed next to her completed winter-white mohair jacket.

"So stop standing over me like that, breathing down my back," Grandmama fussed. Lena wasn't anywhere near the old lady's back. She stretched out on the bed and tried to feign interest in a pattern cover left on the bed.

"Why don't you go in the kitchen and get me a cold Co-Cola, baby? And while you at it, go through the living room and see what that noise is I hear in there. Frank Petersen ain't still sneaking around here, is he?" Grandmama peered accusingly over the top of her reading glasses.

"Nope, it's just you and me, Grandma," Lena said. She had heard it, too: a desperate little noise like the sound of an insistent breeze nipping at the tail of a curtain at an open window. But she had waited for her grandmama to say something about it before she acknowledged she'd heard it. What she had heard could just have been a sound to lure her into the room by herself.

At sixteen Lena felt she knew herself better than she really wanted to. Whenever she looked at her smart new suit, she thought of it as a costume she would wear to masquerade as a normal person for the evening. But she wasn't really like any other person she knew. Not like the girls who still wouldn't talk to her. Not even like Gwen.

She could sit in the parking lot downtown by the auditorium with Tommy Davis, smelling overpoweringly of Jade East, and kiss until her teeth clanked against his perfect straight ones to the sounds of Otis Redding singing "Try a Little Tenderness," the way she had done the week before after the James Brown show, but it didn't make her a normal teenager.

The passion the boy's perfect kisses stirred in her reminded her of how it felt to see visions: her heart beating wildly, her breath short, her skin prickly. She had pulled away from the boy's searching mouth. Instead of seeing Tommy's look of disappointment, in his eyes she saw the heavy eyes of Henry the blind boy. Panicking, she insisted that her date take her home immediately.

She had finally come to the conclusion that she was crazy, truly crazy. As bad as Cliona from Yamacraw. She just prayed that she could hold on and not do anything too bizarre—not walk the streets talking and arguing with herself like Cliona—until she finished college, got a job, and could pay for some professional help. But she knew better than to broach the subject with anyone in her family or even with Gwen. That shit—paying some man a bunch of money to listen to your problems—was for white women and fools, they would say.

Her family didn't even like her to say she had a stomachache, let alone something serious like being crazy. Her mother seemed to dread having to take her to Dr. Williams's office when she was ill and having to answer all old Nurse Bloom's questions about Lena as much as she dreaded seeing her baby in pain.

Sometimes Lena thought Nurse Bloom knew she was crazy,

too, and might say something about it. Lena was starting to dread trips to the hospital herself.

Reassured by her grandmama that there really was a noise in the living room, Lena got right up and went through the music room to investigate. As soon as she entered the living room, she could tell that the source of the sound was in the fireplace. She only needed to glance that way to see what was making the commotion. Quickly she spun around and ran back into the sewing room.

"Grandmama, Grandmama," she shouted to the startled old lady, "there's a bird in the house!"

"Lord, have mercy," Grandmama exclaimed and threw the white skirt across the black body of the sewing machine. She jumped up from her pink chenille seat and ran into the hall. She stopped short of the door to the living room.

"Quick, go get the broom," she instructed Lena, who was hard on her heels.

Grandmama was still standing in the hall peering into the living room when Lena returned at a trot with a broom and dust mop in her hand, her heart racing. Grandmama, whom Lena always thought of as fearless, looked small and unprotected standing in the hall all by herself, her eyes too big for her face, her old hand clutching the lapels of her shirtwaist dress as if they weren't full of straight pins. But the old lady rallied and sprang into action as soon as she spied Lena. She snatched the broom from the girl's hand and took a deep breath, her flat chest puffing out with strength.

"Good," she said, "you brought something, too." Then, without another word, the old lady plunged into the living room. Like a good foot soldier, Lena followed without question.

But she nearly ran into her grandmother's back as soon as she crossed the threshold. The old lady had stopped dead in her tracks the moment she got inside the room. She stood perfectly still by the ottoman next to Jonah's big easy chair, staring at the bird as it struggled in the ashes of the grate. "Lord, have mercy, it's an owl. Dammit, it's an owl." She brought her hand to her flat chest and stood there nervously biting her bottom lip.

The bird was a small thing, probably a baby, Lena thought. She couldn't tell what color it had been originally. It had thrashed around in the ashes of the fireplace so desperately that it was now a dusty gray. And it didn't make any noise that Lena could hear from where she stood near the doorway. Just the flutter of its wings and the sound of its body slamming against the ashy bricks as it threw itself wildly around the cold grate.

"Is it a screech owl?" Grandmama asked herself as she leaned on her broom and gnawed on her bottom lip with her big false teeth. She peered around the spark screen trying to get a better look at the bird. "Now, what in the world is a screech owl doing in amongst all these pine trees around here? I haven't seen one of those in I don't know how long. But it's a screech owl, all right."

Then, seeming to remember she had help, the old lady turned to Lena and said, "Baby, a bird in the house is a sure sign that there's gonna be a death in the family. We got to get him out of here and damn fast. Maybe we can shoo him back up the chimney, the way he came in."

But just as Grandma took a tentative step toward the fireplace in her soft cloth house shoes, her broom extended before her like a sword, the bird found the opening at the top of the screen and flew out into the woman's face, leaving a trail of gray ashes in the air.

Lena and Grandmama both screamed. Lena dropped her mop, fell to her knees, and covered her head with both hands to keep the bird from flying into her hair. Grandmama closed her eyes and swung her broom in the air with all her might, knocking over the tall floor lamp by Jonah's chair. The frightened bird flew to the corner of the ceiling.

"Go open the door to the porch, Lena," Grandmama yelled. "I'll chase him that way."

Lena dropped her mop and dashed to the French doors, but

as soon she got there, the bird flew over their heads in the opposite direction and headed through the door leading to the hall.

"Goddamn his soul!" Grandmama muttered and raced through the door behind him, her broom still held high. The old woman was running back and forth the length of the hall breathing hard and searching in corners, under the telephone table, on the staircase, muttering the whole time, "A bird in the house, we got to get him out of here, we got to get him the hell out of here." They heard a flutter in the dining room.

The bird, most of its feathers sticking out every which way, was caught in the white pleats of the sheers that hung at the dining-room window. It was a pathetic sight, Lena thought, with its long talons hopelessly entangled in the threads of the curtains and a soft sound like a cat's meow coming from its beak.

"We got him now!" Grandmama grabbed the curtains halfway down, trying to envelop the bird in their folds. In her excitement she pulled too hard and the whole curtain rod came crashing down on her head, freeing the bird to fly crazily around the room. "Dammit!" Grandmama freed herself from the curtains and angrily spun around. The bird rested for a moment on the corner of the wide mantelpiece. Grandmama ran to the fireplace and brought the broom down on the spot from high above her head.

"I bet I got your ass now!" Grandmama screamed.

The bird hopped to the middle of the mantelpiece, but the broom swept across the end, knocking a piece of Grandmama's prized wedding china—the large turkey platter propped up like a painting against the wall—to the floor. It crashed into four pieces against the brick of the hearth.

Lena gasped, but Grandmama paid no attention. She swung again at the bird as it perched on top of her beautiful soup tureen, its breast rising and falling as rapidly as the old lady's chest. The bird avoided the falling broom by hopping to the side behind Grandmama's family portrait, but the tureen came crashing down, sending slivers of china and the ladle dancing across the shiny wooden floor and under the big oval table.

Lena dropped her mop, ran over to Grandmama, and grabbed the old woman's hands, now clutching the broom handle in what felt to Lena like a death grip. "Stop, Grandma, stop. You're breaking your china," she shouted into the woman's face.

Grandmama pushed the girl away from her and took another swipe at the bird, knocking over the photograph. It bumped the brass urn containing her husband's ashes next to it. The urn fell over on its side with a metallic clank and rolled slowly to the very edge of the mantelpiece. The urn's matching brass top came loose and fell end over end to the hearth below.

Finally Grandmama stopped. She and Lena watched in horror as the ashes of the dead man, coarse granules of his bones, slipped from the lip of the urn and slowly trickled over the edge of the mantel to the grate. It was the first time ashes had been in that fireplace since the big fire had killed all the teachers thirty years before, leaving only the original fireplaces standing and ashes everywhere.

Grandmama let out a little cry of pain at the sight of the ashes drifting to the floor. "Walter?" Her voice rose slightly as if she were asking the dead man a question.

Lena looked over at her grandmother and thought the old woman might burst into tears. Instead she squared her shoulders and raised her broom again. "That's my husband, you son of a bitch!" Grandmama lunged for the bird as if it were a person who had desecrated Jonah's father's resting place.

Just then a ray of the setting sun glinted in the bank of windows Frank Peterson had recently washed on the opposite side of the dining room. The bird extended its broad wings, took off from the mantelpiece, and flew through Grandmama's upraised arms, headed for what it must have seen as outside.

Lena looked over from her grandmama's contorted face just in time to see the bird career into the pane of glass. The impact made a loud crash, sending splinters flying against the screen outside. Impaled on a wide shard of glass, the bird quivered a few times, then fell limp on its spike. A thin stream of watery blood began to run down the shard of glass.

Once again the girl and the old woman were shocked into silence. Death, the very thing that they had raced around the house crazily to avert, had been thrust into the room as swiftly as the shard of glass had seemed to thrust itself through the bird's heart.

The old woman was the first to move. Lena had seen Grandmama twist the heads off live chickens with an effortless flick of her wrist, but when the woman tried to lift the bird off the window glass, her hands shook so violently that Lena was afraid she would cut herself on the jagged edges. Even though Lena was certain holding the bird in her own hands would ensure that it would soon be flying through her dreams to haunt her, she insisted on doing it.

"Yeah, where the hell is that worthless Frank Petersen when you really need him?" Grandmama blustered, but she couldn't hide her relief.

When Lena lifted the creature off the shard of glass, its plump rounded body still warm and bloody, she had to fight the impulse to scream in sympathy. She was surprised that the thing had weight and shape and was touched by its feeling of just-escaped life. Where the gray ashes from the fireplace had come off, Lena could see that the bird was a beautiful reddish-brown color and that it had small pointed ears.

"What should I do with it, Grandma?" Lena turned to the old lady with the bird held as far away from her body as possible. Grandmama managed only to back off from Lena and point outdoors with a quivering hand.

"It's only a bird. It's only a bird," Lena intoned as she walked around the back of the house and down to the stream. She heaved the carcass as far as she could over the water into the woods on the other side.

Looking at the thicket of trees, Lena thought of her brothers Edward and Raymond, and how they used to tramp through the woods until they smelled like puppies. She missed them so much now that they were grown and out of the house—Edward to an air force base in Texas and Raymond in his own home on the other side of town. Even though Raymond worked at The Place in the evenings, she felt she hardly saw him anymore. Her mother wasn't nearly as high-strung, cursing creatively at every chance, as she had been when they were all living at home, but Lena knew Nellie missed the boys, too.

She felt more and more alone. The girls at school didn't even slip up and speak to her by mistake anymore. And the boys only wanted to see how close they could get to putting their eager hands on her breasts as if it were a game. Even if her brothers didn't understand her any more than anyone else did, they loved her just the same.

When Lena returned to the house, Grandmama was already kneeling at the dining-room hearth, brushing her husband's ashes back into the mouth of the urn. She was frantic to clean up the mess she and the bird had made all through two rooms and the downstairs hall before anybody else came home. "If we hurry up and get this house back into shape," she said, sweeping up the broken pieces of her china with the broom she had just used as a weapon, "we won't even have to mention that a bird was ever in the house."

Without a word Lena fell right to work beside the old woman. She wanted to ask if keeping quiet about it would keep the death the bird portended at bay. But Grandmama's drained face made it impossible for Lena even to say the word "death" in front of her.

"We'll just tell your mama that I broke the window," Grandmama said, straightening her family's portrait on the dining-room mantelpiece. "And your daddy is away so much now he got that other place out on the county line—what he need another old dive for I'll never know—we'll have the window fixed before he even notice it's been broken."

Lena sighed deeply at the thought of another secret she'd have to keep. When I get grown and get myself straightened out, I'm never gonna keep another damn secret as long as I live, she thought as she helped her grandmother put the chairs back at their places at the dining-room table.

"I'm surprised that damn priest didn't show up in the middle of everything, the way he always does at the worst possible time." Grandmama tried to sound like her old self when they finally sat back down in the sewing room.

The house was back in order again. Grandmama picked up Lena's wool skirt, making several stabs at finishing the waistband, but she kept looking over her shoulder as if she felt someone standing there and kept sticking herself with the needle. Then she began rubbing her left shoulder and arm as if to get a crick out.

"Grandma, why don't you go upstairs to your room and lie down until you get your breath back," Lena suggested.

Grandmama looked at the girl as if she had said something outrageous. She sucked her teeth and said playfully, "You must think I'm an old lady or something to have to take a nap in the middle of the day."

After a while she did gather her hand sewing in her arms and move to the sofa in the living room. But her seat there seemed no more comfortable than the one in the sewing room. Still she refused to discard the work altogether and go upstairs to her room. When Nellie blew the car horn for someone to come out and help her with her packages, Grandmama was sitting straight up, looking over her shoulder every once in a while.

Neither Nellie nor Jonah noticed anything out of place in the house except the broken window. After dinner, during which Grandmama tried to put on a face that looked normal, everyone but Jonah, who returned to The Place, went to bed around eleven o'clock as usual.

Lena, exhausted, fell right asleep and, for the first time in years, didn't even awake to go to the bathroom during the night. She wasn't a bit surprised when the owl that had flown around downstairs flew through her dreams, ten sizes bigger than it had been in reality, wreaking havoc on everything its wide wings came in contact with and picking up people like toys in its big curved beak. But the loud screeching Lena heard in her sleep was not made by her dream bird. Everyone in the house heard the pathetic calls made by the mate of the owl that had died that day in her dining room.

TWENTY-ONE

☙ ☙

FUNERAL

Lena awoke to a house that seemed to be in an uproar. But when, still groggy with sleep, she tried to distinguish one anguished scream from another, she realized that it was really strangely quiet.

Nellie had stuck her head into Grandmama's room when she came out of the bathroom that morning. She meant to look in on the old woman and then let her sleep late, even though Nellie knew Miss Lizzie would berate her later on for making her miss the best part of the day. But as soon as Nellie saw her lying there so still, her body slightly contorted, she rushed into the room and gently shook the old woman's shoulder.

"Miss Lizzie? Miss Lizzie?" Nellie repeated a few times, but she knew by the feel of her mother-in-law's body that the woman would never again reply, "What, Nellie? Shit, I can still hear! Hell, I'm just 'sleep.''

Nellie had found her own mother dead in her sleep the same way and knew there was no use rushing to the phone to call an ambulance.

She sat on the edge of the bed next to Miss Lizzie's body and smoothed a few crinkled strands of the old lady's hair back into her hairnet. The two women had spent a great deal of time together in the last twenty-or-so years, especially in the early morning when they both rose together to prepare breakfast for the family and get them out of the house so they—the women of the house—could start their day. It felt right for them to be together for this last time undisturbed with the morning light beginning to break through the satiny curtains. Nellie knew it was the last time they would ever be alone, and already she was missing the old lady.

"As much as we talked and fussed and carried on, Miss Lizzie, you would think I wouldn't have anything else to say. You'd think we had said it all. But now, dammit, I all of a sudden can think of a thousand things I didn't tell you before." Nellie didn't think she would have, but she began to cry. She let her tears fall from her face onto the patchwork quilt that partly covered her mother-in-law.

"You know, Miss Lizzie, I know about you and Frank Petersen." Nellie addressed the corpse on the bed, but she was really talking to the old lady's spirit that seemed to be imbued in the very wood of the furniture in the room that was so much like her. "Not that I thought for a minute that anything happened between you two. To tell the truth, I almost wish it had. Don't get me wrong. I know how much you loved Mr. Walter, but you've been as close to me as a mother. And I know a woman gets lonely.

"It's just that I saw you, how you looked at him, how the two of you picked at each other. I knew he was making you hot. If no one else knew, if he didn't know it, I knew."

Nellie was so used to the old lady breaking in while she talked that she paused for a moment half-expecting a quick retort. Then she half-smiled and continued.

"And another thing. You know, Raymond wasn't premature like I always said. You were right. I was fast. I didn't mean to be. I just always was. It came easy.

"And since we can talk honestly here," Nellie continued, beginning to feel the cleansing that her tears and words brought, "Jonah and I, we got Raymond in your house on that pretty curved-back maroon velvet sofa in the living room. You and Mr. Walter were upstairs in your room. I don't mean any disrespect by laughing here on your deathbed, but I was just thinking about how Jonah insisted that we put all your stuff in storage when you moved in with us. Remember? All he really cared about saving was that old velvet sofa. He planned to make sure Raymond got it some day.

"Lord, Miss Lizzie, I shore don't want to be the one to do it, but I got to go in there and tell Jonah that his mama's gone. He's gonna take it so hard. Maybe it would have been easier if you'd been sick for a while or something, Miss Lizzie. But you were always so damn strong.

"And then—Jesus keep me near the cross—I got to go and wake up our baby and tell her. Now tell me, Miss Lizzie, how am I'm gonna do that?"

"You don't have to tell me, Mama," Lena said from her spot in the doorway. She looked more like six than sixteen in her long thin cotton gown and bare feet.

Nellie held out her hand to Lena, who slowly walked over to join her mother and grandmother on the sixty-four-year-old four-poster bed.

The funeral was held at a church near the top of Pleasant Hill, which Miss Lizzie had attended briefly when her children were small and where she had once been on a program sponsored by the Negro Women's League.

It was an excellent turnout for a winter weekday afternoon. Everyone said so. Even Jonah, who sat in the first pew between Nellie and Lena and sobbed like a baby, his shoulders shaking through the whole short service, noticed that there wasn't an empty pew in the entire church. Nellie, who seemed to have to hold up for the entire family, was just as pleased to see Gloria and Yakkity Yak and Slick and Bovine and the rest of them from down at The Place as she was to see the principal of the black high school, two nuns, Father O'Donnell, and Jonah's business associates sitting there in their dark outfits and funeral faces. Some busy people, like Dr. Williams and some of his nurses and

Miss Rowana from the *Mulberry Clarion,* only put in appearances at the church or cemetery, but they were there.

Other than the sounds of soft sobbing and wailing and the gleaming brass of the coffin, Lena remembered little about the service. Before Lena saw Father O'Donnell there, she wondered briefly if she would have to confess to him that she had gone to a Protestant service. She sat there in the strange church in the high-waisted royal-blue wool dress trimmed in black piping that her grandmother had made for her to wear to serious functions, and low-heeled black leather pumps, and tried to keep a rein on her emotions. She prayed to be made numb, the way her mother said her father was whenever anyone asked, "How's Jonah holding up?"

But Lena feared that she wasn't doing a very good job of appearing to hold up. Nellie must have thought that her baby girl just might pass out or something. At the end of the service, a thin light-skinned man with a notepad in his hand led the family down the church aisle behind the casket, carried by Jonah's poker partners, to the waiting line of black limousines left running outside. Nellie grabbed Frank Petersen's hand as they passed his pew and pressed a nearly limp Lena into his arms.

"Take her home for us, Frank Petersen," Nellie whispered. "We'll be there as soon as we leave the cemetery."

Frank Petersen grabbed his battered hat from the seat beside him and took Lena's arm formally on his own. They headed toward the beat-up blue pickup truck with "The Bluebird Bar and Grill" painted on the side, parked in the lot next door.

Frank didn't say a word all the way down Forest Avenue. Lena felt as if she might never utter a sound again in her life. When they got home, Lena headed upstairs. She was having trouble breathing and couldn't wait to get out of her uncomfortable panty girdle and stockings and heels.

"I'll stick around till your mama and them get back," Frank said as he went toward the kitchen.

In the hush that seems to descend only on a house where a death has occurred, Lena changed hurriedly into a loose-fitting blouse and skirt. Then she rushed down the stairs to look for Frank Petersen. She found him sitting on the back porch steps smoking a Pall Mall. Even though it was cool out on the cement steps, Lena took a seat beside him.

"Just 'cause she's gone, don't mean I'm gonna start disrespecting her in her own house by smoking in there," Frank Petersen said, looking straight ahead.

They were silent for a long while, Lena beginning to feel lost in the cloud of deeply scented tobacco smoke that ringed them. Then Frank spoke again.

"You know me, Lena-Wena, I ain't no liar. Everybody knows me and her didn't get along, never did. So I'm not gonna say a whole lot of mess about what a good woman she was and she went before her time and all that. But I know what she meant to you. And I'm sorry you hurting."

Frank hadn't looked at Lena since she walked out on the porch. While he talked, he kept his bloodshot eyes trained on the woods down by the stream.

Lena laid her forehead against the thin cotton of the man's shirt sleeve below his shoulder and wept as she had wanted to for the last twenty-four hours. She didn't stop until she heard Nellie's friends bustling around in the kitchen preparing food for the mourners. Frank acted as though he didn't feel a thing, but when Lena lifted her head, she saw that his sleeve was soaking wet to the elbow with her tears.

That evening Nellie came into Lena's bedroom one last time before she tried to lay her own weary body down for the night. She was exhausted from the wake, the funeral, and the dinner afterward (more people seemed to tramp through the house than showed up on a Saturday near the first of the month at The Place), but she was so worried about her baby, she knew she couldn't sleep until Lena was asleep for the night. Nellie had felt unsettled all evening, ever since she saw old Nurse Bloom at the funeral.

Nurse Bloom had to be older than Miss Lizzie was, but she still looked the same as Nellie remembered her when Lena was born more than sixteen years before. The strange old woman wore the same brilliantly white nurse's uniform she always wore, but for the funeral she had added a matching white net veil covering her face and falling to her shoulders and chest. Nurse Bloom had taken Nellie's hand in her white gloved one as they all walked back from the gravesite, and forced Nellie to fall in step with her. Then she leaned forward and spoke conspiratorially.

"It is such a blessing to have a child like Lena in the house at a time like this," Nurse Bloom said softly. "Children like her— born with a veil, who can see beyond the grave—are such a comfort when the rest of us are trying to understand the death of a loved one."

Nellie hadn't even tried to hide her repulsion and indignation at the old woman. *I don't give a damn how old she is. There are certain things any fool knows better than to go around at a funeral saying,* Nellie had thought as she snatched her hand away from Nurse Bloom's grip and hurried away to join the others in the family. *And who does she think she is, saying that about Lena as if my baby was some kind of crazy voodoo woman? What in the hell would Lena know about death? Miss Lizzie was the first person close to her who ever died.*

Nellie had vowed that afternoon to forget all about the old nurse. Just thinking about the woman made her so angry she couldn't see straight. But at the same time, Nellie couldn't shake the eerie feeling that somehow the nurse really knew what she was talking about.

Lord, I hate funerals, she said to herself as she stopped climbing the stairs to stand awhile on the landing overlooking the woods. *All those flowers crowded into that little space—I thought for sure I was going to throw up right up there in that front pew each time the heat came on and blew that warm wet air over those roses and carnations right into my face. I never could stand heavy odors.*

Even from outside her bedroom door, Nellie could hear the

soft whimper of Lena's sobs muffled in her pillow. She knocked and walked in without waiting for a reply. Lena was curled into a ball in a corner of her bed nearest the wall.

"Oh, sugar," Nellie said as she rushed over to Lena's bed, "don't be in here all by yourself crying like this."

"Mama, I should have said something," Lena cried.

"Said what, Lena, baby? What could you have said? That Grandmama was old and her heart was giving out? What did you know, baby? She didn't tell any of us what Dr. Williams had found when he checked her out."

"Oh, Mama, I know 'bout stuff like that. What's gonna happen and stuff like that. You know that."

"Lord, your grandmama know she can reach from the grave," Nellie said with a sigh and not a little admiration.

"Mama, you know," Lena said, too tired to continue fighting an enemy too big and powerful for her to deny.

"Lord, Lena, what in the world made you mention that tonight? You sound just like . . ."

"I sound like who, Mama? Grandmama?"

Nellie hesitated and hurriedly said, "Uh-huh, you sound just like your grandmama."

"Well, I don't deserve to sound like her," Lena said harshly. "I don't deserve anything 'cause I know I could have done something and I didn't and she died."

"Oh, Lena, baby, please don't start talking crazy tonight. I'm just too tired. I swear I can't take it tonight. If you got any God in your heart, you will not put your mama through this shit tonight."

"But I can't help it, Mama, I can't help but talk crazy. Everything that comes out of my mouth is crazy."

"Lena, you got to stop that," Nellie said sternly. "You've got to stop talking about being crazy and all that. Before you know it, you'll really be acting crazy. It's nothing to play with."

"I'm not playing, Mama. I am crazy. I know it."

"Lena, life is gonna be hard enough for you as it is. It's hard on all us, without you making it more so by acting crazy. You just not allowed to act any way you want to in this world. I know we raised you like there ain't nothing you can't do, but, baby, acting crazy is one thing me and your daddy can't fix. The world'll make you pay for acting crazy."

"Mama, how can I help it? I'm just crazy."

"Sugar, you're just overwrought and upset about your grandmama. We all are. But you got to try to calm down. Just feel your forehead. You already getting warm. When you were a little girl you'd do this, get yourself so worked up that you actually got sick. Now, you too old for that shit," Nellie said, getting exasperated at Lena in spite of everything. It had been a long day, and because Miss Lizzie had not been her mother, everyone in the family had expected her to be strong and take care of all the arrangements. And everyone knows how damn delicate I am, Nellie thought.

"Now, don't you go getting sick on me," she said as she stroked Lena's warm forehead.

When Lena didn't seem capable of controlling her sobs, Nellie just held her tighter in her arms and said softly, "This my baby right here."

The familiar words dried up some of Lena's tears.

"This my mama right here," Lena said finally and they nestled up against each other the way they had when Lena was a baby.

Nellie stayed in Lena's room until she thought the girl had fallen asleep. Then she got up, covered Lena with one of the quilts Miss Lizzie made for all the beds, and quietly left the room. As soon as she had closed the door, Lena opened her eyes.

Lena longed to turn back time. If she had had any sense, she thought harshly as she lay in bed, she could have protected her grandmama in some way. Many nights, even after she became a teenager, Lena had gone into Grandmama's room and checked on her, and the old lady had asked her to come lie beside her on the big old-fashioned bed, as she had when she was little. Happy not to sleep alone with the apparitions that visited her in the night, Lena would jump eagerly into the high bed and nest against her grandmother's old thin bones under her heavy quilt.

But I wasn't lying there when it counted, she thought ruefully.

Whether she was crazy or not, she knew that she did see things, real or otherwise. And if she could see all these other dead people—a slave on a beach, her infant aunt in the picture—then she damn well ought to be able to see her beloved grandmama.

Lena lay awake, waiting.

TWENTY-TWO

❦ ❦

HOME

For the first couple of hours, Lena lay awake in the dark, the covers pulled up to her chin, listening to the house creak and settle. The image of her grandmother sitting at the sewing machine rubbing her left shoulder kept sleep away.

She remembered how years ago her grandmama would say to her, "Don't worry, baby, Grandma ain't gonna let nothing happen to her little puppy."

That memory made Lena bury her face in her pillow and heave dry sobs. But she sat up at the sound of a tree branch brushing against the window near her bed.

Then she noticed a heavy odor. At first she thought it was the scent of the Joy perfume that her mother had left there. But as soon as she took one deep breath she realized that what she smelled was not Nellie's perfume, but the heavy scent of moonflowers. As Lena sat on her bed taking in big gulps of flower-scented air, it became stronger and stronger. Soon the smell lay on the room like a cloud of smoke and made her drowsy.

Lena seemed just to have drifted off to sleep when she felt the bed jostled as if someone had sat on the mattress right by her shoulder. When she opened her eyes again and raised herself up on her elbows, she recognized the figure immediately.

"Grandmama!" she screamed and threw herself into the familiar arms.

All Lena wanted was to feel the spirit of her beloved grandmother envelop her like a gentle mist, but Grandmama seemed frantic to tell her something. In what looked to Lena like slow motion, Grandmama held the girl at arm's length and looked into her eyes.

"Oh, baby, baby, Grandma so sorry," the spirit said over and over. "Baby, Grandma so sorry. I shoulda known better. If I'da been any kind of grandmama, I would of known something was wrong. I've seen plenty of country folks who never been off the farm who had enough sense to know about a child like you and to make sure everything was done that should be done."

Lena didn't understand what she was being told, but she didn't care. She was so happy to have her grandmother again. Dead or alive.

"Grandma, can you hold me again? I been so alone."

Grandmama's ghost enveloped Lena like a soft warm mist. "Alone? You *alone?*"

"The girls at school stopped speaking to me," Lena said. "And I never had anyone I could ever really tell about the things I saw."

"Lena, don't you know you ain't never been alone? No matter how bad it got, there was always some somebody, dead or alive, trying to help you."

"Help me? Grandma, don't you know what it's been like for me? I thought you said you knew what it's been like for me."

"Baby, didn't you always have all your family's love? We may a' been foolish and blind not to see you were special in a way other than just being our baby. But didn't we love you with all our hearts? And your friends Sarah and Gwen? Didn't you have Mamie all to yourself for more than three years? What would you have done without that old lying wino Frank Petersen? Baby, you wasn't never really alone. And you shore ain't alone now.

"I tell you, Lena, baby, it's been some kind of job to get to you. It seems like three or four lifetimes I been trying to get back to this house. But them other spirits—the scary evil ones—was too strong."

"Oh, Grandmama," Lena moaned. "What's gonna become of me?"

"Shit, baby, I'm just dead. I ain't no fortune teller. But you, you can do more than me and four others like me put together if you let yourself."

"Grandmama, I don't know what you're talking about."

"Come with me, baby," Grandmama said as her wispy form seemed to rise from the bed and waft out the door.

Lena jumped out of the bed and followed her to the hall.

"Girl, go back in that room and put on your slippers and a robe," Grandmama chided when she saw Lena's bare feet. "Walking 'round like that in that flimsy little gown, you'll catch your death of cold."

Lena couldn't help it. She had to smile. She stumbled back to her bed in the light streaming from the bathroom. For once she felt lucky to be able to see ghosts.

"Now, come on," Grandmama said and floated down the stairs. Lena followed quietly in her soft slippers. She could hear her brother Edward, home for the funeral, snoring through his bedroom door and her father, across the hall and two doors down, joining in as if on cue.

It was a cloudy night, with the moon barely a glow in the sky. But Lena had no problem seeing the luminous figure of her grandmother. Besides, Lena seemed to be trailing the scent of moonflowers, long since out of season, as much as she was following her grandmother's spirit. She was glad Grandmama had insisted she wear shoes and a robe. Lena could see her breath as she bounced down the back kitchen steps toward the incline leading to the stream. She felt as carefree as a two-year-old.

At first Lena thought her grandmother was going to lead her across the brook into the forest. Since the night she had awoken shivering in the woods, she had been afraid even to look in the direction of those trees. But Grandmama stopped at a charred spot just before the stream, where the family had always burned yard and garden debris. Even dead and cold, the place still had the heady smell of burnt leaves. Scents seemed to be so strong whenever ghosts appeared, Lena thought.

"When you were born, and Dr. Williams caught you, Nurse Bloom was right there. And she did right by you, I found out. Right there in the hospital she gave Nellie two things. One was a bottle of tea made from your birth caul. The other was the actual thing, the caul.

"Your mama poured out one, and the other, your caul, she burned in this spot." Grandmama looked at the chunks of coal and ashes and sucked her teeth in disgust. "While we were up there in the house making over our newborn baby girl, Nellie was down here destroying your priceless, precious caul. I still can't believe that Nellie was foolish enough to do something like that. She disrupted two rituals, Lena, that you were lucky to even be connected with. They would have helped you in living the kind of life a child like you should have lived. If you had drunk that tea, baby, it would of weakened those scary spirits. Instead, you been scared of what you should have understood."

"Grandmama, I thought I was mad. I thought I was crazy like Cliona from Yamacraw."

"My poor baby. I know it's been hard. But don't you know, Lena? We all mad in our own way."

"But, Grandma, I really saw all that stuff, all those things . . ." Lena paused a moment. "Grandmama, I see you."

"For God's sake, baby, just 'cause you see a few ghosts and such, you think you crazy? What you think the rest of us—those that come before you, those that's living now—done been through? Don't you think we 'bout crazy, too? All us colored women in this here country crazy as betsy bugs. Life done made us that way.

"Crazy ain't all bad, child. Sometimes it's the only thing that protects you. This world you living in can be so mixed up, so ass-backwards, that not fitting into it, being what some folks call crazy, is a blessing. And you, Lena, you got the power to do something with your craziness."

"Do something *with* it? I don't want to do anything *with* it! I want to get rid of it."

"Don't never say that, Lena. Don't never let me catch you saying that again. What if your powers can heal people? Don't you remember how you could put the magic on stuff? Or, baby, what if your craziness can just bring a little succor to some tortured soul? Even those old roustabouts at your daddy's place seek you out to tell you some little ole thing 'bout their lives, just to share it with you. Don't you think that means something?"

"I don't care, Grandmama. I don't want to have to keep living like this. With no friends and seeing strange things and hearing and saying all kinds of things." Lena bit her lip and shuddered. "Grandmama, if I can't get rid of it, can't I just be with you for good? Is that why you're here? Am I gonna die, too? Did you come to take me back with you?"

"Go back with me?" Grandmama said. "Hell, no, baby, you just starting out. You got a whole lot to do before you over on this side. That's what you was made for. That's why you had that veil over your face when you was born. That was a sign of the things you can do, things you can be."

"Tell me, Grandma, what was my veil a sign of?"

"That's what you got to find out yourself. Baby, if you don't know yourself, then you ain't never gon' find no peace.

"There's someone who can help you. I want you to see Mother Bloom."

"You mean Nurse Bloom? You want me to go to the hospital?" Lena asked.

"Yeah, you can probably find her at the hospital. Tell her that what she thought was done to protect you at birth wasn't done."

"What? Grandmama, I can't just walk up to her and tell her something like that."

"Nurse Bloom can't bring back your birth caul or change what you been through. Your caul is gone forever." Grandmama looked down at the charred spot on the ground with such an expression of loss that Lena felt the old lady's spirit might cry. "But she can tell you things about yourself. She got a lot of experience with children like you and that can help you."

"And after I do this, after I go to see Nurse Bloom, then I'll be normal, Grandmama?"

Grandmama chuckled. "Normal? Baby, you ain't never gon' be normal."

In the pit of Lena's stomach it felt as if a storm were brewing. Suddenly gusts of wind set the woods across the stream dancing and swaying in the moonlight.

The wind whipped through the trees and brush like a chorus. Then it seemed to collect itself, whiz over the stream, and whistle around Lena, lifting her gown and robe above her waist. The gust of wind eddied up her body. As it blew past her face, Lena noticed a scent she hadn't smelled in nearly a decade . . . the raw briny smell of the ocean.

The salty wind was soft and warm, but Lena was beginning to feel the dampness of the ground through her thin slippers. She shuddered and Grandmama said, "Let's go back inside."

When they got back to Lena's room, Grandmama sat on the bed beside Lena and looked at her granddaughter's crestfallen face. "Lena, there're things you have to know about yourself. And it's time you did something to start finding them out. Baby, you can't run away from what you are. You was born a special child. Now you got to claim what is yours."

Tears started to well up in Lena's eyes.

"You believe what I'm telling you?" Grandmama asked.

Lena opened her mouth a couple of times to reply, but no sound came out. The simple question threw her into such a state of confusion that she was actually dizzy. How can I believe in all this? Lena thought.

"I ain't saying it's gon' be easy. But listen to me, Lena, no matter what you see or what you hear, I don't want you afraid anymore. Now, that's your grandma talking, you hear me?"

Lena nodded her head.

"I got to go now, baby," Grandmama said.

"Wait, Grandma! I *am* scared. I don't want to do all this alone. I don't even know what I'm doing. Going to Nurse Bloom. Talking 'bout teas and veils. Don't make me."

"Ain't nobody *making* you, Lena. What you are, baby, it's a gift. It's like in the Bible. It's your birthright. There's gifts that you're given in this world that you just can't throw away. If you do, it's like telling somebody who love you to kiss your ass."

Then she took Lena in her arms one more time. "And no matter what, me and others who love you, we'll always be with you." Grandmama paused and added, "Baby, there's just some things you have to take on faith."

Then she gave Lena one last squeeze and evaporated into the darkness along with the scent of moonflowers.

Lena sat watching the empty space her grandmother's ghost left in the middle of the room. She had to rub her throbbing temples to try and settle her thoughts.

She finally got up, turned on the light, and went to the closet. For a while she stood staring at the image in the mirror hanging on the door. She bunched her gown up tight and pulled it in the back to show her figure. Leaning close, she examined her face: the faint line of hair above her lip, the beginnings of freckles on her cheekbones like her mother's. She stared so long into her eyes that her pupils began to dilate.

Then she switched off the light and went back to bed. She pulled the quilt her grandmother had made for her up around her waist and sat up in bed the rest of the night.

HARVEST AMERICAN WRITING

Diana Abu-Jaber
Arabian Jazz

Tina McElroy Ansa
Baby of the Family
Ugly Ways

Carolyn Chute
The Beans of Egypt, Maine
Letourneau's Used Auto Parts
Merry Men

Harriet Doerr
Consider This, Señora

Donald Harington
The Choiring of the Trees
Ekaterina

Randall Kenan
Let the Dead Bury Their Dead

Dan McCall
Messenger Bird

Lawrence Naumoff
Silk Hope, NC
Taller Women: A Cautionary Tale

Karen Osborn
Patchwork

Jim Shepard
Kiss of the Wolf

Brooke Stevens
The Circus of the Earth and the Air

Oxford Stroud
Marbles

Sandra Tyler
Blue Glass